# KARMA'S REVENGE

## SALINA HARRIS

**KARMA'S REVENGE**

Karma's Revenge is a work of fiction. Names, characters, places, and incidents are a product of the author's imagination. Locales and public names are sometimes used for atmospheric purposes. Any resemblance to actual people, living or dead, or to businesses, companies, events, institutions, or locales is completely coincidental.

Published in the United States by RIA JAY Publishing
3355 Lenox Road Suite 750 Atlanta, GA 30326
www.riajay.com

ISBN 978-0-615-30827-2 (Paperback)
ISBN 978-1-955727-27-3 (Hardback)

Manufactured in the United States of America

This book is dedicated to my parents. You are my guiding light, and you have supported me in all I've pursued. You were there for many of my firsts and now I must dedicate my first book to you both.

You gave me the strength to push on when no one else did. You gave me the courage to be brave and different. You enabled me to chase my dreams. You gave me support when I needed to be supported. Thank you for encouraging me.

# Prologue

I never expected my life to be over at the age of twenty-eight. Gurgling my own blood wasn't the way I envisioned going out, but it should have been expected since I lived such a tumultuous life.

I was naive to think that there was some divine explanation to our existence, but really, there's many eminent flaws in the grand scheme things. I thought that the rich had it made and being at the top was life's goal. But I learned that climbing the ladder does not bring happiness. In fact, the higher the climb, the harder the fall. I played the game, and I played it well, but even the best players lose sometimes, and it was my turn to experience the ultimate loss.

Maybe I shouldn't have put so much effort into trying to make it— into trying to make something of myself. Maybe I should have changed my actions so I would not have been labeled a bad person... a malicious person... a deceitful person. Maybe, *just maybe*, it would have changed my fate. I don't know. I just know that I'm scared right now. I'm afraid to let go of my family that I appreciated too little and material things that I valued too much. I'm scared of letting go of the future and all of the 'what ifs' that came along with it. I'm literally terrified to let go of my life. I don't want to die, but at the same time, I'm not certain I deserve to live.

Now, I'm gasping for air like a fish out of water. Panting, as blood surrounds me like the air I once breathed. The last kiss I will feel is the cold kiss of death as I drift into another dimension. I can't believe that my greed led me to this – led me to this misjudgment, this self-destruction.

I thought I had it all – the money, the car, the looks and the clothes. I had men catering to me left and right, feeding them spoonfuls of lies just to make sure my plate was full. I made sure I got whatever I wanted, whenever I wanted it. I didn't care about the cost or how I obtained it; one thing was certain... if I couldn't get it myself, I made sure someone got it for me.

I definitely had everything I needed and more, but that still wasn't enough. I wanted it all, I *needed* it all. No one could stop me, no one could tell me anything different. I was on a high and I didn't want to come down. I always craved the next big thing. If it was more expensive, I wanted it. If it was on trend, I had to have it. If *he* was most powerful, I wanted *him* too.

I didn't want a mediocre, middle-class lifestyle. I wanted to pop the finest champagne every day. I wanted to do what I wanted, whenever I damn well pleased. I wanted to ball with the ballers and rub elbows with the elite. I wanted to be the one everyone looked at and whispered, "I want to be her." I wanted to be the envy of everyone who ever thought less of me and the woman that all the men ogled over. I craved the flashy lifestyle, but now my life is flashing before my eyes.

In scheming my way to the top, I failed to realize that every choice has a consequence. Although it was hard to determine what the results of my actions at the time, my fate was inevitable. I expected merciless perils to present themselves clearly, but that was not the case. Death has no face. He can be white or black, a next-door neighbor, a nickel-and-dimer, a bum, or a millionaire. Truth is, when it's your time to go, it's your time. There is no guaranteed date for your life's end. Good looks or money can't save you from the reaper. There's no escape and no rescue.

You live with many, but you die alone. Your accomplishments and material things must be left behind because when you are holding on for your life you can't grasp onto anything else. When your time is up, friends don't matter, family don't matter, *nothing matters*. The only thing that matters is if you have made your peace with your maker. From there, you better pray that your ass doesn't end up getting scorched by those eternal flames.

My sister forewarned me that one day my conceit and egoism would catch up to me one day, but being the bullheaded person that I was, her warning went unheeded. Sometimes words of wisdom can be spoken right into your ear, but you're just too deaf to listen.

I'm convinced that life works in mysterious ways. I guess you can say that my sister was an angel in disguise. But, sometimes in life it's difficult to distinguish the demons from the saints. She tried so hard to let me know that there was no light at the end of the tunnel I was traveling down. Maybe it was that the truth hurt so bad I didn't want to hear it, or maybe I was just too damn stubborn to listen. Like a lot of people, I felt no one knew what was best for me, but me. Now, far too late, I realize that outsiders can provide constructive criticism; sometimes it's best to heed their advice. In my case, frivolous, trivial things clouded my vision. And like many, I became my own worst enemy.

I suppose the clichés "What goes around comes around" and "What's done in the dark will someday come to the light" are not understatements. What is done in the dark will *always* be exposed, and deceitful actions can also cost you your life. Unfortunately, my first brutal lesson was my last. There are no second chances for me.

I've done wrong for so long that I guess God is fed up with my shenanigans. Now there's no time to go back and fix things; what's done is done and nothing can rewind time. So, with the last breaths that I take, I will tell you this – do not let greed rule your life. Appreciate what you have and build on that because karma's a bitch and she will find you and repay you for what you've done. I am a firsthand (and dying) witness. Too bad I realized it all a little too late.

Karma hit me in the worst way possible. There's nothing I can do about it now but wait for my spirit to separate from my limp body and await judgement. My time is up now. My name is Aisha Carmichael, and this is my story.

# Chapter 1

## Walk of Shame

Waking up in a stranger's bed wasn't my style, but if I could potentially gain from it, I was game. This was the case with Neilson. From what I recall, his sex game was weak, but he did provide an exhilarating night out on the town and kept me from potential Friday night boredom.

He spotted me sitting alone, having an after-work cocktail at a lounge that I frequented on Wabash Avenue. I noticed his gaze from across the bar, longing to gain my attention. His dark, deep-set eyes were hard to miss.

It was early evening, so the place was still pretty desolate. Just a few stragglers in suits stood near the bar with loosened ties and full pockets. Some of them indulged in a glass of bourbon, while the remaining gents partook in a few shots for solace before retiring to their suburban homes that consisted of a spin-cycling, cake-baking, stay-at-home-wife and a pair of seemingly perfect kids.

The usual flock of pre-gaming hipsters hadn't flooded the scene yet. These were the ones that were living off of 'Daddy's Money,' which allowed them to inhabit swanky condos downtown. They pretended to be independent and sophisticated, though they were completely opposite. Like clockwork, they would pit stop at the lounge in their designer clothes before hitting their favorite nightclub and becoming a drunken stupor. Soon enough, those same fancy threads would be covered in vomit, and the next day would be sent to the cleaners to be refreshed and pressed. I had my fair share of encounters with these types of people. Their false sense of intellect and entitlement made me cringe. I was in my latter twenties. I had no interest in politicking with new age twenty-one-year-olds who thought they knew it all. We were cut from two totally different cloths. I was ready to make my exit before they arrived.

With the absence of patrons, it was difficult to dismiss the stranger's intense interest in me. Unlike the other corporate men there who chatted amongst peers, he was sitting alone, same as me. Our eyes locked briefly, but I immediately disengaged. I was often approached by a suit, wearing a ring, looking for a 'good time' in efforts to escape his mundane sex life with his long-term wife. I was always on guard, ready to unleash my bitchy speech to suggest they keep it moving. I figured this fella staring at me was one of those fellas— one in a suit, with a ring, looking for a fling. I wasn't in the mood to entertain a married man, and even if he was unmarried, he didn't appear to be my type. But no mattered how many times I looked away, this guy continued staring and smiling— bobbing his head to the music being performed by the lounge's live band.

I can't lie, the ambiance that evening was more soothing than usual, and the music was quite alluring. I too couldn't help but to sway to the rhythm of the melodic saxophone, which washed away my workday woes. My relaxed movements must have suggested an open invitation for conversation, because before the selection was over, he gulped the rest of his drink and meandered my way. I skootched in my chair to position myself where my back was slightly towards him. He inched a bit closer, placing his elbow on the bar mere inches away from me. I immediately covered my drink with a napkin. He was way too close for comfort.

*Here we go.* I thought.

"Hey baby. What's your name?" He raised one of his thick, untamed eyebrows and bore a slight grin.

He was a tall, lanky black guy— the only black guy in the place, actually. Maybe he felt like we had some type of connection since we were the only people of color there. However, two brown people sitting alone in a lounge didn't constitute for instant chemistry, just like two specks of pepper in a saltshaker don't make for perfect seasoning. Hell, I wasn't even feeling a spark. I was more so feeling my inner bitch yell out '*Get the fuck back,*' but then, I thought that would be a bit much for the upscale setting. Being a young, professional female of color meant not being too loud, or too ghetto, or too over-the-top, or too aggressive. When in Rome, do as the Romans do.

"Well, my name is definitely *not* baby," I sniped, tilting my nose up.

By this time, the band was in between sets, so my words echoed off the walls of the barren lounge. I snatched the napkin from my drink before downing it. I wanted to make sure he fully grasped my annoyance. His head shrunk into his shoulders with embarrassment, almost like a wounded animal. A couple of older gentlemen close by turned and chuckled, hinting that they'd been in the same boat before in their younger days. One lifted his glass and nodded at him as to say, 'Try again, young man.' Then he watched us for a bit. I assumed he was interested in how it would all pan out.

"I…" he stopped, searching for words. "I apologize. I see that's the wrong approach for a lady such as yourself. I don't blame you for that reaction. Let's start over. My name is Neilson. Pleasure meeting you."

His hand slowly extended towards mine. By the look in his eyes, I didn't know if he wanted to shake it or kiss it, but he was a fool if he thought either was going to happen. I left his hand dangling midair, then tapped on my glass and told the bartender I wanted another… on Neilson's tab. She winked an, '*I got you girl*' wink and started shaking up a fresh drink immediately. Neilson smirked and casually lowered his hand to his side. Then he let me know that I could have whatever I wanted as long as I told him my name.

Fair enough.

"Aisha," I blurted before taking a quick sip of the new Martini sitting in front of me.

"Oh, like the continent?"

"No, like A-I-S-H-A." I snubbed.

"Sooo, like the continent? It's still pronounced the same way." He shrugged. "Regardless, that's a nice name. I like it. And I like… *you*."

Annoyed, I took an exaggerated breath before turning up the corner of my lips and staring off into the band's direction. Suddenly, I had a full-on interest in whatever they were doing. Anything was better than talking to this man at the time. However, he was obviously unbothered that I was ignoring him, because after several minutes of awkward silence he uttered…

"Did you hear me? I said, I like you."

I couldn't believe he was still hanging around. I thought that my brashness would, well, push him away. He was persistent, which was kind of a turn on, but the physical attraction just wasn't there, and I wasn't about to cave that easily.

"You like me? You don't even know me." I retorted.

"This is true, but I do know enough."

I shot him a look that pushed him into further explanation.

"Well, I know your name is Aisha. I know that you are a beautiful woman. I know that you don't take any bullshit. I know that you like Martinis. And even while sitting down I know that you're wearing the hell... out of... that... dress." He grunted the last words like he was savoring the first morsel of a perfect steak.

I couldn't help but crack a smile. I could tell his compliments were genuine and one thing that he didn't know about me was that I was a sucker for an authentic compliment. I found my eyes unintentionally wondering down to his hand and searching for a ring, then I took another swig of my drink. The combination of the two loosened me up a bit—the stiff drink and the absence of a ring.

"Now there's a smile. I knew you had it in you. You should do that more often. It's more..." he paused, rubbing the few hairs he had on his chin, "...inviting."

A look of concern crossed my face.

"Well, I definitely don't want to be that." I declared.

"Be what? Inviting?" His forehead wrinkled, forcing his thick eyebrows into a unibrow. "Why not?"

"Why not?" I questioned back. "Because of this. This right here is a prime example of why. I didn't look like I was inviting, and you still came over here, right? Could you imagine what would happen if I actually looked pleasant? My God! The type of attention I would attract? Who wants all that?"

His eyes widened, a little taken back.

"Woah, con-fi-dent!" He enunciated.

It was then I realized how absurdly cocky I must have sounded. My mouth opened, but no words came out. He put up his hand to stop any explanation that I was about to give.

"Hey, it doesn't matter. You have every right to be. You *are* truly breathtaking."

I exhaled slowly. He was quite the charmer.

He stared at me for a few moments. It was the type of stare someone does when they are trying to figure someone out. The kind of stare he did from across the bar not long before. The kind of stare that I previously disengaged from, but now had my full-on attention. And I reciprocated. I stared back… deeply… attentively. Although Neilson had this fake Miami Vice swag to him that was a bit overwhelming, he seemed okay. He seemed… safe.

I smiled and crossed my legs towards him. My dress bunched up around my waist, making the four-inch slit that once rested near my knee, slide up my thigh. I didn't attempt to pull it down or readjust it, I wanted him to see— to be teased a little. By this point, I was buzzed, and he looked a lot better than he did half hour prior. Plus, I knew an expensive suit when I saw one, and his was far from cheap.

"So, Neilson, what do you do for a living?"

I leaned my side against the barstool and hung my arm over the back, in a relaxed interview sort of way. He seemed excited I wanted to know more about him and responded before I could get my last word all the way out.

"Well, I own a few luxury dealerships around the city. Been going strong for eight years now." He nodded proudly. "So, if you know anyone that's looking for a Benz, BMW, Maserati, Ferrari, Lamborghini, something of that nature, just let me know. I only sell the best of the best."

"Is that right?" I asked with full-on interest.

"Most definitely." He confirmed, nodding again.

I took a moment and took a sip of my drink before proceeding.

"Well," I paused, letting my tongue rest between my teeth for a second, "I'm in the market."

I stared at him while circling the rim of the Martini glass with my finger.

"For?" He nearly whispered.

"For a car, of course." I flashed an unconvincing smirk.

His lip curled at one corner— his facial expression matching mine.

"Tell you what. Let's see where this night takes us and maybe I can take you off the market. For looking for cars that is," he smiled.

"I just copped me a new Lambo to add to my personal collection. You should check it out. See if you like it."

"Ohhh." I instantly perked up.

"In that case, why don't we get out of here and take it for a spin then? I wouldn't mind...riding." My lips hung open after the last word.

Neilson gulped hard before clearing his throat. His noticeable Adam's apple climbed his neck and then fell before he responded.

"You really don't bullshit, huh? Straight to the point," he answered coolly, although I know I was making him hot. I smiled and nodded. He continued.

"Well, I like it. You ain't said nothing but a word, beautiful. Let's get out of here."

He raised one finger to get the bartender's attention. After paying both of our tabs, he stretched out his hand to assist me from my seat. Upon standing, I realized how tall he truly was. Even with stilettos on, he had me by a foot, at least.

"Can I?" He asked while placing his hand at the small of my back. I didn't give him permission, but the look in my eyes told him he didn't need to ask.

I was keeping it sexy and cool, glancing up at him every few seconds flirtatiously. I was strutting in my brand-new Louboutin Undessins, hips switching and all. But every two of my steps I made only equated to one of his. We were halfway to the door and my right heel slipped to the side and my knee buckled. I looked like a bad version of Rip the Runway. Thank God no one else noticed, but Neilson. Nevertheless, it was still embarrassing.

"I swear to you, I'm not drunk." I confirmed.

"Its fine," he laughed. "I got you. I'll carry you out if I have to."

Neilson inched his hand around my waist, pulling me in closer to him. It was comforting, even though I knew this wasn't the start of anything serious. I was a realist, and reality was that he was just a friendly giant looking for a good time. I obliged because I liked a man who knew how to handle a woman with a little sass, and it didn't hurt that he had money. That was reality was the reality of it all.

Nothing more, nothing less. Before long, the valet fetched his Urus and we were cruising shoreline.

In the looks department, Neilson was a four out of ten— thin body, no muscle tone, a slightly lazy eye, and a patchy beard. However, by the looks of his car and designer clothes, I knew he was well-off, which for me, bumped him up to a solid eight.

During our ride, he invited me back to his condo for a nightcap. My initial hesitancy must have thrown him off.

"What's wrong?" He asked.

"Oh nothing, it's fine. I'll swing by. Just need to grab my car first."

"Oh, yeah, sure… of course." he said, grabbing my hand reassuringly.

He seemed harmless, but I learned to never be too trusting of anyone. Hell, I barely trusted my damn self. I didn't want to be stuck without a car (or without my pepper spray and stun gun, which was inside of my glove box) at a guy's place that I just met a couple of hours prior, just in case. Even the devil used to be an angel. Can never be too sure.

One nightcap turned into a few. The drunker I got, the better he looked and the drunker he got, the more he built himself up to be some Big Kahuna in the bed. We wanted each other, no doubt about it, but I should've known better. In my experience, men that talk the most shit tend to have the least to offer. If I wasn't so tipsy I would've taken my ass home, but I had an emergency overnight bag in my car and his California King seemed comfy enough to stay. Night soon turned into morning, and I found myself sleeping a lot longer than intended. That did not suppose to happen.

"Damn it," I mumbled with half-hatched eyes. I

raised my arm to shield my face from the sun as it danced over the Chicago skyline and through the sheer curtains. I didn't mean to stay so long. I wanted to slip out before the sun came up, but then there it was, telling me good morning. The warm bed enticed me to snuggle back under the comforter, but my sober senses told me it was time to go.

My night at Neilson's place was a bit of a blur due to the excessive drinking. I held my head, having a slight headache and took a few blinks to bring the room into clear view. Everything was white— stark white. Sheets, blanket, headboard, throw rug, even the chaise near the window… white. I instinctively turned to look at the pillowcase. *Shit.* Makeup heavily smeared cotton surface and it looked like my entire face was eternally morphed onto the pillowcase. Probably would've been so noticeable if the case was another color.

I turned my head to see Neilson's mouth wide open, breathing heavily. Crust as white as his linens encompassed the corners of his mouth. Most people look peaceful when they're asleep, almost like a cute little baby. But he was definitely, *definitely* not cute at this point. His score quickly fell from a solid eight, back down to a four and after the awful sex we had, he was close to being in the negatives. Alcohol couldn't even coax me into thinking that it was any good. I couldn't even begin to imagine what it would be like if I was completely coherent. I don't even think I would've let him finish.

One of his long legs was draped over mine, making it hard to slip out of the bed without waking him. I slowly pulled my leg towards my chest, stopping every few seconds. With the last pull, his leg flopped onto the bed. His snoring ceased, and I froze in position. I was certain his eyes were going to pop open, which was the last thing I wanted to happen. But, once he let out a loud snore, I realized he was just having an apneic episode. I went limp noodle and slid out the bed onto the floor. I held my breath and paused again, making sure he was still sleep. Soon, I was tip-toing to the bathroom where I purposely remember leaving my overnight bag. What I didn't remember was how white his bathroom was as well.

*What is he, some type of got damn psychopath? Who has this much white in their house?* He took being neat, tidy, crisp, and clean to a whole other level.

I looked through is linen closet to find a towel to erase the remaining makeup on my face. Again, all white. I already had my mind made up that I'd never see this guy again, but I wasn't ratchet enough to mess up his pillow *and* towels. I did care, a little.

His bathroom was pristine. Modern white towels hung from the towel bar and a fluffy, white rug laid in the middle of the floor. White orchids in a clear vase sat upon the Calacatta countertop. The only colorful things in his bathroom were the array of colognes, beard oils, and beard balm that was held in a clear vanity tray. *Thank God he's trying to fix that patchy bit of hair on his chin*, I thought. That's when I spotted some face wash and helped myself.

After splashing a handful of cold water onto my face, I quickly scavenged through my bag to piece together some sort of outfit. It had been a while since I used my emergency bag and didn't really know what was in it. The options were a set of gym clothes, torn jeans, and a short-fitted dress. The dress matched with my heels that I wore the night prior, so it was a no-brainer.

After dabbing on a bit lip gloss, I dusted my face with

bronzer and let down my tightly wound bun, unleashing caramel-streaked tresses. I gently ran my fingers through the bouncy locks to loosen them into soft, free-flowing waves.

I carefully tipped down the stairs, hoping not to wake Nielson. Once at the bottom, I put on my heels. Every few seconds I looked at the top of the stairs. Still, no Neilson. My eyes were redirected to the door. Only a few feet separated me from ghosting this guy. I stood up, juggling my large, overnight bag, while balancing myself in the five-inch heels. But just when I thought I was making a smooth getaway, my heel snagged on the carpet and my bag landed on the floor with a loud thud. Damn those shoes! The prior night, I blamed the slippery lounge floor for nearly busting my ass, but then I realized, maybe I just couldn't walk in the damn things. I anxiously looked around hoping I could still make a clean escape, but it was too late. His voice stopped me in my tracks.

"Hey, baby," he yawned. "Where are you running off to so fast?"

Bothered, I threw one hand in the air, as to say 'hello' and 'goodbye' at the same time. He was still waiting for an answer.

"I got this appointment and…"

"It can wait, I'm sure. I didn't even get my round two in. Last night was *sooo* good," he emphasized, swerving his narrow pelvis in a circular motion, and licking his lips.

Now, he just seemed like a perv, which gave me even more reason to want to make a quick exit. I'm glad he was satisfied; too bad I didn't feel the same. My favorite part of our fling was when it was over, so I definitely didn't want to partake in any of his "round two" shenanigans. I regretted even getting slightly damp for this dude. I wiggled my foot back in my stiletto and scooped up my bag.

"I'm flattered Nielson, really, but I gotta go."

"C'mon. You can have a cup of coffee with me at least. Let me order some breakfast and..."

"No!" I blurted, cutting him off.

There was a long pause. He aimlessly stood there looking like Lurch. Guess he didn't have anything else to pull out of his bag of tricks.

"Ok, well if you really got to go…"

"I do. Just call me. Maybe we can do lunch sometime."

I fumbled with the large wooden door. I don't know if it was nerves or me moving too fast, because I couldn't get the damn thing open. Neilson rushed to assist me— junk jiggling as he galloped down the stairs. Most times I was turned on by a man in a nice expensive pair of boxers, but not when his junk looked like a Vienna sausage.

"I got you." He smiled. His face was a little cuter the night before. Guess I had my drunk goggles and Lamborghini blinders on.

I rushed out the door without saying thank you or goodbye. With flat carpet in the hallway, I was able to speed walk to the elevator. The bottom of my dress kept hiking up and I kept tugging it down. I imagine I looked like the Hunchback of Notre Dame— one shoulder hunched up to keep my bag from falling off and the other arm hanging down to keep my ass from showing. But I already had my mind made up; he'd seen more than enough; he didn't need to see any more.

"Hey, I don't even have your number," he yelled from the doorway of his condo.

He was right – he didn't have my number, and he

didn't need to have it either. I didn't want to do lunch… I didn't want to do anything more with him at all! In the end, his pleasures were fulfilled, but it was a pleasure he would *never, ever* experience from me again. I couldn't get the repulsive image of him swirling his narrow hips around out of my head – like he really put it on me. That image alone was enough to ruin any future rendezvous for me.

Once inside the elevator, I repeatedly pressed the ground level button until the doors closed. I saw him looking confused from a distance, yet I was also confused as to why in my late twenties I was still doing the walk-of-shame. Finally, the elevator doors shut, and I planted my back against the wall, sighing with relief. *How did I let that happen? Why did I even give him the time of day? I should've gone with my first mind.*

I was so angry and disappointed in myself. I knew I should have trusted my gut and shut it down at first glance. But for once I let my heart soften a little… I shouldn't have done that. Was he attractive? No. Was he nice? Yes. Was he accomplished? Seemed like it. Did that matter in the end? Hell no.

*Ding.*

The opening of the elevator doors broke my mental conversation, and I snapped back into reality. I scuttled my way out before the doors could fully open. Thank God the lobby wasn't far because I was over the awkwardness of lugging the large bag in heels. Upon reaching the lobby, I nodded and smiled at the concierge who was engaged in the phone call. However, instead of returning the kind gesture, he cleared his throat, pulled the phone away from his ear, and cupped the receiver with his hand.

"Excuse me, Miss Aisha?"

24

"Yes?" I said confused, wondering how he even knew my name.

"Mister Nielson would like to speak with you," he whispered.

*Seriously?!* This pushed me to my wits end and I was ready to clean my hands of Neilson once and for all. I see he was the type you couldn't beat around the bush with.

"Look… Sir." I said brashly with a hard 'k' and an overly pronounced 'S.'

"We *just* spoke. I told him *I* would contact *him*." I pointed first to myself and then in the direction of the phone. I continued.

"But, since he obviously has a hearing problem, maybe he'll listen to you when you tell him… *just forget about me*. I wish him the best."

The concierge's eyes grew big, and his bottom lip dropped, mouth slightly parted. There was silence and a short stare down. I wasn't leaving until he properly relayed the message. And he did…reluctantly.

"Thank you, sir," I sassed before making my way toward the valet.

The click-clack of my stilettos on the marble floor resonated through the lobby. Luckily, there was no wait, and the attendant was able to fetch my coupe in record time. Before he could close my car door completely, I had already shifted into drive. I wanted to leave zero chance of Nielson coming down to stop me.

I stared into the rearview several times, envisioning him running behind my car with his flopping, little sausage. Thankfully, that vision never came to pass. I made a sharp turn out of the premises and onto the busy street, disappearing into the city's traffic.

With minimal congestion, I was able to weave in and out of lanes on I-94. My Saturday mani-pedi appointments were the highlight of my week and I wasn't going to miss it for some lame, one-night stand that wasn't even worth my pussy juices. I was ready for total relaxation. I couldn't get there fast enough.

With the warm breeze brushing against my skin, it seemed like the start of a great day. But, while I was busy revving my Jag, I neglected to see the police clocking cars from the side of the road. By the time I noticed, it was already too late. *Damn.* Busted.

*Whoop, whoop!* The siren startled me, and I immediately pulled to the side of the highway. I carefully considered what I was going to do when the officer approached me. I decided playing dumb was best. If there was one thing, I was good at, it was lying. I know that's nothing to be proud of, but in this case, it was my only option.

"I'm sorry, is there a problem?" I slid my window down and put on my best dazed face. Rule #1 in lying: innocence is key.

"Yes, ma'am, there is a problem, but I'm sure you already know what that is." The officer spoke in a monotone voice as he looked at me over his dark shades.

He was short and muscle-bound with a buzz cut. He looked like he was born to be an officer — like he busted out of the womb with a baton and badge.

"Actually, no I don't. That's why I'm asking you. After all, *you* were the one who pulled *me* over." I retorted.

"Being a smart ass definitely isn't going to help your situation. I suggest you calm your tone."

"I'm not being a smart ass. I was simply wondering

why you pulled me over." I said innocently.

He paused, giving me time to change my response. After a brief stare-down he continued.

"You were going twenty-seven miles over the limit, which constitutes as reckless driving? I hope the rush was worth a citation."

"Well, to be quite honest, sir, I—"

"License and registration please…"

He cut me off before I could rebuttal. That's what put a bad taste in my mouth about cops – they are always so invasive. I grabbed the necessary documents out of the glove compartment and handed them over.

"Here you go…"

"Proof of insurance," he stated before even glancing at my license and registration.

This fool could have asked me for my insurance the first time around. I wanted to tell him to piss off but thought better of it. I presented the insurance card as requested.

"Be right back, just need to run this." He walked back to his car with documents in hand.

After several minutes of tapping my unmanicured nails on the steering wheel, I was growing impatient. With all the technology the world has at hand, I've always felt these stupid pricks could be faster. With him moving at a snail's pace, I knew I would definitely be late for my appointment. I pulled out my phone to call the salon. No answer. I started to dial again, but then he reappeared.

"Ma'am. Get off the phone, please."

"I'm sorry, it'll be just a moment." I stared down at my phone holding one finger in the air.

"No, get off that phone now! I won't ask again." He demanded. His stance was staggered with his hand on his holster.

He acted like I just robbed a convenience store. And all over speeding? I knew that he was doing his job, but if he raised his voice one more time, I was liable to put the smack down on his punk ass. Whether he had a gun or not, it was about to be WWE on I-94. However, I respectfully held my tongue and stowed my cell. As soon as I put the phone down, he resumed talking.

"Did you know your license was suspended?"

"What? Suspended? How is that?!" I was truly shocked.

"Why don't *you* tell *me*? Then we can move on as to why you were speeding."

"To be quite honest, I don't know why or how it's suspended. If I knew there was a problem, I would've definitely taken care of it. I mean, whatever the cost, I can fix it right now." I rummaged through my purse to find my wallet.

"Oh no, no, no. You'll have to settle this in court. You were driving recklessly on a suspended license. To be frank, you shouldn't be on the road at all. So, turn off your engine and get out of the vehicle now!" He lashed out.

"Step out of the vehicle? You gotta be kidding. Do you see that Chicago PD sticker on my window? Do you know what that means? That means I support y'all asses. And you're trying to take me to jail?" My fierce diva attitude kicked in full force.

"Honestly, I wouldn't care if you had a million stickers on your window, that doesn't change the fact that you broke the law. Now I'm not going to ask you again, turn off your engine. You can either have someone pick your car up or have it towed. If I were you, I'd use that phone of yours to have someone come pick it up. Trust me, I'm the nice guy here. Most officers wouldn't even give you that option."

His voice was tight like that of a drill sergeant. This Major Payne wannabe was becoming a major pain in my ass.

"Look, I work for a big firm. I know how these things work. There's no legal situation that can't be fixed. C'mon. Name your price." I pulled out my checkbook and a pen, already pre-filling the date and my signature.

"Now you're bribing an officer? Get out!"

I stared at him a moment, wondering how I was going to get out of this. I couldn't go to jail. I'd end up being everybody's girlfriend and I couldn't let that happen. I've never been in a situation I couldn't buy or talk my way out of, but I knew he wasn't going to back down. I had to come up with something quick — something outrageous. If I was going down, I was going down with a bang. I cleared my throat, softened my tone and spoke with the most seductive and teasing voice I had.

"Are you sure there's nothing else I can do? Is there anything else you need to see officer?"

"That's it!" He fiercely yanked my car door open and attempted to snatch me by my wrist.

"Wait!" I wailed in desperation.

"Are you sure there's nothing else I can offer?" I proceeded to spread my legs to show the officer my pantiless crotch. My heart was beating through my chest, but I tried to not look too wild-eyed. The seductress in me took over. "You can always see this. You want to touch it?"

"Miss Carmichael! I…" He unleashed my wrist and stared in awe. He looked confused, interested, and guilty all at once.

"Call me by my first name. It's pronounced like *Asia*. I might like the way you say it." I licked my lips and gave him a wink. I could tell he was uncomfortable, but I also saw that I was breaking him down. Glancing at his badge, I addressed him by name.

"So, Officer Denning, do you want it or not? Just remember, if I'm in jail, you can't get any of this. You won't regret it, I promise. So, what's it going to be?"

The officer nervously fumbled with his wedding ring. I could tell he was weighing his options. He moved his glasses to the top of his head. I could see he was trying to be stern but couldn't withstand temptation.

"Hmmm, gray eyes, huh? Nice," I complimented.

"Look, I don't think… I mean, I don't know. You're an attractive woman and all but..." The officer took a step back from my car and stood up straight.

"But what? C'mere. What are you moving away for?" I purred.

Slowly, the officer moved closer to my car. He leaned in like he was going to hear a dirty little secret. I had his attention.

"Yeah, that's right. Don't be scared. Come closer." I insisted. "No one will know except you and me. Now, let's just forget about this situation, and in return… I'll do you an unforgettable favor."

"A favor? I… I don't know if I can do that," he stuttered.

"Why not? I'm not convinced that you're 100% sure about that. Even if you are, I think I can help you change your mind," I said, touching myself seductively. I pulled out all the stops and it was working.

He cleared his throat, attempting to go back into

officer mode. "I have to abide by the law, Miss Carmichael. I cannot accept your offer. Now, please, step out of the vehicle."

"Officer Denning, I told you to call me Aisha." I paused dramatically, still eyeing him.

"Oh, I get it. You must be a new to the force. Trying to do everything by the book, right? I see you over there fiddling with that little ring of yours... contemplating. Well, let me tell you something, Officer Denning. I don't give a damn about your wife or who she is. I'm sure I don't know her but even if I did, I never kiss and tell. That's the *only* rule I abide by. So why don't you just hop into that little car of yours and follow me around the corner to that abandoned warehouse? The parking lot looks empty; it's pretty secluded. No one will even know we're there and we can take care of business then. We'll just say its tit for tat."

I continued to look him up and down.

"Don't worry, you're in good hands. Not a soul will ever know... I promise."

The officer looked around suspiciously and bit his bottom lip. Suddenly his whole demeanor changed.

*Got him!*

"Okay, I'll follow you. You show me a good time and we'll act like none of this ever happened."

"Alright, Mr. Officer, let's go."

He followed me around the corner, and I did what I had to do – no vaginal sex, due to the awful freak session with Nielsen mere hours prior, but I did put my mouth in motion in ways that he probably hadn't felt before. He must have been pretty excited, because things went fast, if you know what I mean.

It didn't faze me much; I was just glad to be free as a

songbird rather than locked up like a jailbird. As soon as his car pulled away, I called to make sure that I could still make it to the salon and not have to wait. They said I'd be fine, so I wiped my mouth, popped a breath mint, reapplied my lip gloss, and was on my way.

# Chapter 2
## Diva Status

"A-sha! Ha you dis mo-ning?" Lee immediately ran to greet me, speaking his usual broken English. He took my right hand into both of his and shook it enthusiastically.

He and his wife owned the small salon, which was located in a shopping plaza on the Southside where I grew up. Some considered it a hole in the wall, but I'd been going there since I was a teenager, and they always treated me like royalty. Great service with a genuine smile; that's what I liked.

"We did not think you come. You late."

"I know. I got stopped by a cop and…"

"You always late, but this time, you *real* late," he laughed.

His accent made me chuckle.

"I'm sorry."

"No worries A-sha. You good. All good. Glad you make it. We not busy. You want SNS today?" Lee's words were short, almost staccato-like, as he pronounced each and every syllable.

"Yeah, I think it's time. Also, eyebrows, upper lip and a deluxe pedicure." I gave my feet a quick glance, turning them side-to-side. It was a fact – I needed the works.

"Ok. Pick out color for toe. We bring nail color to you for SNS."

"Ok, thanks Lee." I grabbed a nearly nude, pink polish and handed it to him. I loved a simple, clean look.

"Eh. Dis boring color. Pick bright color," Lee urged looking at the pale polish.

"Now Lee, you know I work in a professional setting. I can't be all flashy like that. Gotta look the part."

"Professional A-sha, no fun. Old A-sha wear lime green, hot pink." He said passionately, grabbing a brightly colored polish.

"Old A-sha not make money either." I laughed. "New A-sha need to be grown up."

"Ok, ok. Boring color for you today. But next time you get bright color, ok?"

"For you Lee, yes. Next time I'll try it." I smiled.

Lee assisted me to the cushioned pedicure chair. I relaxed, immersing my feet into the tub of warm bubbling water, allowing it to swish freely between my toes.

One at a time, Lee took each foot out of the water, exfoliating and massaging my feet and calves. Lee's wife Lin always pitched in when they were slow; she started on my nails.

"Hold one min, A-sha. Put feet in tub. I be right back," Lee said before sprinting off to assist another young lady.

I leaned back and closed my eyes, soaking up the warmth of the water and freeing my mind of Neilson and the officer. I heard a woman say that she was getting a pedicure, but I shut my eyes before I could catch a glimpse of her. Lee walked her over to my area and directed her to sit in a seat opposite me.

"Oh, no. I'll sit right here next to her. Thanks."

The lady nestled down in the chair adjacent to me. I slyly peeked one eye open. She appeared to be in her mid-thirties and her auburn hair was swept up into a neat, tight bun. Aside from her overly tanned skin, which was leathery in appearance, she was beautiful. Her authentic Birkin bag screamed "kept woman." She was dripping in diamonds, apparently drowning in money.

"Oh, my God, I needed this," the woman spoke aloud as she leaned back and closed her eyes.

"So, what do you think of this place?"

"Who me?" I asked.

"Why, yes. Who else would I be talking to?" she asked snobbishly with sealed eyes.

"It's okay, I guess. I come here often. But I'm pretty sure it's something that you may not be 'accustomed' to."

"Why would you say that?" The lady perked up; her bright, blue eyes now wide open. She looked somewhat offended. However, after I ogled at her bag, she got the hint.

"Oh, well, yes. My ex is very wealthy. When I'm in town visiting, I stop wherever it's convenient for me, and this was convenient for me today. But you're right, I am used to something a little more upscale," she sighed. "But this will just have to do for now. I've been to salons all over the world, flown in private jets, and been waited on hand and foot. Money is never an issue. So, in retrospect, you're right. This is a bit beneath my standards, but it's okay," she bragged.

Although I didn't appreciate her tone, I kinda liked her. She reminded me of, well... me. She was one of those people I wouldn't mind having as a friend. Sure, it would be a love-hate relationship, but it could work. I couldn't knock her style; she was the epitome of what I wanted to be. I envied her, but I refused to show it. My silence must have made her uneasy. She continued.

"Someone told me this was a good place to come, so I came," she said nonchalantly.

"Oh, okay. Wealthy ex, huh? I'm trying to get me one of those."

"Believe me, it is delightful. I've been everywhere, spending *his* money. I have my own yacht, a home in the Hamptons, and vacation property in Nassau, and a condo in Miami. The key is learning to play the game. You know, figure men out like a puzzle. After you put together all the pieces, it's easier to see the big picture. But it takes lots of work – work and power."

"Power?" I inquired. Obviously this chick was playing on a bigger field than I even imagined... one where I wanted to be a star player.

"That's right. It's important to know that we, as women, have the power. Not only *here*... but *here*." She pointed between her legs and then to her head. She spoke slowly to give me time to digest what she was saying.

"We have to use both to our advantage, especially if we want to get ahead. No matter if you have to scheme, manipulate, or lie your way to the top, all that matters in the end is that you *are* at the top. If you don't remember anything else, remember that. These men are just waiting to give their money away, most don't even know it. Our job as women is to figure out how to get it. So, just learn how to get it. Some may call it being a gold digger, but I call it being smart." She winked.

Those were the last words she said to me before taking a call. Lee started working on her pedicure after finishing mine. I spent another half hour or so in the chair while Lee's wife finished my nails and brows. I was silent, thinking about the woman's words. They were direct and ignited me. I knew I needed to step my game up; I needed to get on her level.

"Ok Aisha, you dry." Lee said, leaning over to touch my toes. He sprinted to grab me a pair of flip-flops to put on to prevent smudging. I picked up my things and shuffled my way to the counter.

"A-sha, ninety-fi dolla fo you," Lee announced as he got up and walked to the counter. I followed behind him, pulling out a platinum Visa.

Lee squinted, pulling the card close to his eyes. "This is no you, A-sha? You no Jim Bearing." Lee questioned the credit card that I had given him.

I huffed and rolled my eyes. My mood suddenly changed; I was instantly irritated. *Please don't question me today, Lee— and especially not in front of Ms. Money Bags. Just take the damn card.*

I pulled out a business card that read, "Jim Bearing, Senior Partner: Bearing and Bearing Associates," then slapped down another that said, "Aisha Carmichael, Office Manager: Bearing and Bearing Associates."

"That's where I work, Lee. They haven't given me my bonus check yet so they're letting me use a company card for all of my expenses instead. So, go on… Finish processing the payment." I allowed him a quick glimpse before I swiftly snatched the card from his sight.

"Oh, I so sorry, A-sha. I did not know you work there. I thought you work someplace else. You never paid with this cred-card before." Lee apologized and ran the card through the reader. When he returned the card, I forcefully stuffed it back into my Prada bag.

"Damn right, you thought. Well, you know what? You thought wrong, Mr. Lee. Oh yeah, you might want to make sure that it's not counterfeit before you take it."

I threw a fifteen-dollar tip on the counter before flinging the door open and flouncing out of the building. He put the money in his pocket and sprinted toward the parking lot.

"No hard feelings, A-sha. So sorry. Please come again." He waved.

Lee's words fell on deaf ears. I jumped in my car and blared the music. The only response Lee got from me was the bass from my subwoofers. I skidded off so fast, I left tire marks in the street. He pissed me off with all of those questions. And it was definitely embarrassing that he said it all in front of the diva I'd met over pedicures. Why did he care whose credit card I used as long as he got paid? He was right, no hard feelings though, just an attitude for the day. I knew I'd still go back the following week for my usual pedicure.

After driving for a few minutes, I decided to grab a bite to eat and head to my sister's house. I turned the music off and rode in silence. I couldn't stop thinking about what that woman had said… *Just learn how to get it.* She was right – I needed to up my strategy. Game on!

# Chapter 3
## Tonya

When it came to sibling rivalry, Tonya and I was the textbook definition of it. Though it was more prevalent during our teenage years, it still lingered as adults. I was the bossy, older sister, and she was the baby girl that was the apple of Momma's eye. She got away with nearly everything. In Momma's mind, Tonya could do no wrong, while I was the hell raiser. This created a rift in our relationship. I was convinced that though we were older, Momma still viewed us this way.

Tonya was two years my junior. She was a stunning thing to behold and that alone was enough to stir a constant jealousy within me. She stood around 5'7" with a complexion embellished with yellow undertones. Her warm chestnut eyes always sparkled as they reflected the light. Natural cherry-colored streaks provided just the right amount of shimmer to her dark brown hair. She usually wore it gather back in a low ponytail with soft baby hairs framing her perfectly round face in which a deep dimple was carved into each cheek. She had a playful, youthful look to her, which was very inviting. I suppose this is the way Neilson suggested I look, but I preferred the resting bitch face, just like I preferred to ward off people like Neilson.

I had an older brother who died in a car accident when I was sixteen. The car was mangled, and his body was unrecognizable. We never knew the root cause of the accident. The only thing the police told us was that it seemed he lost control, causing him to ricochet off a building and into oncoming traffic. It devastated us for years and a lot of things changed after we lost him. After all, he was the man of the house. Even though he was young, he always made it his duty to watch over us and take care of the house to the best of his ability. He made sure that he kept us girls in line, including Momma.

We all had different dads, but that never diluted how close we felt. All four of us (Tonya, Drew, Momma, and I) were each other's strength and we often leaned on one another for guidance. After Drew passed, everything changed. Momma was lonely, even with Tonya and me there. I changed too, turning from a naïve teenager to a bitter, bitchy, broken chick. I was angry at the world. It was an anger I never fully worked through and that I unintentionally took out on Tonya. Something that I know she didn't deserve.

Fourteen years later, I still thought about my brother every day. He was my best friend, and although Tonya and I grew closer despite our differences, there was no bond greater than the one Drew and I had shared. Momma still cried a lot, visited his grave every chance she got. Kind of like an old friend, except for this friend couldn't talk back. She would go to the grave site and sing to him, talk to him, and even eat there with his favorite meal. Yes, it sounds morbid, and I initially thought she was losing it, but everyone deals with death in their own way. I lost a brother. I couldn't imagine how Momma felt losing a son—a child that grew inside of your womb and that you raised from a baby to a man. I don't think she'd ever got past his death. Frankly, I knew none of us ever would.

"Come on in, girl. You're letting all the air out," Tonya said while ushering me into her mid-century bungalow. She usually chose tops that revealed her cleavage to best display "Jordan" tattooed on her perky right breast. On this day, she wore a tube top accompanied by a floral wraparound skirt that covered her thick toned legs and hugged her tiny waist. I envied her; she had two kids and a flawless physique. I had no kids but had to work out constantly just to maintain what I had. She was perfect with minimal effort.

Upon entering the house, my niece immediately ran up to wrap her tiny brown hands around one of my thighs. She looked like a replica of my sister with the exception of her cocoa-brown skin. Her long wavy hair was braided back into several cornrows. I kneeled and held out my arms to embrace her and I examined her head and began fiddling with her braids.

"Who did her hair, Tonya? It looks nice," I complimented.

Before Tonya could respond, young Sicily blurted out the name *Denise*.

"Denise? Who's Denise?" I asked my sister.

"Denise is Daddy's girlfriend," Sicily said with her hands on her hips as she tilted her head side to side with each spoken word. Kids tend to get cocky when they're saying something they know they have no business saying.

"Now that's enough, little girl. Auntie A was talking to me, not you. Stop acting so grown… gossiping. Your daddy might let you do that at his house, but you won't be

41

doing that here. Understood? Now go to your room and play. I don't want to hear another word out of you."

"Yes, Mommy." Sicily complied.

"So, who's this new girlfriend Jordan has?" I questioned.

"Correction, she's not his girlfriend anymore – she's his wife." Tonya leaned back on the couch, crossing her arms. She pursed her lips and rolled her eyes.

"Oh! That's the chick? You never told me they got married."

"Yeah, they've been married ever since Gracie was born. I thought you knew that." Tonya paused and turned her head slightly, diverting her attention to the back of the house. "Hold on. I think I hear Gracie crying."

Tonya leaped from the recliner and began a tiptoe sprint toward the baby's room. Tonya returned holding my chubby caramel-colored niece. Her dark gray eyes were glossy from sleep, her light brown hair slightly mussed, and her face was pink. She didn't look like Tonya the way Sicily did, but she did have her mother's dimples. Grace held on to her momma like a baby koala. Tonya sat back on the couch and rubbed her back soothingly as she whimpered, sending her back to sleep.

"Oh my gosh, Grace is looking more like Jordan every minute," I whispered.

"Yeah, it's kind of funny. Sicily looks like me but she's dark like Jordan, and Grace looks like Jordan, but she has my complexion. Either way, there is no denying these kids."

"So, how has Jordan been acting lately?" I pried.

"Same old, same old. He throws money around like it's nothing. The girls have everything they need, and he pays my rent, which helps while I finish school. But money isn't everything; he needs to be a father. Before Gracie was born, he'd come get Sicily all the time. She'd spend the night, and he'd make sure he had her a few days every week. After he got married and I had Gracie, he stopped coming around as much... I don't know what's wrong with him lately but I'm sure his wife plays a part in his absence. I know she's probably upset about Gracie. He said that they've been trying to get pregnant. Then here we go and have another one. She probably hates me for that."

Tonya slid down on the couch and nestled a pillow under her head with Gracie still on her chest. She played the mid-century design well, so her couch was not a plush one. She moved around a bit to get comfortable before continuing. I felt like her shrink.

"He shouldn't have married her in the first place. She just sits around the house doing nothing, according to what he says. I know he's not happy. He doesn't say it, but I can tell. He should have just married... Never mind." Tonya stopped.

I knew she was itching to say that he should have married her instead, but Jordan was a cheater, and she knew that. If he would have put a ring on her finger, she'd be more heartbroken than she already was, guaranteed.

"Tonya, of course he's gonna act like he isn't happy with her; that's what men do. They lie and tell you what you want to hear."

"I honestly doubt that." She shook her head in denial. She took a deep breath and looked at the ceiling in silence, getting lost in her own thoughts. Jordan was the love of her life; she was blinded by him. But I knew Jordan better than she thought and I knew he was no good. However, for the sake of her sanity, I decided not to dig any deeper. The silence was getting uneasy. I could see I was hitting a nerve.

"Look, Tonya, as long as the kids are taken care of, what else is there to worry about? If I were you, I wouldn't even sweat it. Most men are dogs anyway; they're just built like that for some odd reason. I refuse to sit around being the doting housewife while my man is sticking it to another chick when he wants 'something different.' That's why I get what I want from them and that's it. Just think of it like this: men are like toilet paper; no matter if they're an off-brand or a cushioned double ply, somebody's bound to use them. I figure, why not me? Personally, I prefer the double-ply. And for you, my dear sister, Jordan is double ply. He got the looks and the money. Can't go wrong there." I winked.

"And so what if he's married? You see who he keeps coming back to. You were his first love, and you have his kids. His wife doesn't even compare. What you need to do is put your assets to work and play these guys like I do – including Jordan. I know he's your girls' father, but you need to get over the whole jealousy thing. Let him do his married thing and you get his money."

I held my arm in the air and rubbed imaginary cash between my fingers.

"Aisha, you're a nut. I'll never understand how your brain works." Tonya chuckled causing Gracie to squirm. Tonya rubbed the baby's head, gave her a kiss, and went to put her back in her crib.

"Hey, isn't your ten-year high school reunion creeping up on you soon?" she asked when she returned to the living room. She started straightening scattered books and magazines on the coffee table.

"Yeah, it's in three weeks. I'm trying to find that

perfect outfit to make all the heads turn. It's imperative that I stand out. I plan on grabbing me one of those nice fellow classmates who's well off. You know there's always one that makes it out of the bunch. I don't care what he looks like, as long as he's paid. I can see it now… Me using his credit cards to go shopping every day. What a life!"

"You ain't ever gonna change, are you? You're getting too old to be acting like that. Do you ever plan on settling down or getting married one day? Don't you want kids or something? Give me nieces and nephews, dammit." Tonya playfully slapped the edge of the coffee table.

"Please, Tawnie," I scoffed. I stood up and did a slow turn. "And mess up this body? How can you insult me like that?"

"Look at me… I had two babies and I still have a banging body," Tonya confirmed as she smoothed over her curves.

"Yeah, well, we also have different dads, which means different genes. Have you seen the women on my father's side? It's a scary sight. After kids, it's all downhill. Having pancake boobies and a potato-shaped booty doesn't sit too well with me. Aside from that, marriage is for the birds. Prime example? Jordan. He just can't seem to keep his dick in his pants."

"All men don't cheat, Aisha."

Tonya seemed irritated that I called Jordan out on his bullshit, but I figured if she heard the truth enough times, she would get her mind and heart off of him.

"That's bull crap. According to who?" I asked, eyebrows raised and hands on my hips.

"I guess what I'm saying is you're getting older, and you need to slow down a little."

"Slow down? Don't even start with that again. Those are like cuss words to me. I told you before that I am a P-I-M-P."

"No, you're not. You're more like a W-H-O-R-E," Tonya mumbled.

"Oh, whatever. There's easy money to be made. My looks and my body aren't going to last forever, you know."

"Sure, Aisha. Whatever works for you."

"Damn right. Oh yeah, speaking of what's working for me, I've been able to have all my beauty and shopping expenses paid. Like I said... P-I-M-P."

"Oh, God, whose card are you using now?" Tonya shook her head, not shocked at all.

"It's Jim's. Remember, the one I met a few months ago when I was at that luncheon? Well, I got in his head and his wallet quicker than I expected. He may not be the youngest, but he's cute and he let me use his card for whatever I want. I teasingly pulled out the card and waved it in front of my sister.

"On top of that, he made me a business card with my name on it from his firm; it makes me look like I work for his company. You know, just in case I have issues. For instance, Lee questioned me today when he realized my name wasn't on it. So, I just whipped out the handy-dandy business card and *voila*! Everything was A-ok."

"A-ok, huh? Well, you could get into some real trouble falsifying information like that. You and Jim. And you could both lose your jobs. You could lose your *real* job. Like I told you before, using all these men is going to come back on you one day. Karma is real. Besides, you know God don't like ugly."

"Well, if God don't like ugly, I shouldn't have a

problem because I'm oh-so-sexy and beau-ti-ful. God must love me."

Tonya sat back down on the couch and rubbed her temples. She knew she was beating a dead horse. "We all know you're gorgeous, but I will tell you this, A… Looks are not going to carry you through life."

"Says who? It's working for me and obviously it's working for you too, so quit your yapping," I combated.

"Yeah, but I'm also in school trying to make something of myself too. I don't want to have to depend on Jordan for the rest of my life. I guess what I'm saying is that you'll never find a good man with that sort of mindset. If you do, it'll be for all the wrong reasons, and that's not right. Reality is, you just need to grow up."

Now offended, I plopped down on the couch next to my sister to square off face-to-face. "First off, don't talk to me like that. I'll whoop your little ass no matter how old you are or how many kids you have. Remember that. Also, look who's calling the kettle black; before you had Grace you were the biggest gold-digger out here—"

"You're right," Tonya cut me off. "The key words are, 'used to be.' There's more to life than using people and being used. Eventually, you'll get tired of sleeping with these men for money and materialistic things. Besides, you're getting old. You don't think that these men are going to move on to the next pretty young thing who's ready to give up some ass for a little money? If you don't think so, then you're pretty dumb."

Tension and silence fell over the room. I glanced up at the ceiling, avoiding eye contact. I knew what she was saying was true, but I was trying not to hear it. The room was quiet for a short time while we basked in our own thoughts.

Suddenly, the doorbell rang, breaking the awkward silence. Tonya sprang up from the recliner, stumbling over her own feet to answer the door.

"Daddy!" Sicily yelled when she heard the bell ring. She hopped out of her room toward the door like a kangaroo. She began leaping around the living room, twirling around in circles. "Daddy! Daddy! Daddy's here," she screamed.

More excited than Sicily, Tonya adjusted her skirt and tube top. She smoothed her eyebrows with her index fingers and draped her ponytail over her right shoulder. The tip of her hair dangled next to her tattoo. She turned the knob slowly, closed her eyes and took a deep breath. She opened the door calmly as if she wasn't anticipating his arrival.

"Hey, Jordan." Tonya remained calm and relaxed.

"Hey, what's goin' on, Tawnie? And how is Daddy's little girl?" Jordan knelt to hug Sicily, who immediately jumped into his arms and grabbed him around the neck. Her tiny hands knocked his hat to the ground, revealing his short wavy hair. Jordan picked up his hat and placed it on Sicily's head. She laughed hysterically, excited to see her father.

Jordan held his daughter out from his body to adjust his button-up that had been twisted in their bear hug. His designer denim complimented the rest of his attire, and his shoes always looked brand new. Jordan was very muscular and had distinguished features – smooth skin, sparkling, straight white teeth, and good looks. He looked like a model but had taken the path that had led to a career in marketing where he was very successful.

"How is my favorite big girl doing? You've been a good girl for your momma, right?" He squeezed Sicily's cheeks, twisting her head from side to side.

Tonya responded to the question before Sicily could

open her mouth to answer. "Yes, she's been a very good girl." Tonya smiled at Jordan then kissed Sicily on the cheek.

"That's always great to hear. Now where's my baby girl at?"

Jordan walked toward the back of the house where Grace was sleeping. Tonya followed closely behind. When he reached Grace's crib her eyes were slightly opened. She had just awoken from her nap. He scooped her up into his free arm.

"Here are Daddy's only two angels." He kissed both of his daughters while Tonya smiled with admiration.

"Okay, now go to your momma, honey." He handed Grace to Tonya and put Sicily down.

"Alright! You ready to leave with Daddy?" he asked Sicily.

"Yeah, Daddy, I can't wait. I couldn't sleep last night because I want to go swimming in your pool."

"Oh, is that right? So, you're using Daddy for his pool, huh? You little rascal. I thought you wanted to be with me because you love me."

"I do, Daddy, and I love your pool too." Sicily giggled uncontrollably.

"Okay, good enough. Well, go get your things," he instructed.

Sicily ran to her room to get her overnight bag.

"I have her stuff all packed up and Gracie's diaper bag ready too."

Jordan cleared his throat. "Um, baby, I didn't plan on taking Grace with me."

"Wait, you're not taking Gracie? Why not?" she asked.

"I thought we'd already discussed this. You know,

I've been really busy lately. When Sicily is over, I can still work, but when Gracie is over I have to devote a lot of time to her; time I just don't have right now. You understand, right, sweetie? My job can get very demanding at times. You know how it is."

"No, Jordan, I don't know how it is. I'm here all the time with these kids. That's bull!"

Tonya's top lip started to quiver, which often happened when she was really upset and on the verge of tears.

"Okay, Tonya. Calm down. You win; you're right. I didn't think of it like that. But you do have to understand that I have business that I need to take care of. How am I gonna pay the bills here and keep everything in order if I don't handle my business? I'm trying to hold it down here and at home…"

"*Psshhh…* at home," Tonya huffed as she mumbled with a scowl.

Jordan ignored her jealous mumbling and continued. "I'll do whatever it takes to take care of you and the girls, you know that. So as a compromise, I can take Grace for a few hours today to give you some free time, if that's what you need. Then I'll drop her off later tonight. How does that sound?"

"You don't have to worry about taking Grace anywhere. If you don't have time to deal with her, fine! I'm just tired of going through this with you, Jordan."

"Look, Tonya, I have a lot on my plate right now. Please understand that. I'm working hard now so you and the girls don't have to later on. Okay?"

"Whatever. Can you at least spend time with her after you drop Sicily off at school? It would be nice if you actually *spent time* with your youngest daughter. I just don't understand why you treat her differently. You never treat Sicily like that."

"That's nonsense, Tonya. The only reason I treat Grace differently is because she's a little bitty baby. Of course, I can spend time with her Monday. Then later that night we'll all go out to dinner or something. Will that make you happy? Damn!"

Frustrated, Jordan left Grace's room without giving Tonya a chance to disagree. He came back to the living room where I'd been pretending to watch TV. (I was eavesdropping the entire time.)

"What's up, A? How have things been on your end? When I pulled up, I just knew your gold-digging ass was here." He chuckled. "I saw those rims sparkling from down the street. Those new? I see you got some sucker to get them for you, cuz you damn sure didn't buy them yourself."

I cut my eyes at him and sucked my teeth. "You're real funny, Jordan. No, I didn't get them myself. Gotta play the game, right?" I paused. "You should already know how I do it."

"Oh, yeah, out of all people, I know." He gave me a half-smile.

Sicily ran out of her bedroom, interrupting her father's smart remarks. She was anxious to leave.

"I'm ready, Daddy."

"Okay, ladies. Me and my little angel will see you guys in a few days. Oh, and I'll call you to see if we're still on for Monday night," he said to Tonya while giving me a goodbye hug.

He proceeded to walk over to Grace and gave her a gentle kiss on the forehead. Then he pulled Tonya close and whispered in her ear. Although I'm sure he thought he was being discreet, my eavesdropping skills were a force to be reckoned with.

"Maybe Monday when I come back over *we* can get together after the girls go to sleep. You know, spend a little *quality* time. What do you think about that?"

Tonya pulled away, trying not to acknowledge his proposal. He pulled her back to him and kissed her passionately on the lips. Tonya acted like she didn't like it, but I know she did. Just like I knew he was still sexing her up, but she'd never admit it.

"Don't do that again," she said with attitude.

"Yeah, okay, Tonya. I hope you're in a better mood Monday." He smirked. "Tell your momma goodbye, Sicily. Give your baby sister a kiss."

Sicily gave Grace a kiss and skipped out the door. She waited for her father to open the car and buckle her into the backseat of the pearl-colored Navigator. Tonya and I stood in the doorway and waved goodbye. Soon they were out of sight.

"Hmmm? What was all of that about? Look like you got a married man who's doing more than just taking care of his kids. Seems like he's taking care of some other business too. And you were talking about *me* earlier? What a joke. What was Jordan saying about Monday again?"

Tonya ignored me, like she usually did when I asked her private questions about her and Jordan. I knew she was just cringing inside.

Embarrassed, she walked back to the living area, slouched down on the couch with Grace, and turned on the TV. Apparently, she wanted to be left alone.

I didn't say another word, but my point was proven.

We were one in the same.

# Chapter 4
## Pop-Ups

Sundays was my prime time to sleep in. No work the day before and getting well-rested for work the day after. My new position at work was demanding, but the pay was satisfying and more than expected. That alone was enough to keep me going.

I was deep in my Sunday slumber when I was awoken by a rapid knock at the door. Clumsily, I jumped out of bed and threw on a pair of shorts from the floor. With eyes half-open, I stumbled to my closet to grab a t-shirt from the shelf and headed downstairs to answer the door.

"Who is it?" I yelled as I approached the door. I couldn't believe that someone had interrupted my beauty sleep. I didn't know which I hated most – people screwing up my money or screwing with my sleep. Needless to say, I was pissed.

"I said, who is it?" I repeated with full attitude in tow. I leaned forward when I reached the bottom of the stairs, trying to catch a glimpse at who could be standing outside.

Having a modern home with clean lines had its drawbacks—like the glass door my designer Marta thought to incorporate into the design. "Lots of natural light," she said. "More inviting."

But on this day, I didn't want to see any type of light and I damn sure didn't want to invite anyone in.

Then a voice yelled out. It was Tonya.

"What do you mean who is it? It's me," she yelled from the opposite side of the door. I hastily let her in, barely able to open the door before she barged in with two baskets of clothes.

"What in the world are you screaming for," she asked. Her voice echoed through the two-story foyer; my stained concrete floors didn't help cushion the sound. She quickly made her way to the great room, unable to balance the baskets any longer.

I followed.

"I'm screaming because you're banging on my door like some crazy person. I thought you were a crazy pop-up. I hate when people just pop up. Besides that, I was trying to get some much-needed sleep. There's been a lot of long days at the office lately now that I have a senior marketing spot." I yawned.

"Well, I told you I had to wash today. The girls don't have any clean clothes for tomorrow and I sure wasn't about to go to the laundromat."

"Yada, yada, yada." I yawned again.

Tonya always had some excuse as to why she had to do her laundry at my house.

"Let me ask you a question: Why hasn't Jordan bought you a washer and dryer? If that was me..."

"But you're not me. That's the problem. You always want to give someone these scenarios, but you're not even in my situation. He does enough for us already. I want to feel slightly independent, ya know? I don't need him for *everything*."

"Yes, you do," I sassed, even though it was too early in the morning to be arguing.

"Now, like I was saying, if it was me, I would've had a new washer and dryer... possibly even a weekly housekeeper. Why feel bad about it? He can afford it; he takes care of two households. Hell, he could take care of three if he wanted to. He's a married man anyway. He just wants what he wants from you, so you better get what you need from him. You know that man will do anything for his girls. So, if he knows that you've been going out your way to do laundry for them, I guarantee he'll buy you a washer and dryer. Speaking of the girls, where are they at anyway?"

"They went to church with Momma. That's why I thought you'd be up already. Momma said you were gonna be meeting her at church this morning."

Tonya paused, eyeing me. "Don't tell me you forgot?"

I shrugged and playfully fiddled with the bottom of my shirt before answering. "Well... I... um... Let's just say I got a little tied up last night and didn't get any sleep. I'll go next week though."

My sister raised an eyebrow and twisted her lip. "Yeah, right. Don't explain it to me... Explain it to Momma. I'm surprised she hasn't called you yet. You know how upset she gets over broken promises and she sure ain't gonna believe you when you tell her that you're gonna go next week."

"I think she may have called me. My phone is on silent—I didn't want to be interrupted. But if you're so concerned, why aren't you at church with her? Huh?"

"Because I don't wanna be," she said bluntly.

"Well, hell, I don't wanna be either," I added matter-of-factly.

"Well Aisha, the difference between me and you is that I actually have things to do today."

"Well, I don't have a damn thing to do because Sunday is my day of rest. So, you see, I'm still honoring God on the Sabbath. Thank you Jesus for my day of rest. Amen." I sarcastically through my arms in the sky and shook my hands with open palms.

"Not funny, Aisha."

I smirked.

"Besides, I should've figured you were occupied when I saw an extra Jag sitting outside. Day of rest my ass," she mumbled.

She continued sorting clothes, making piles of whites, darks, and delicates.

I said, 'Day of Rest' not 'Night of rest.' So due to my wonderful time last night, now I'm resting." I flopped down on the armless couch, propping a throw pillow under my head for comfort.

I used my forearm to shield my eyes from the bright morning rays. Again, 'Floor-to-ceiling windows,' Marta said. 'Tons of natural light,' she said. I was kicking myself in the ass for this concept

"Whatever, A, I'm sure you have an earful coming." Tonya scooped up a large load of clothes into her arms and headed to the laundry room, which was adjacent to the kitchen. Socks and undergarments made a trail from the great room through the open-concept kitchen. She was a modern-day Hansel and Gretel—with clothes being the breadcrumbs.

A few moments passed before she returned to pick up the stray clothes. She paused and I could feel her standing over me. I slowly pulled my arm from my face to acknowledge her presence. The sun was blinding, and I squinted one eye, seeing only her silhouette.

"What the hell are you looking at?" I asked.

She gazed at me strangely without answering.

Tonya pointed to my shorts, and I looked down in disbelief. *Boxers*! I'd picked up the wrong shorts when I rolled out of bed. I looked around slyly and whispered as I proudly pointed at the pair of Gucci boxers.

"This one... this one upstairs is taking me shopping today and on vacation next month. I'm definitely taking him to the reunion with me."

Tonya mumbled the word *slut* under her breath and prepared the next load, this time putting the clothes in a basket to prevent stragglers.

Before she could make it to the laundry room, she let out a frightening squeal and dropped her basket of clothes. I leaped from the couch to see what was wrong and found her face to face with my overnight guest.

Tony was a professional light-heavyweight boxer. He stood about 5'10" and was a medium-built, dark-skinned man. The small towel wrapped around his waist revealed his toned legs, chiseled abs, and rock-hard chest. His features were very masculine and well-defined. A permanent scar was carved above his right eye. He tightened his towel before bending over to help with the clothes now on the floor. He was indeed a stunning man.

"Oh, I see you met my sister," I said with my hand out as an informal introduction. "I thought you were still asleep."

"Well, I was on a mission to find my boxers, but I see you got to them before I did." He looked me up and down before flashing a million-dollar smile.

I looked down at the boxers I was wearing and back at him with sexy eyes.

"Oh, yeah, these. I was in such a rush I threw the closest thing on. If I didn't have to come downstairs, I wouldn't have anything on. I'd still be in bed with you."

I flirtatiously twirled a curl around my finger, attempting to divert the attention from my sister. Focused on helping pick up the rest of the clothes, he paid me no mind.

"I am so sorry. I didn't mean to startle you. I came down the back stairs and I didn't know anyone else was here. This is a weird introduction, but I'm Tony." He held his towel tightly with his left hand and extended his right one to shake Tonya's hand.

Seemed to me he had a sort of "come hither" look in his eyes. I glanced at Tony, then at Tonya. Before she could tell him her name, I interrupted.

"This is my little sister, Tonya. Oh, baby, and no need for apologies. You wouldn't have run into her if she didn't have to come over so early."

I softly grabbed Tonya's shoulder and forced a smile. "She's over here washing her kids' clothes because her idiot baby daddy hasn't bought her a washer and dryer yet. Isn't that right, Tonya?"

"Well put... in true Aisha fashion." Tonya shook her head, snatched up the basket, and marched toward the laundry room.

Tony sneered at me.

I didn't care. He wasn't going to be all flirty with my sister. I knew that look; he gave me that look all the time.

"What? What did I do?" I attempted to look confused and innocent at the same time.

(Back to Rule #1 when it comes to lying: Feigned innocence is key.)

"C'mon, you know that wasn't necessary. Go talk to your sister." Tony gave a nod as if to say *get to moving*, before he walked away to head back upstairs. I huffed and went to the laundry room. I guess I had to make it right.

"What's your problem now, Tonya?" I needed to remain firm. I didn't think there was anything wrong with what I said, but I guess both of them disagreed.

"You. You're the problem. Why do you feel the need to belittle me in front of your own man? I don't want him, so you don't have to down me in front of him. You always feel the need to be one step ahead of the game, huh, Aisha?"

"What're you talking about? What do you mean?"

"What do I mean? I mean that little comment you just made. He doesn't need to know all my personal business. You tried to embarrass me because you felt insecure, but you made a fool out of yourself instead I've been around you way too long and I know how you think. When the attention isn't on you, you trip. Point blank."

Tonya's words offended me, but I kept my composure until she took it too far. I lowered my voice before addressing her—arguing through clenched teeth. My finger was mere inches from her face. Although I lowered my voice, I want her to really *hear* my words.

"Let me tell you one thing. If you're saying that I'm a jealous person, I'm not. Who do you think you're speaking to? Who do I need to be jealous of? You? Please. I'm overly satisfied with being me, thank you. I can have any man I want, whenever I want, and however I want. I don't give a damn if Tony was paying attention to you or not. I just want his money, that's all. No strings attached. So that little attitude you caught out there was unnecessary because you're the one who got things twisted," I hissed.

"No, you got things twisted. It ain't that serious. You're the one who's taking it to another level, Aisha. You…"

A knock at the door interrupted our spat. I peeked around the corner of the laundry room. The open concept kitchen gave an A-line view to the front door. A small, short figure peered through the glass. It was Momma. I knew what I needed to do. I immediately reconciled with Tonya, diffusing the argument.

"Okay, whatever. You're right, I'm wrong. Just go answer the door. It's Momma."

"What? What's she doing here? I guess I'll go get the door," Tonya huffed with frustration.

"Wait," I whispered frantically. "I don't care what she's doing here, but you know that I was supposed to go to church with her today, so let me go upstairs first so I can tell Tony to stay up there. Just act like I'm asleep. I don't want her saying anything crazy to me about not being at church."

I slid against the wall ninja-style to get to the back stairwell. At this point I was thanking God that Marta suggested adding it. I sprinted through the hall upstairs to get to the front stairwell, where I perched down behind a large planter at the very top, ready to spy.

By this time, the knocking was insistent; Momma was practically beating down the door. Tonya moseyed out of the laundry room to give me time to vanish. Momma impatiently continued knocking, even when Tonya was in clear view.

"Bout time you came to the door, movin' round all slow." Momma said when Tonya opened the door.

"Well, hello to you too, Momma. You're early. Where are the girls?"

"They're knocked out in the car, all tuckered out. All that hoopin' and hollerin' at church today scared poor Gracie. She cried her lil' self right on to sleep."

"Are you dropping them off now? I thought you were keeping them all day."

"Well, Sister Houston wants me to help her set up the baptismal. We have a baptism this evening at five. I don't know if I can take the kids with me."

Momma peered over her oval-shaped glasses like she always did when she talked, while speaking in her southern vernacular.

Unlike Tonya and I, my mother did not have a long lean body; she was short and round. Momma had a thing for tall men back in the day, so Tonya and I ended up being five-seven and five-eight-ish. My brother had been six feet tall, a whole foot taller than Momma.

Though my mother was short and plump, she was an incredibly beautiful woman; she was mixed (half black and half white) and her dark reddish-tan complexion reminded me of an island girl. On this particular day she was dressed in a red and black suit and wore fiery red lipstick. Her long wavy hair flowed from beneath the big red hat she had paired with red lace gloves. It was really too hot outside to be dressed in all that, but that's just the way Momma got down.

Tonya's words were whiny and drawn out. "Mom-maaaa... I just started washing, Ma. You know that Jordan acts like he's always busy, so I won't have anyone to watch them. C'mon, just this one time? I don't even ask you to babysit that much." Tonya clasped her hands together and bounced slightly on her toes like the whiny little brat she was.

"Alright," Momma said, "those puppy dog eyes of yours remind me of when you were little. I can't say no to that. But I'm bringing them back to you before the baptismal service. I can't concentrate on the Lord with chil'ren running round. Make sure you're at home on time, you hear?" Momma said sternly.

Tonya obliged and mumbled a faint *mmm hmm* to hurry her on her way. Just when I thought the coast was clear, Momma pushed past Tonya and was now standing in the foyer. I knew she wasn't going to let me off the hook that easy.

"Where she at?" Momma stretched her neck to look into the great room and into the kitchen.

"Who?"

"Chile, you an owl all the sudden? You know who, the fast-tailed one."

By this point I was stiff as a board, hoping not to ruffle the leaves of the foliage in the planter.

"Oh, Aisha? She's upstairs sleeping."

Tonya was now doing double duty—looking outside to supervise her sleeping daughters in the car and inadvertently guarding Momma from moving further into the house.

"Um, huh. I don't believe that for a second. You know the Lord don't like liars, and I hate a liar. Why she tell me she was coming to church today and didn't?" Momma yelled up the stairs so I could hear her loud and clear.

"Little fast ass, I know how you are. The devil sho-nuff busy."

Momma walked up two stairs at a time like a police dog sniffing out drugs.

"Momma," Tonya yelled, stopping our mother in her tracks.

"Girl, you ain't got to tell me. I ain't goin' up those stairs. I know the girls are in the car, gonna get back to them in a moment. But I do know this... it smells like you-know-what up there. I ain't gonna say it because I'm a Christian woman, but I will tell you this: You need to spray some air freshener up there and wash out your coochie... with some bleach... and probably your mouth too!"

Tonya sniggered. I know this felt like ultimate payback for the whole Tony ordeal.

Momma was little, but boy, was that lady gutsy. There was no stopping her once she got started; one embarrassing comment after another.

"Well, it's the truth. Tell the truth and shame the devil, is my motto. What's done in the dark will surely come to the light. My good Lord makes sure of that. She's just as brazen as she wants to be. She's been fast ever since she was little. You better be glad one of my knees is bad because I'd come up there and tell you off face to face. I'd tell that rusty man you got up there the same thing too because I know you got one up there.

"Now I'm all worked up. I'm not even gonna waste my time or breath on that little heffa. *Wooo!* She got me sweating in my good church clothes and my new hat. You know, Tawnie, sometimes I wish I had waited for your daddy to come along to have all three of you. She got so much of her daddy in her, it's ridiculous. He was just as barefaced too, but worse. And my baby boy, rest his soul, was no saint. Oh, this is too much, Lord... Just too much. My blood pressure is gonna go up, doing all of this screamin' and carryin' on. I'm leaving. Not wastin' no more breaths on this foolery."

Momma wiped her forehead with a small napkin and gave Tonya a kiss on the cheek before leaving. She was such a drama queen.

Thank God Tony was in the shower… he hadn't heard a thing. Tonya walked her to the car and checked on the kids.

Once I heard her come back in the house, I ran down the back stairs, just to play it safe. I'm glad I did, because no sooner than Tonya had come back to the laundry area to share a laugh about our crazy momma, when a series of knocks came from the door again.

*Shit, what does she want now?*

Assuming it was Momma, Tonya sprinted off to open the door while I hid in the laundry room, hoping the conversation would be quick. Instead, I heard a man's voice. I quickly popped my head out to see who it was.

*Fuck…* it was Jim.

Jim was a tall Caucasian man, very tan and well-groomed, in his late forties or early fifties. (He told me how old he was but once he'd given me his Visa, I forgot about all of the little conversations we'd had.) His slightly spiked salt and pepper hair showed his modern style. He wore a fashionable Italian suit with glasses to match, and his nails were always neatly manicured. Before he spoke, he took off his shades to expose crystal-blue eyes. His extraordinarily good looks left Tonya in awe.

"Well, hello there. Is Aisha home?" Jim asked politely.

"Oh, I'm so sorry. I'm Aisha's sister and I thought

you were our mother. See, she just left a second ago." Tonya pointed down the street.

"Oh, okay. I see." Jim nodded.

An awkward silence followed.

"Unfortunately, Aisha isn't here at the moment. Do you want me to give her a message when she comes back?"

Jim turned around and looked at the multiple cars sitting in the driveway. "Hmmm... I see," he said in a particular voice.

"Oh, yeah, her car. I dropped her off at our cousin's house this morning. They're all hanging out over there today... barbecuing and stuff. I used her car to come over here to do laundry, you know, getting it out of the way early."

Tonya gave him an innocent grin. She wasn't usually a very good liar, but suddenly, she became a natural.

"Oh, okay, very well then. I'll just give her a call later. Tell her that Jim stopped by to pick something up. It's urgent, so if you can please give her that message for me as soon as possible."

"Sure, no problem. I'll be sure to tell her," Tonya assured him as she waved goodbye. He stuck his hands in his pockets and walked back to his car.

I slid down the wall and sat on the floor (talk about pop-ups).

Tonya returned to the laundry room.

"Whoa, that was a close one. I'm glad Tony's upstairs getting dressed. You know, he thinks he's the only one I'm dating. That damn Jim would have ruined everything." I sighed with relief and rubbed my temple.

"I'm not going to keep lying and covering up for you, Aisha. That's the second time in five minutes! I'm not gonna be here every time you need to get out of a jam. You need to be more careful. But I have to admit, he's hot. I'm just surprised he's white. You usually go for the chocolatey brothas... Case in point, the one upstairs. Why the sudden interest in white men?"

"You know I don't discriminate – black, white, yellow, I don't care. The only color I care about is green – If he's got green, I'm fucking him. Jim is the one whose credit card I have. He's borderline stalking me, trying to get it back. But he's not gonna get it back until I feel like I'm done using it, and right now, I'm not certain when that'll be. He shouldn't have given it to me if he was gonna keep pestering me about it. If he's gonna keep harassing me, he won't get it back at all. He might as well just cancel it."

"Well, if he had any sense at all, it should've been cancelled. Why don't you just give the man back his card before he gets crazy with you?"

"Crazy with me? Jim? No, he's not like that. He's a softie, and softies like to be used. It gives them a sense of worth in this world, like someone needs them or something. Besides, he has lots of money... He won't miss it. He just needs to keep paying the bill and I'll be happy. He's supposed to be happily married, but obviously now I got the dirt on him. He better not mess with me. I'll go to Lilly Path Way and tell his wife everything I know and ruin his happy little marriage," I retorted.

"Okay, Aisha, all these games you're playing aren't right. I hope you wake up before one of these guys goes Mike Tyson upside your head. I know I would if I were one of them. That's why I am glad I was born a woman; if I were a man, I'd probably have numerous domestic violence cases just because of chicks like you. I just pray that God has mercy on you."

"All of that church talk is making you sound more and more like Momma. Seriously, you don't have to worry about me; I'm a big girl. I know what I'm doing. I know how to play the game."

# Chapter 5
## Face-off

"Hello?" Tonya answered the phone slightly out of breath.

"What is the deal-i-o? Jordan must be over there," I said. "Am I interrupting something?" With all the heavy breathing I figured she must've been in the middle of some sexercise.

"Ha, ha, ha, very funny. Trust me, if you were interrupting something, I wouldn't have answered the phone. I'm just running around trying to get the kids situated for bed. Why? What's up?"

"Girl, you wouldn't believe what happened to me today."

I barely gave Tonya a chance to respond. "I said, you would *not believe* what happened to me today," I shouted, this time overly excited.

"Must be something juicy. Hit me."

"Okay, so Tony and I went on a little shopping spree today. The day was going perfect—had a nice little lunch, went to the Riverwalk, and headed back to my place to unwind. But when we got back, Jim was sitting in the driveway."

"Nooo…" Tonya gasped.

69

"Oh, yeah, but that's not all. So, I told Tony to stay in the car while I went to talk to my 'travel agent.' I know… that was weak, but it was the first thing that came to my mind. I mean, it was too late to turn around; that would've seemed too suspicious. So, I got out of Tony's car and went over to talk to Jim. Girl, do you know he had the audacity to ask me who I was riding with?"

"So, what did you tell him?"

"I told him the truth. I told him that it was none of his damn business who I was riding with. He went ballistic. He got out of the car and started yelling, 'You bitch, you little scandalous bitch! You max *my* credit card out and then want to ride around with that… that nigger? I'll show him a thing or two!'"

"What? That's crazy. I know he didn't go there."

"Oh, yes, he did. I was just waiting for him to call me one, but he didn't get a chance to. He was screaming and yelling so loud that Tony heard him. Before he even got a chance to walk over to the car to challenge Tony, Tony got out of his car."

"Uh oh. Then what?" Tonya inquired.

"Well, Tony said, 'What did he call me?' and I told him to ask him for himself. Tony asked Jim, and he was stupid enough to repeat what he said. He was yelling, 'Yeah, I said it. I called you a nigger because that's what you are. What're you gonna do about it, buddy?' Then Jim took two fingers and pushed Tony's shoulder. I was thinking, oh damn, Jim messed up now. There were no more questions after that. Tony beat him to a bloody pulp like he was in the boxing ring or something. Poor Jim hardly had a chance to swing back. I was screaming for him to stop. I thought he was gonna kill him! He gave me the craziest look and kept

70

drilling him. Hell, I thought I was gonna be next. But after the last blow, he just walked to his car and left Jim lying in the driveway. He threw shopping bags out of the car and yelled, 'Take this, you piece of trash! I can't believe you. The only thing you were good for was sex anyway. Don't call me. Don't come over. Don't ask me for a damn thing! I don't want to ever see your face again.' Then he slammed the door and sped off.

"Now, Jim's all messed up. I think his jaw is broke or something. I know he had blood gushing from his head; I didn't really get a good look at him but from what I saw, he was done for. Jim must've been scared to death because at first he was threatening me, saying he was gonna call the police and that I was gonna be held liable since it all took place on my property. But when the police arrived, he told them someone tried to rob him. Maybe he said that so that his wife wouldn't see what really happened on the police report. I don't know. I just know Jim's in the hospital right now and Tony is MIA."

"Damn, that's deep, A. I told you something crazy was going to happen. You better be glad you didn't get hurt. So, your neighbors didn't say anything to the police?"

"Well, you know the old black man across the street ain't gonna say anything and the Asian people next to him don't speak a lick of English. My neighbors to the right of me are on vacation and the lady to the left works evenings. With all the tall trees around my house, it's hard to see anything anyway. The police asked me if I saw anything and I told them I'd heard some noise, but by the time I came outside, the guy was gone."

"And they believed that?" Tonya asked.

"Yeah. What else would they believe? We both said

the same thing and no one else saw anything. Why would they think we'd lie about something like that?"

"Well, apparently you both *did* lie. And you better quit playing folks or the next time it might be you getting a beat-down. It might be a good ass-whooping though. They might knock some sense into you."

"Whatever... Like that would ever happen. Who would want to mess up this pretty face?"

"Aisha!"

"What?"

"So, you're not even concerned with what happened to Jim? Shouldn't you try to see him at the hospital?"

"He's alright. Even if he wasn't, that's not my problem; that's for his wife to worry about. He needs to be beat on for cheating anyway. Giving away all that money that he should be spending on his family," I scoffed. "Shame on him. From this day forward he'll think again before he tries to get something back from me, that's for sure. You know, bad things happen to bad people, Tonya. That's the way this world works."

"What makes you so much better? Using people and sleeping with a married man...."

"Hah! And you would be the one to talk about sleeping with a married man? You have no room to talk. You can't give me advice on something that you do yourself."

"Look, my situation is different, and you know that," Tonya attempted to justify her own actions.

"Wrong is wrong, Tonya, and *you* know *that!*"

# Chapter 6
## White Lies

It was a few days before the reunion, and I was preoccupied with perfecting my ensemble. I picked up each piece and adorned my body like I was preparing for a grand ball. I slid the black, satin halter dress over my head and wiggled it over my hips. It was already well steamed, but I smoothed it from top to bottom until the last little wrinkles fell free. The dress cinched my waist perfectly and had a daringly low neckline that stopped right above my naval. A large faux ruby rested at the peak of a high slit as the rest of the material swept the floor. I delicately slipped on my stilettos, which were detailed with red satin straps that tied around the ankle and a small black satin strip across the top of the foot. I accessorized with a classic black satin handbag, small ruby stud earrings, and a matching bracelet. I modeled in the mirror for a few good minutes before disrobing. *This is it. This is perfect.*

After I stowed my dress, shoes, and accessories away, I was ready for a bubble bath. I swaddled myself in my white cotton robe and entered the master bathroom. Hot water filled the oval-shaped tub causing the bathroom to steam up with a misty haze. I pinned my hair to the crown of my head, eased into the water, and closed my eyes. The bubble bath quenched my skin with delight. Moisture beads and oils from the body wash soothed every inch of me and by the time I got out, my fingers and toes were pruned. Slightly damp, I massaged oil over my entire body, leaving my skin silky smooth. I blew out the scented candles.

As soon as I walked out of the bathroom, the house phone rang. I grabbed it and flopped down on the bed without looking at the caller ID.

"Hello?"

"Yeah," a deep male voice responded from the other end.

Not knowing who it was, I hesitated and looked at the caller ID, attempting to match the voice with the phone number. It read an unfamiliar number.

"Yeah? What do you mean, 'yeah'? Who is this?" I demanded.

The man took a deep sigh. "It's Tony."

"Who?" I asked again. I was unable to make out his muffled voice.

"I said, Tony! Damn, you don't know my voice anymore? I'm at my sister's house, so if you're screening calls, like I know you do, that's why you don't recognize the number. I thought maybe you'd still be able to recognize my voice though. Do you have *that* many men calling your house phone?"

"No, sweetie. I know your voice, I just—" Before I was able to produce a lie, he interrupted.

"Cut the act, Aisha. I know you're full of games and lies. What happened the other day could've been avoided if you'd have just kept it real. I know you knew that man when we first pulled up. I could've gone to jail, or someone could be dead right now. Did you ever think about that, or do you only think of yourself? The only reason I stepped in is because he said something about me. So, don't flatter yourself by thinking we were fighting over you. Hell, he had the right to cuss you out. He must be one of your sugar daddies."

"No, it's not like that. I'm sorry, baby," I attempted to calm my current money source. (Rule #2 when it comes to lying: Stick to your story.) No matter what he said, I wasn't going to stray from saying that I was wrong, and he was totally right. Like the lady in the salon had said, sometimes you have to scheme, manipulate, and lie your way to the top. I was trying all three in this case.

"Man, stop being so phony and don't baby me. I'm done with you. The only reason I called is to set you straight and let you know how I feel before ending this, so there's no confusion. Yes, I may be a flirt, but it's just my nature. Your nature is to be a gold-digging bitch. I thought you were different, but you turned out to be *worse* than these other girls. So, find some other trick to take you out to eat and shop, because I ain't doing it anymore. Oh, and as far as that reunion of yours goes, you can shove it. Go with one of your other dudes."

Tony's words left me speechless, my mouth open in disbelief. I didn't get a chance to respond to anything he said because the only sound I heard from the other end was the echo of the dial tone.

"That bastard. That's alright, he's right. I don't need him," I shouted.

I couldn't believe he dissed me. I couldn't believe he wasn't going to my reunion. I wanted so badly to show up with someone of his caliber. I guess that was ruined now. I knew everyone would know who he was. Entering the event with him would've made me a superstar for the night. I took a few deep breaths and called Tonya.

"What's up, my cutest, most favorite little sister? What are you doing?"

"I'm your only little sister, Aisha, so what do you want? I know that conniving voice from anywhere."

"Well, I was wondering if you wanted to go to my reunion with me. I was sitting in the bathtub thinking, and I realized something: I was going to take Tony with me, but why do that when there are going to be other men there? I might meet someone who sparks my interest, and I won't be able to engage the way I want with Tony tagging along. So, I told him I was going to take you instead. He was a little heartbroken, but he'll get over it. What do you say?"

I knew it was a little white lie, but I wasn't about to admit to the rejection. Plus, if she knew she was a last resort, she wouldn't go.

"Hello?" The silence was killing me. I needed a wingman, and I anticipated her accepting my proposal. My heart was thumping and the five second pause was killing me. I knew she wasn't convinced, and I had to sweeten the deal.

"We can go out shopping to find you the perfect dress tomorrow when I get off work. My treat," I added.

"Oh, alright, I'm game," she said.

*Bingo!*

"Oh shit."

*Oh shit?*

"I forgot Jordan and Denise are going to be out of town this weekend to visit her family. I won't have anyone to watch the kids."

"That's what you're 'oh shitting' about? Those are

76

his kids too. He can take them for a couple of days; they're all part of Denise's family no and whoever doesn't like that, well, screw them. But if worse comes to worst, there are such things as babysitters you know."

"I know. The only thing is, Gracie has a cold, and I don't…"

"That girl's gonna be okay. She'll be in good hands, don't worry about it, we'll work it out."

"Okay, okay. Let me just give Jordan a call so he can watch the girls tomorrow. Pick me up around six?"

"Sounds good, I'll be there."

~

The next day rolled around, and I was exhausted after work. Long days in my new role left my fried. All I wanted to do was to go home, nestle up in my plush bed with a bowl of Ben & Jerry's, and watch a cheesy chick flick. But at the same time, I knew it was imperative to get Tonya a dress. It was the only way she'd go to my ten-year soiree. So instead of retiring for the evening, I headed to her place as planned.

In a rush, I hastily parked crooked, half in the driveway and half in the street, and sashayed up to the house and urgently rapped on the door, cigarette in hand. My new position had me resorting to my old ways; puffing the little nicotine stick put my mind at ease. To my surprise, when she answered she also had something in her hand – Grace. I was bewildered.

"I thought you said Jordan was coming to pick them up?" I said as I walked in the house.

"Aisha," she admonished, staring wide-eyed at my lit cigarette.

"What?"

Tonya stared at Grace and then glared at the cigarette now dangling from my mouth.

"Do I really need to say it?" she replied.

"Oh, get over it. She ain't supposed to be here anyway. Besides, we have smog and pollution all over this city. You think a little secondhand smoke is really going to *kill* her? Which do you think is worse? Smoke or smog… Smog or smoke? You choose." I teetered my hands in the air in a scale-like fashion.

"Aisha… Really!" Tonya yelled.

"Okay, okay, I'll put it out. But if they spend the night over my house, they won't be exempt from the Smoke Monster." I took a few quick puffs before putting it out.

"And that's why they'll never spend the night." She watched to make sure I actually put the cigarette out before continuing the conversation.

"Okay, so here's the deal. Jordan came and took Sicily, but he said that he couldn't take Grace because she's sick and he wouldn't be able to take care of her like I can. So, he figures it'll be best if she stays with me."

"He figures? Well, it seems like Mr. Jordan is making a whole lot of decisions on his own. Didn't you tell him we had a reunion to go to this weekend?"

"Yeah, that's why he gave me money for a sitter, just in case."

"A babysitter? Wait a god damn minute. Did you hear what you just said? This doesn't make sense. He thinks his daughter is too sick for him to watch, but it's okay for someone else to watch her? Uh-uh, that's not right, Tawnie. Now what're we gonna do? What about finding a dress today? What about the reunion this weekend? How come that wife of his can't help out? That's her stepdaughter, you know. That's alright… Imma call his black ass."

"What? Wait, what are you calling him for?" Tonya wailed.

"I wanna know what the hell's going on - why he can't watch his own daughter. I'm the auntie; I have a right to know."

"No, A. It's not even that serious. I'll just have Momma watch her."

"No, uh-uh… He needs to man up to his responsibilities. If you want him to keep her for one night, *one funky night,* he should be able to do that."

"Calm down, girl. I'm going to the reunion regardless. I mean, I can kinda see it from his point of view. Besides, I'd rather care for her myself than have Denise watch her. I don't even talk to that woman; we've never had a real one-on-one conversation. I don't know what she's about and she doesn't know me. Sicily says she's nice, but she can talk and tell me what's going on; Gracie can't. You know what I'm saying?"

"Yeah, I get you. You're right, I guess. You know Momma will watch her. But, in the meantime, you need to stop making excuses. Stop taking up for that man. He shouldn't always have excuses on why Grace can't spend the night or come over. He shouldn't have favorites between his kids. That's what it seems like to me," I said with my hands on my hips.

Tonya looked offended. I knew she would be, but I had to let the truth be known.

"He loves both his girls the same. He just doesn't want to keep Grace when she's sick. He knows he can't care for her like I can. Plus, he's taking Sicily a few places and I don't want my baby out being exposed to all those germs. She'll get sicker than she already is. Besides, what makes you think you know him that well, saying that he chooses favorites?"

I rolled my eyes and strutted into the kitchen to raid the refrigerator. "Whatever, Tonya. I know Jordan better than you think, and you know as well as I do that he ain't right."

Tonya waved me off and walked away.

"Gotta get Grace's diaper bag and stroller," she yelled from the other room.

I shrugged my shoulders and made myself a ham and cheese sandwich. I plopped on the counter and scrolled through social media to pass the time.

Several minutes went by, giving me enough time to finish my sandwich and more than enough time for Tonya to gather Grace's things.

"You ready yet?" I bellowed impatiently.

"*Umpf!* Yep, ready," she yelled from the family room while fumbling with Grace's diaper bag, her purse, and a stroller, all while Grace was on her hip.

I jumped off the counter and walked over to assist her. "Give me this… What you got in this thing?" I scoffed. "You look like a damn… *Umpf…* Fool. *Umpf!* Put this down… All she need is a bottle, some diapers, and a pacifier. Never mind, give me the kid."

"Come here, Gracie… Come to Auntie so Mommy can put some of that shit down." I spoke in a babyish voice and held out my hands to help minimize Tonya's load.

"Aisha, don't use that language in front of her." Tonya turned to shield Grace, muffling her ear with her free hand.

"Girl, whatever. She can't even understand what I'm saying yet." As soon as I touched my niece to take her, she started crying uncontrollably. (I guess she didn't like my cursing either.) I quickly threw my hands up in the air in surrender. I don't do crying babies.

"Alright, guess I'm stuck carrying the diaper bag. Let's roll."

# Chapter 7
## The Reunion

The day of the reunion finally arrived, and Tonya decided to spend the night at my house after a hard night of partying. Since Momma ended up keeping Gracie, Tonya had a free night and didn't want to waste it. We decided to go to a swanky lounge spot in the city and club-hopped a bit after that. It was 5am before we made it back to my place and I was so tired. Nevertheless, the ringing of the clock pierced my ears at 10am.

"Ummm, not yet. It's too early." I smacked the snooze button and rolled over. Seconds later, Tonya sprinted from the guest bedroom to make sure I was up.

"Aisha! Did I just hear that clock go off?"

My only response was a loud snore. I didn't care what time it was or where we had to be – I didn't feel like getting up yet. Tonya insistently tapped me on the shoulder and started yelling.

"Hello! Wake up. We got hair appointments at noon, remember?"

Her yelling startled me, causing me to leap from the bed. I was sleeping so hard that my hair was stuck to the right side of my face, and I had pillow imprints on my face.

"Dammit, girl. You scared me. I'm up, I'm up. How

did you hear that clock from in there anyway?" I swept the stuck hair from my cheek and rubbed the side of my face.

"It's called 'a mother's ear.' It's time for you to get your drunk ass up. We got stuff to do today. Nobody told you to get drinks from everybody in the club."

"Correction, I didn't accept drinks from everyone in the club; they were practically forcing them down my throat."

"Aisha, the only reason they were getting you all liquored up is because they wanted to take you home. Thanks to me, Captain Save-a-ho, you're lying in your own damn bed. Now get up or we're going to be late for our hair appointments."

"I almost forgot. Alright, I'm going to jump in the shower." I walked to the bathroom rubbing the sleep from my eyes.

Tonya went downstairs to get ready, pulling her hair to the back and applying a dab of lip gloss. She threw on a t-shirt, blue jean capris and flip-flops, and sat on the couch to watch TV until I was finished.

I pulled my hair into a tight ponytail, allowing curls to dangle from the nape of my neck and on both sides of my face. I put on a halter top, a mini skirt, and a pair of pumps. My makeup was flawless, including eyeliner, shadow, and lip gloss. I met Tonya in the living room, and she raised an eyebrow in confusion.

"Took you long enough. Why are you trying to look all supermodel? Your hair doesn't need to be done – we about to go *get our hair don*e.

"Well, you know I got to look fly." I shimmied. "There's no telling who you're going to run into."

I grabbed my Gucci bag and looked in the mirror.

That was my philosophy: *Never get caught slipping.* When you live in a big city, you must look your best at all times, even if you're going to get your hair done.

"Girl, you're a mess. Let's go." Tonya ushered me out the door and we took off in my car.

Traffic was smooth as butter—just the way I liked it. No tension, no horn blowing, no crazy asshole cutting me off. We had about forty-five minutes to kill when Tonya suggested we grab a bite to eat… at McDonalds.

"McDonalds? I don't think so. You know I don' eat that crap. "

"What do you mean, we don't eat that crap?" She confronted me with somewhat of an attitude.

"You know I don't eat that fast food stuff – especially McDonalds. I'm on my keto and counting my macros…"

"Keto? Macros? Really? I could've sworn you were just eating a ham and cheese sandwich at my house the other day, and let's not talk about macros after those drinks you had last night… That was about five cheeseburgers worth."

I rolled my eyes, flying past an exit that clearly had McDonalds listed.

"Seriously? I know you don't think that you're too good for McDonalds," Tonya sassed.

"Yes. Actually, I do. I'm too good for a lot of things," I fired back looking directly at her, hands still on steering wheel She shot me a look that said, 'eyes back on road,' then continued to blab off.

"You're too good? Are you serious? We grew up eating pork-n-beans and hot dogs. You don't have room to say that you're too good for this or too good for that."

"Yes…. I… do," I over-annunciated. "I have options now. I have expensive taste in everything, including food. If you don't like it, that's your problem."

My sister rolled her eyes.

"Damn you and your expensive taste— I'm hungry. We always go wherever you want to eat, but when I want to eat it has to be a big hassle. I just want something quick and easy. I want McDonalds!" She went into full tantrum mode.

"Alright, we'll stop at the Golden Arches. Quit whining like a little kid. You want a Happy Meal too? Damn!"

I veered off onto the nearest exit. I never thought I'd say it, but I'd never been so happy to pull into a fast-food joint. But by that point, anything to stop her bitching was worth it.

~

It was 9pm and after putting the finishing touches on our makeup and slipping into our evening wear, Tonya and I looked like caramel Barbie dolls. I knew no one would be fresher than us; how could they be? I kept peering out the window like a kid looking into a candy store. Tonya was looking at me crazy, as usual. She didn't know what I had in store for us that night, but I spared no expense and pulled out all the stops.

"It's here," I yelled.

"What's here?" Tonya said, still in the process of putting on the rest of her jewelry.

"Our ride. You're going to love it. Come on, Tonya!"

I stood up straight, fixed my dress, grabbed my handbag, and promenaded to the door. I opened the door with grace and ease as if I was a chauffeur. As Tonya approached the open door, she saw the black stretch

Hummer outside and stopped in her tracks.

"Ooh, Aisha. You didn't tell me we were rolling out like this…"

"I know, I know. I knew you'd like it. It almost feels like prom." I shrugged and gave a half smile. I didn't get a chance to go to my prom and I was making up for it.

"Let's stay in good spirits, shall we?" Tonya nodded. "How much was it? This had to be a lot."

"Actually, I don't know; I had Brad pay for it."

"Who's Brad?"

"Well, um…." I stalled, not wanting to explain right at that moment. I think she got the hint.

"You know what, A? Tonight, I don't even care. This is too nice for words. Let's go!"

The driver opened the door and assisted us in where a bartender and a masseuse were waiting for us. We drank champagne and received hand and foot massages on the way. I felt like I owned the night.

Upon arriving, people were scattered everywhere outside the convention hall. Cars in the parking lot ranged from hoopties to Benzes, and Wal-Mart hubcaps to custom rims. Regardless of the cars, everyone was dressed to impress. They were either dressed in creased-up jeans and crisp button-ups or decked out in full-fledged three-piece suits and evening gowns.

Despite the raucous crowd, all heads turned when Tonya and I pulled up in the limo. Fingers were pointing as people rubbernecked, trying to get a glimpse as to who was behind the tinted windows. The crowd's anticipation was finally satisfied when the door of the black beauty swung open. The driver took each of us by the hand and ushered us out of the limo. Whispers echoed through the crowd as I dramatically swung my hair and pulled my black designer glasses from my face.

I really felt like a superstar. This was the way I dreamt my reunion would be. It was fantastic.

As I'd imagined, everyone looked different from the way they'd looked in our high school years. A lot of skinny cheerleaders were now fat blobs, most of the ballers somehow fell off and were broke, and the chunky butts had dieted and looked great. A few people were just skinny because they couldn't take the stress of the world and turned into crackheads, looking lifeless, jittery, and bug-eyed.

Yet still, I was the center of attention. Many people commented on how I still looked great over the years and how I'd kept my shape. The single men were getting me drinks and the wives of the married men seemed jealous since most of their husbands looked at my sister and I with flirtatious eyes.

Like a dynamic duo, Tonya and I single-handedly captivated the crowd with our beauty and style. After a few drinks and a couple of dances, we decided to catch some fresh air on the balcony.

"It's dull as hell in here; I think I'm ready to go. We can hit up an IHOP or something."

Bored, I pulled a cigarette from my clutch, slumped over the balcony, and began puffing away. I was tired of the music, and I didn't see anyone who caught my eye. I showed my face and all of my awesomeness. Since my mission was complete, it was time to wrap things up.

"Well, it ain't all that bad; it seems cool to me. Honestly, I don't care if we stay or go, but while we're here we might as well enjoy ourselves. This is your ten-year reunion. You need to be in there having fun instead of being out here moping and acting like a big baby."

Tonya's words came to a sudden halt as she directed her attention to the door. She was stunned by the arrival of the most debonair man at the reunion.

"Aisha, who is that over there? He looks scrumptious."

"I don't know, but he got a swagger and charm about him that just won't stop. He's making me wet just looking at him," I said in a voice that sounded like I was going to orgasm. "Ooh, you can tell he has money too. *Jackpot!* I'm hitting that tonight."

My eyes lit up as the diamonds from his necklace and pinkie ring sparkled. Strangely enough, the man eyeballed me from afar. I quickly chucked my cigarette over the balcony and into the pond below. I didn't want his first impression of me to include a cancer stick hanging from my mouth.

He walked directly over to me and greeted me with a hug. I don't usually hug strangers, but his embrace felt so good. I could feel his muscles through his shirt, and they were begging for my attention. The mystery man had no strikes against him yet; I was ready to slide into home base.

"You know my sister? Well, well, well… I think I need to go over here and mingle. I'll be back." Tonya winked at me and excused herself, giving me alone time to get acquainted with the stranger.

The strange man drew me toward him as he whispered in my ear, inhaling my sweet perfume. "It's been so long. I didn't think I'd ever get to hug you like this, at least not in this lifetime. You know you're the most beautiful woman in here tonight, maybe even on this earth? I could never forget you. I can't believe I let you get away. Let me take a look at you. Turn around." He took my hand and spun me around gracefully.

Mesmerized but confused, I pulled back and gazed at the man's unfamiliar face. "I think you must be mistaken. I don't think I know you. Don't get me wrong, I'd like to get to know you, but I don't think we've met before. Have we?"

"Aww, come on, A. I know I changed over the years, but with all the hell you put me through in high school, I thought you'd at least remember me."

I began to stutter with embarrassment. "Uh, uh, ummm. I don't remember. Believe me, I don't think I would've forgotten you."

The man leaned toward me. "*Chunky Chucky*. Remember? But you can call me Charles now."

I gasped and drew a blank stare. I couldn't believe it – Charles Proctor, a.k.a Chunky Chucky, was no sight for sore eyes in high school. Instead of eye candy, he actually looked like he ate the entire candy store. He had been tremendously fat and greasy. He looked as if he just got finished eating a cheeseburger every time you saw him. The top of his head once resembled a psychedelic afro gone wrong; it was uneven and nappier than a sheep's ass. On a good day, his clothes were straight from the thrift shop and his shoes were tattered and old. His teeth looked as if he'd been munching on rotten cheese all day and his breath didn't beg to differ. But *this* was not *that* Charles Proctor.

Scrolling through my memories I couldn't recall him having a car, even after we graduated high school; he always rode an old-school ten-speed that his grandfather had given him in the ninth grade. He was the butt of all jokes, and I used to frown upon his very existence. How could someone be so sloppy, so nasty looking?

I coined the name "Chunky Chucky" given his appearance. He disgusted me, even though I knew he was secretly in love with me. At lunch I would pour his milk on the floor or knock his food off the table. I'd tell him, "You're too fat to be eating that." (I know that was mean, but he was. Hell, I was trying to help him out.) Sometimes I'd trip him when he went by. I also put crude notes on the door of his locker. I knew it wasn't right. I don't know why I took it to those extremes. I guess I figured since I was the most popular girl in school that I could get away with anything. I often pushed my limits, just to see if I could get away with it.

"Oh my gosh, I… I…" I stumbled over my words, recollecting my mean girl acts in high school. I didn't know how to address this man. There's no way he'd forgotten how much of a bitch I'd been.

"Wait a minute. This has to be a joke or something, right?" I still couldn't believe my eyes. There was no way that this man was Chunky Chucky.

"Nope, no joke. This is all me, baby… in the flesh." Charles flashed his suit and his jewels. He turned around in a circle to show off his new physique. It was obvious he was proud of the man he'd become.

"You sure have changed. And boy, it's a good change. You look so… so different. I don't believe it's you!"

"I know it's hard to believe. I can't believe it myself sometimes." Charles stroked his goatee.

"I'm so sorry about the way I treated you in school. I don't know what to say or do to make up for that." I nervously fumbled with my fingers. "I feel horrible. I was young and dumb."

I rambled on idiotically, apologizing for the torment I put him through. If I'd have known he was going to turn out so sexy, I would've given his fat, weird, broke ass a try.

Charles chuckled with arrogance, and I loved it.

"Stop, Aisha, don't sweat it. No apologies needed. We've all done things in our past that are just skeletons now. We were kids then. It just happened to take a 120-pound weight loss, braces, hitting the gym three times a week, designer clothes, jewelry, and lots of haircuts for me to look like this. We've all grown to be very different people. You know what I mean?"

Even though I agreed, I really didn't know what he meant. I was the same beautiful girl who always got her way and whatever she wanted. I really hadn't changed too much since high school. I never felt the need to.

"So, I see you're still looking as fine as ever. You've definitely blossomed. Was that your little sister who was just over here? She hasn't changed a bit either. I can still see her dimples from a mile away.

"You and your sister should hang out with me and the fellas after this. I'll make sure you girls have a really good time. I can show you how I'm living now."

"Sounds good, I'd like that." I grabbed his hand and caressed it so that he knew for certain I was interested.

"Hey, CP! Come on and get some of this drank," a man shouted from across the crowd. He was just as handsome as Charles but still as ghetto as he wanted to be. The man held up two bottles of Dom Perignon, motioning Charles to come over.

"Excuse me, miss, but I'll be back for you at the end of the night." Charles softly pulled my hand to his full, sexy lips. He stared deep into my eyes and simultaneously kissed my hand. "Don't leave; I'll be back for you. We've got a lot of catching up to do."

I nodded, in a trance. Charles disappeared into the crowd to meet up with his friend.

"Damn! Who was that?" Tonya emerged into the spot where Charles had been standing. With the noise of the reunion and us talking so low, Tonya couldn't eavesdrop to get all of the details.

"Girl, that was Chunky Chucky," I said in amazement while staring in his direction.

"Chunky Chucky? Are you talking about *the* Chunky Chucky? No way! Now you know you're sitting there just telling me a big ole lie." Tonya laughed.

I shook my head. "Nope, that is the God's honest truth."

"Really?" Tonya asked in disbelief as she eyeballed me, waiting for a snicker or any other indication that I may be fabricating the story.

I looked at her straight-faced and nodded.

Tonya began to speak slowly as she squinted her eyes, trying to make sense out of the transformation. "Well, I'll be damned. I guess there *is* a God. If I was ever a skeptic, now I know that miracles really do happen. I guess he was never an ugly guy, just fat and unkempt. Yep, he was in desperate need of a makeover."

"Girl, you know I never apologized to anyone in my life. But as good as he was looking... ooh wee! I had to apologize for the way I acted back in the day.

"Tonya, he's the total package. Even though he was lame in high school, he still graduated sum cum laude, so you know he's smart. He has a lot of money too. He has to; the boy has a tailored suit and he's dripping in diamonds. He must be rich. His skin, nails, and hair are perfect. He has charm and charisma too. I'm gonna get a piece of that. I got to be on his team. Or more so, he needs to be on mine." I spoke with certainty.

"I heard that. Now he's worth giving it up to. You know how crazy he was about you in high school. You got to make it up to him now." Tonya nudged me and smiled. "Now, that one, he's a keeper. Matter of fact, see if he has a friend for me."

"You know I will. He told me not to leave. Maybe we'll hang out later or something. I swear I'll suck the meat off the man's bones, he looks so delicious."

"Oh, now you don't want to leave?" Tonya chuckled. "You're nuts. I'm pretty sure if he looked good but wasn't iced out, you wouldn't even give him a second glance."

"Yep, you know me. Even though he's the finest man I ever seen in my whole life, money still makes the world go 'round. He still needs to have that dough or I ain't messing with him. I can't ever go out like that. I need somebody to take care of me. I'm too high maintenance to do it alone," I boasted.

"Okay, Miss High Maintenance, I'm about to go to the bathroom. I don't think there's enough room over here in your area of conceit. I'll be back," Tonya joked, and headed to the restroom.

Shortly after she left Charles spotted me in the crowd. I migrated to the other side of the hall where the refreshments were. I acted like I didn't know he was walking up, but I had actually spotted him before he saw me.

"Hey, Aisha, sorry to keep you waiting. My boy had a little too much to drink and he was acting a little ignorant. He's in the bathroom right now coughing up his guts. I think I'm about to take him home, but here's my number. Make sure you use it. Don't diss me like you used to in high school."

Charles handed me a slip of paper with his cell number on it. I gripped the paper tightly as he walked away.

"What about tonight?" I blurted out.

He stopped in his tracks and smiled as he turned around. He confronted me with a straight face. "What about tonight?" He acted puzzled as he took a few steps closer.

"I mean, after you take him home, what are you doing?" My voice had a nervousness that had never been in it before.

"I'm not doing anything. If you and your sister want to slide through, you're more than welcome. Like I said, I'll have a few friends over if she wants to come. There'll be a couple of them to choose from." Charles laughed as he headed back to the bathroom.

"Wait! I don't know your address," I wailed in desperation.

Charles winked. "It's on the back of the paper."

Tonya passed Charles coming back from the ladies' room. She scanned the crowd and found me in the corner sipping on a glass of wine. "So, what were you guys talking about?"

"He asked me if I wanted to come over tonight, practically begging. He said he would've asked you to hang out too, but he'd like to chill one-on-one since we haven't seen each other in so long."

I lied like a spy caught in enemy territory. I wanted to spend some alone time with him. His friends were expendable. I was sure if I went over there alone, he would make them go home.

"Well, that's understandable. Just have the driver

drop you off at his house. Then I guess I'll go home after that."

I knew that if I got dropped off first and Charles came outside, he might ask Tonya if she wanted to hang out too. Any other time it would've been fine, but that night I wanted this one all to myself without distractions.

"No, it would be out of the way if we did it like that. We'll just drop you off first."

"Whatever floats your boat, A. Just see if he has any friends who are coming over to hang out. I have no kids with me and I'm not ready to call it a night yet."

"Yeah, sure," I said in a less than reassuring voice before walking away. Tonya followed as we made our way out of the reunion while saying our farewells.

We climbed into the limo and headed to Tonya's house. While enroute, I decided to call Charles to see if he'd made it home yet. I pulled out the slip of paper and dialed the number.

"Hey! How are you? Have you made it home yet?" I asked.

"Yep, I'm here waiting to see you."

The simple words he spoke sent chills down my spine.

"So, is Tonya coming with you?" he inquired.

"Um, I don't think so." I tried to avoid answering the question.

"The reason I ask is because I don't have anyone here yet, but I can call someone over if you like," he said.

"No, that's not necessary. We're almost to her house now."

I quickly glanced at Tonya, hoping she didn't catch on. She was looking at me inquisitively, trying to figure out both sides of the conversation. I swear, that girl is too smart for her own good.

"Alright, sweetie. I'll see you in a minute. Oh, and don't change clothes. I like the dress you had on tonight."

I giggled and sighed as I hung up. "I think I'm in love already."

"I bet you are. So, what did he say? Are we kicking it over there or what?" Tonya asked.

"No, he was just asking me if I wanted him to come pick me up. I told him that wouldn't be necessary because we were almost to your house. That would be somewhat stupid. About time he makes it over here, I could almost be to his place."

Tonya didn't believe a word I was saying. Sometimes I think she knows me better than I know myself. She crossed her arms and looked out the window.

"What's wrong with you?"

"Nothing's wrong, I just know how you are. It's actually kind of funny but pitiful at the same time," Tonya retorted.

The limo soon came to a halt, stopping in front of Tonya's house. The driver got out to open Tonya's door. My sister got out without uttering another word to me and strolled to the house.

I didn't care if she was mad or not. I sighed in relief, happy to be alone and on my way to Charles.

# Chapter 8
## Charles

The rest of the drive felt like an eternity. Dark curvy roads and scattered groves of trees framed the trip to Charles' house. I nodded off for a brief moment; it was late, and I had consumed a significant amount of alcohol at the reunion. I awakened to find that we were *still* not at Charles' house. I was flush with anticipation.

"Excuse me, but how much further is it?" I asked the driver through the partition.

"Not too much longer, ma'am, maybe ten minutes. That's it," the driver responded in a deep, Jersey accent.

Now on edge, I started fixing my hair and re-touching my makeup. I needed to look perfect when I arrived.

"Okay, ma'am. We're here." The driver stepped out to open my door.

"What? This is it?"

"Yes, ma'am. According to the address you gave me. Right this way, ma'am." The driver extended his hand to help me out of the car.

"Naw, I got this playa."

Charles sprinted to the car to escort me. "Welcome to mi casa."

"This is your place? You've got to be kidding…"

"Nope, no kidding. This is my comfy little abode. I hope you like it. There should be enough room to kick your feet around." Charles smiled. I couldn't help but notice the hundred-dollar bill he tipped the driver before ushering me into the house.

I looked back at the tall, elaborate gate at the end of the long driveway as the limo vanished. I was so busy primping, that I didn't realize the driver had passed through it.

The estate was like a dream. The massive white mansion had towering columns on either side of the double-door entry. Though most everything was white, the doors were a deep mahogany, which warmed it up and made it very inviting. There were four large urns of colorful flowers placed just-so on the porch. The blooms provided a nice pop, making it feel like a home rather than some cold and sterile place. It reminded me of a modern southern plantation home, but on steroids. I couldn't stop looking around, my eyes capturing all the property's beauty. It was breathtaking.

"Wow, that's a nice car. I like Maseratis." I instantly took notice to the Gran Turismo Sport parked in the cul-de-sac in front of the house.

"What do you know about Maseratis, girl?"

"I don't own one, but I know all about them. Is it yours?"

"Of course, it's mine. It's parked in my driveway, isn't it?" Charles smiled.

I felt a little embarrassed. "That was a dumb question. That's a very fine car though. I guess it matches its owner."

"Well, thank you. I wanted something stylish and

sporty, so I figured it fit the bill. I also have a Maserati Quattroporte as well. I usually drive that one when I do business. I chose that so when my son is in town he has room to pile all of his toys in." Charles laughed.

"Come on, this way."

He opened one of the double doors revealing the interior of the home. The foyer was dressed in exotic plants and the walls were a warm chestnut color. High-end art framed the walls throughout the long hallway.

"Wow, Charles. This is just fascinating. What did you do, hit the lottery or something?" I walked slowly, examining every nook and cranny.

"No lottery. I'm a business owner, hun. I got my hustle on, started investing, built on what I had, and made it grow. Now I have businesses all over the United States, Europe, and Asia. This is my main home, but I have a condo downtown Los Angeles, and I have a vacation home in the Bahamas. Not bad for a fat geek, huh?"

"Not bad at all." I nodded.

I was looking like a foreigner in a different country for the first time. I touched on and stared at everything in my path. His house was immaculate.

He gave me a tour of the main floor, which consisted of a large great room, family room, den, kitchen, formal dining room, a child's playroom, two bathrooms, and an office. We then took an elevator to the second floor, which had two guest rooms, a child's room, a study, and the master suite. All of the rooms were en suites, aside from the study.

"This is where I spend most of my time when I'm not working; it's my favorite place in the house," he said referencing his bedroom.

The master suite had a jacuzzi near a glass sliding

door that led to an outside balcony. The wall that divided the sleeping area from his meditation room was comprised of an enormous built-in fish tank and a fireplace nestled one foot beneath.

On the other side of the wall was his Zen room. He said the room possessed a tremendous amount of positive energy, flow, and light... he was right. Even though it was nighttime, I felt lighter, even happier in this room. I couldn't help but smile when he said he named the room Zion, which was also his son's name. It showed that this place was the happy reflection of his heart, of his son, Zion. He used the Zion Room to meditate, pray, and read.

The master bath had an oversized claw-foot tub in the middle of the floor and the shower was like something that resembled a rainforest. Traces of pebble-sized water was still beaded up on the seamless, glass enclosure. I briefly envisioned him in the steamy, hot shower— his chiseled body lathered in bubbly soap, with water trickling down his back. This made me smile again.

Everything was elegant, not overdone or gaudy. We soon left the upstairs, and he continued the tour to view the lowest level of the house. This area was complete with a full kitchen, gym, theatre, and studio.

"I didn't know you were into music." I peered at the fully equipped studio through the large picture window. I'd been in a few studios in my day, and this one by far was more professional than the "professional" ones I'd visited.

"Well, that just shows how much you really know about me?" Charles responded. "In high school, I was a nobody to you. You didn't care anything about me, Aisha, so truthfully, you wouldn't know if I was into music or not." He gave a nonchalant shrug, stuffed his hands in his pockets and rocked back on his heels. He looked through the window with me and an uncomfortable silence fell upon us like a stranger's shadow.

I was stunned. I wasn't expecting *that* type of response. I didn't know what to say and stumbled to gather the right words. But no words in my mental dictionary could reconcile how badly I treated him in the past.

"Well, I apologize. I don't know what else to say." I uttered. He took a deep breath but didn't reply. I grabbed his hand and stepped in front of him.

"Charles, I deeply apologize. You have to believe me."

After a lengthy gaze, he smiled warmly.

"You don't know how long I've been waiting to hear those words… in that way."

Relieved, I smiled back.

"Well, now that we're past that little bout of awkwardness, let me tell you about the studio." He chuckled, breaking the ice. "The studio is for my son."

"Your son? Oh, that's nice. How old is he?"

"Five."

"Five! That's it? That's funny. A five-year old with his own studio? That's unheard of."

"Well, I believe that greatness is cultivated, not just born. He loves music, so I created a studio for him. If he doesn't want to do that in the future, he doesn't have to. I just want to give him the tools to be all he can be while he's here on this earth. You feel me?"

"While he's here on this earth? That's a dramatic way to put it."

"Not in my mind it isn't. You just never know. I guess I meant, until he or I are no longer on this earth. I know it sounds weird, but that's reality. So, I get my son whatever he wants; that's daddy's little boy. He's the one and only. Don't plan on having any more kids. Always wanted a girl… a cute, little, sassy princess to spoil, but that's not in the cards for me. That is, unless I adopt."

"Oh, why not?" I asked.

"Why not what?"

"Why don't you want to have more kids? Why do you want to adopt? Is it because you haven't found the right woman yet?" I brushed against him seductively.

"You're a funny woman, Aisha. No, it's not that at all. I really don't want to be with anyone anymore. Society puts such an emphasis on being with someone and getting married; I just think there's more to life than putting your all into a mate. It's not like I don't think about it sometimes, but I don't think that life is for me. I've been there and done that already."

"You must have had your heart broken, or you're a player – one or the other."

"To be quite honest, I had my heart broken once. It was in high school to be exact, by a skinny long-haired girl named Aisha…" Charles gazed into the air rubbing his chin, reminiscing. Then he nudged me.

"Oh, whatever, Charles. You're full of it."

He smirked. "No, but really… The reason I would think of adopting is because I'm celibate and I don't plan on getting married. So, if I'm celibate, I guess adopting is the only option, right?"

I laughed until tears ran down my face. "Celibate? This night just keeps getting crazier and crazier. No one's celibate these days unless they're a monk, a priest, or a nun. Hell, even some of *them* ain't celibate. I don't believe this celibacy mess for one minute. A fine man like you in a big mansion like this? I don't believe it. You're kidding, right?"

Charles shook his head with a straight face. "Everyone responds like that, but I really am celibate."

"No man on this earth is celibate. No way. Given how successful you are I'm pretty sure you have a lot of free pussy coming your way.

"Wait a minute. Are you gay? I knew it. All the nice-looking, well-groomed, well-off men are. Well, I can always be your shopping buddy."

"Naw, sweetie, believe me, I'm far from gay. I love women too much. But not all pussy is good pussy. I learned that the hard way. Sometimes people grow up and realize which lifestyle suits them. This lifestyle suits me just fine. I'm content, so other people should be content with me too. I don't judge the decisions of others. That's why we all have our own brains, to make our own decisions. What's best for me may not be good for someone else, but it makes me happy and that's all that matters. Anyone that don't like it, well, that's their problem. If anything, I'd rather have a soulmate - someone to be best friends with; someone to show that there's more to life than just sex."

"I guess I can respect that."

Charles smiled and grabbed my hand to lead me upstairs and out the back door. "Let me show you the outside of the house. You're going to love it."

Tropical plants engulfed the space, and a beautiful rock garden surrounded part of the stream.

"This is what really sold me on this place. Everything else was already here – the pool, the basketball court, and the little Zen Garden. The only thing I added was that stream over there to complement the garden. That was my inspiration for my Zion room upstairs. I'm busy, so when I get home, I just like to relax. It's so peaceful out here."

"I bet. This is absolutely stunning. I know you put a lot of money into this place."

"Yeah, it was initially out of my budget. I was only worth a few million dollars when I bought the place, but what can I say? You can't take it with you, so you might as well live it up."

"So, if you don't mind me asking, how much... uh... never mind."

"Come on, speak your mind. I've never known Aisha to hold her tongue about anything. Don't start today. What do you want to know? How much did I put into the house? What's it worth now? How much did I pay for it? What? I'm an open book."

"Umm... it's not about the house."

"Well, what is it? Ask away..."

"Well, I mean... I don't mean to pry, but I was going to ask if you were worth a few million *back then*, then how much are you worth *now?*"

My face was scrunched up like a kid who'd just cursed in front of their parents. I felt like I was way out of line, but I wanted to know... I *needed* to know.

"Oh, you want to know how much *I'm* worth. Let's just say this: my son's mother doesn't ever have to work again thanks to court-ordered child support. She's a millionaire. I never married her, so all that money is strictly from child support. The messed-up thing about it is that I take care of my son *and* his mother very well. But she still went behind my back and ordered child support. I guess what I was doing just wasn't enough for her. She still wanted more. Greedy!"

"Damn, that's crazy." I paused and thought about it for a second. "Oh, I see now."

"You see what?"

"That's the reason you're bitter against women."

"I'm not bitter. I'm celibate. Don't confuse the two." He sounded a bit offended.

"Sorry, I just figured you're bitter because your baby momma did you wrong and that's why you're celibate."

"No way, that's not it at all. I never said I was *bitter* against women. I don't know why you think that just because I choose to be celibate. I bet if a woman said she was celibate you wouldn't think she was bitter."

"The hell if she's not! Somebody did her wrong or else she didn't have good sexual experiences. That's what I believe."

"Okay, I won't argue with that, but I'm going to tell you what I believe. I believe that having sex with random people is for the birds. People should be in a committed relationship and not just have sex buddies. Since I choose not to include myself in relationships, what's the purpose of having meaningless sex? My time is valuable. I don't like to waste my time lollygagging. It's a long story, A, but I have my reasons. I'll tell you one day."

"I thought you said your life was an open book?"

"Even books have covers, Aisha."

"So, there's no one who could possibly change your mind about that?" I looked at him with big puppy dog eyes.

"About what? About the reason I don't want a relationship?" He looked confused.

"No. About being in one. Possibly with someone like me."

"Hey, don't get me wrong. You're as sexy as you

wanna be, but right now I want to be strictly friends. That's it; nothing more, nothing less."

"So, does that mean that you really just have friends... never friends with benefits?" I pried.

"You're really trying to get something out of me, huh? How can I have friends with benefits if I don't have sex? Girl, you're crazy. Most of my so-called friends are friends with me because of my benefits. That's why my friendships don't last long."

"Well, I'm your friend to the end," I said. "Even though we weren't anywhere near being friends in high school, we are now. Everything happens for a reason. That's why we ran into each other tonight."

"You know what, Aisha? You are absolutely right. Come on, let's go back inside."

I smiled.

Before reentering the house, I pulled a cigarette out while searching my clutch for a lighter.

"Oh wait. I'm sorry, before we go inside, do you mind?" I asked with a cigarette in one hand and my lighter in the other.

"Oh, no, no, no, Aisha. Actually, I do mind. I hope you're not hooked on those nasty things. You're too classy for that. My sister died of lung cancer. I don't allow smoking at my house, *at all*. If you want to kill yourself, do it on your own time and at you own place, not mine."

I felt like a grade-school kid getting scolded by the principal. I hung my head and put my things back in my clutch. I had no words.

"I'm sorry. Too harsh?" Charles had an apologetic look on his face.

"No, you're totally fine - your house, your rules.

Let's go in, sweetie."

I grabbed his hand as he led me to the kitchen.

"Would you like something to drink? I have beer, wine, or champagne if you like."

Charles must have sensed that I was embarrassed after his comment outside, but he made me feel so comfortable that I immediately loosened up.

"Sure, champagne will do me fine. Thank you, baby." (It just felt so natural to call him *baby*.)

"No problem, miss. Let me get that for you," Charles said as he popped the top on a bottle of bubbly and proceeded to pour us each a glass.

"You're so charming and refined, Charles. Too bad more men aren't like you." I sipped my Moet. The bubbles tickled my throat as it went down.

"Thanks for the compliment, but as we both know, it's not like I was born this way. I'm telling you the truth when I say you don't know the half of it. I may have been a nerd in school, but I hustled on the block to pay my folks' bills. You didn't know that did you?"

"No, I didn't. That is interesting – interesting and funny at the same time. I guess I couldn't imagine you doing that."

"Yep. It was good I was a nerd; helped me keep a low profile. I used to be with your brother on the block. He taught me a few things."

"Don't lie on my brother like that. He didn't do that stuff," I snarled.

"Yes, he did, rest his soul. When you guys went to sleep, he'd leave out of the window because he said your mom worked third shift. He had his little pager, went to work, and got back before she got home."

"Wow, I never knew."

I tried to remember ever going into Drew's room after dark, but I didn't recall doing so. I'd been too busy sneaking out too, so it was probably true.

"It was really tragic how he passed. I was right there at the corner store when it happened."

"You were? Well, what happened to my brother? We never knew the details because most of the eyewitnesses left the scene, or they didn't want to talk about it. You know how things are in the hood."

"Well, all I know is that I came out of the store from buying a pop and I saw Drew driving your mom's car on the sidewalk trying to run some man over."

"Trying to run someone over?" I was taken aback, trying to make sense of it all.

"Yeah. I don't know who the guy was, but he ran like hell. He was tall, about 6'4", brown skin, had a mini afro, maybe in his forties. All I know is that Drew was mad as hell at him for some reason. Maybe the guy owed him money or something; I don't know. He was screaming out the window, something like, 'I'm gonna kill you for what you did!' The man leaped out of the way, Drew lost control of the car, and well, you know the rest."

"Damn, that's crazy. I wonder what he was doing trying to run a man over."

"I'm not sure, but the guy was long gone by the time the police got there. I didn't want to say anything to them about Drew trying to run a man down. I wanted his name to be clear, you know?"

*Wait a minute,* I thought. *Tall, 6'4", brown-skinned, mini afro, in his forties? That had to be my dad.* It finally made sense.

A week prior to Drew's death, I told him how my father used to molest me. For years I'd told no one. Then Drew asked why I hated my father so much and I told him. He was so furious that day that he didn't eat. He went around the house punching walls and doors, saying if he ever saw my father again, he was going to kill him. I guess he was serious. After Drew's death I never saw or spoke to my father. He left town without explanation and never returned. Now I knew why.

Charles started talking again, interrupting my thought process.

"Drew said he was gonna hustle for a little while and then stop. He wanted to own some businesses too. To be honest, he was my role model. He told me I had the mindset of an entrepreneur – said I should stop hustling and start my own business. Now look at me with all this legal and legit money. It feels really good."

"See, that's the thing. Drug dealers are really just entrepreneurs, but they go about obtaining their money the wrong way. They don't realize that they're not just destroying lives and families in the process, but also themselves. All those illegal activities are just detrimental in the end. There's only three ways out of that lifestyle - death, prison, or just giving it up and going 100% legit. Most people on that path only know one way of making a dollar, but I'm sure if given the right tools, knowledge, and opportunities, more people will learn how to use their entrepreneurial talents. Your brother taught me how to do just that."

"It's nice that you would say that about my brother; that means a lot. You just didn't look like someone who hustled. I can't imagine it."

"Well, like they say, looks can be deceiving." Charles chuckled.

"Well, if looks are deceiving, what are you hiding now? You seem pretty perfect to me." I looked him up and down.

"There are a lot of things you don't know about me. Some you will never know, and others will come to know in due time," he said, sounding serious.

"Ooh, always so intense. Loosen up, baby."

"I'll be loose after this, believe me." Charles looked at his champagne glass, which was almost empty, and chugged the rest.

"Well, I'm already feeling loose. What do you want to do now?" I put my glass down and jumped up to sit on the counter. I straddled the area where Charles was standing.

"Well, we can take a dip in the pool if you want," he suggested.

"That means I'm going to have to get my panties and bra wet. I didn't intend on coming over here to swim. I don't have anything to wear."

"You don't have to worry about getting your things wet; you don't have to wear them."

My eyes sparked.

"Ooh, skinny dipping, huh? Naughty! Yeah, that sounds like a plan to me. I love showing off my body and I can't wait to see yours." I wiggled from side to side.

"Sweetie, as much as I want you to skinny dip, and believe me, I do… I'm a gentleman. So, I've made sure to have a bathing suit available for you."

"A bathing suit? From where? I'm not wearing no other broad's swimsuit, if that's what you're thinking."

For some reason Charles found my combativeness

amusing and began laughing so hard, he grabbed his stomach like Santa Claus.

"Oh, man, let me catch my breath. Seriously, Aisha... What do I look like, having you wear someone else's clothes? Don't insult my intelligence, woman. I have people in high places. I got one delivered here before you arrived just in case you wanted to swim."

"Nuh uh." I turned my lip up and twisted my mouth.

"Okay, don't believe me then; you'll see. I'm going to go get it. If I did get you a swimsuit, what do I get?"

"What do you want? Me? I can give you that. That's all I got to give right now."

I smiled, laying it on thick. I wasn't used to working so hard to break a guy down. Matter of fact, I usually didn't have to put in any work. Charles was a tough nut to crack—he wasn't biting at all. I still wasn't giving up, celibate or not.

"Aisha, you're too much. I'll be right back."

I poured another glass of champagne while Charles went into his office. He returned after a few moments with a box.

"Here you go," he said handing me a package laced with beautiful pink ribbon.

"Aww, you were serious. Thank you." I tore into the box like a kid on Christmas.

"This is really nice. Satin? I've never owned a satin bathing suit before."

"Yep. When it gets wet it's nice and clingy, just how I like it." Charles smiled.

"See, I knew you wanted to see my body." I winked. "I'm going to go change. I'll be right back."

"Alright, I'll go get my trunks on and meet you by

the pool then."

Charles went to change and after putting on his trunks, he stepped onto the diving board and went in headfirst. He was able to get a few laps in before I arrived poolside.

"Hey, pretty boy."

I struck a pose in the barely-there satin suit. The one-piece suit Saran-wrapped my body and the color blended with my skin, revealing all my curves. Charles' mouth dropped wide open.

"*Mmm, mmm, mmm...* I guess I picked the right size."

"Yes, you did. You have good taste as well. This is very nice, I must say."

I eased into the shallow end and walked a few steps into the water to meet him. I wrapped my arms around him and kissed him passionately before pitter-pattering my lips along the perimeter of his right ear.

"Oh, my, that's my spot right there. I don't think you should do that," he said as I kissed his ear. He closed his eyes, lost in the moment.

"I think I should," I responded. I continued kissing him and he seemed to be enjoying it. I slipped the swimsuit off my shoulders and let it fall to my waist. Then I took his hands and ran them across my nipples. I continued to shed my swimsuit until it was floating nearby.

"Whoa, there, little lady. You're getting me a bit excited, and I think you're getting excited too. Let's slow this down a bit; it's our first night getting reacquainted."

"Well, I told you if you were right about getting me a swimsuit then I'd let you have me. You already said you were getting excited... I know what that means. Just don't fake it, Charles. I know you're a self-proclaimed born-again virgin or whatnot, but I know you still want me. I felt how hard you got when I started kissing you."

I grabbed his manhood and began stroking him slowly. Charles took a deep breath with every stroke. I put my other hand on top of his and guided him to caress my body. Then I took his index finger and thrust it inside my warm cavity. Abruptly, he pulled away.

I moaned. "C'mon, are you serious?"

"Yes, I'm dead serious," he said. "This is too much for me right now."

Annoyed by his answer, I threw my hands in the air.

"This is just too weird. I don't know what's up with you. I never had a man treat me like this before." I scowled.

"Treat you like what, A? Take you to his mansion? Show you a good time? Buy you a twelve-hundred-dollar designer swimsuit?" Charles snatched the suit from the water and shook it angrily.

"Don't be a smart ass. You know what I'm talking about. You're acting like you don't want me. Why is that?"

"It's not that I don't want you, because I do. It's just that I'm not one of these idiots out here who would take advantage of you."

"But I *want* you to take advantage of me. I want your hands all over my body." I grabbed his hands and placed them on my waist. He firmly pushed me away.

"Look, I'm serious now. We can be cool, we can hang out, and we can see each other whenever I'm in town. But you have to respect me in the same way I respect you. If you don't want me to do something, I won't do it.

"I told you I'm celibate, and you act like you don't know what that means. If you're kissing all over me like that,

113

of course I'm going to get hard. What man wouldn't? But you lack respect. Usually, it's the man trying to push sex, but you're acting like a thirsty, horny trick who hasn't had dick in ages. I mean, what are you trying to prove?"

"Don't you talk to me like that. Quite frankly, you should feel lucky I even want your ass. Just because you look good and you're rich don't dismiss the fact that you were a nobody in high school. Then you have the audacity to say *I'm* acting like a thirsty trick? Trust me, I could be with anyone tonight, but I chose to be with you. So, if I just wanted to get some, then I would have left a long time ago."

"Oh, that's the way you feel, huh? Well, why don't you just leave now and go grind up on someone else? They *cannot* and *will not ever* treat you like I can. I'm a multi-millionaire, baby... I don't have to take your shit. If you were looking to freak someone for the night, you came to the wrong place. There's free dick running around everywhere. So why don't I just get you an Uber so you can go find the nearest dick to jump on?" He clenched his teeth as he talked. He turned to the ladder to get out of the pool.

"Sorry bastard," I blurted.

"What in the hell did you just call me?"

"I called you a sorry bastard. You think you can just talk to me any kind of way and have me not say anything to you about it?"

"Wow, no home training. Ghetto-fabulous at its finest. You know, Aisha, I may have said some things, but they were the truth.

"Still, no matter what I said, I didn't call you out by name. You were the one disrespecting me. I don't hang around women who don't have class, so I think it's time for you to go."

114

"Wait, Charles, this conversation is getting blown out of proportion."

I attempted to grab his arm and pull him back in the pool. He snatched his arm away and marched into the house with the bathing suit. I submerged my naked body into the water, hoping he'd cool off and come back out to talk.

He returned a few minutes later.

"Look, we need to talk," I asserted.

"Aisha, please, I think we've done enough talking for tonight. I was going to throw the suit away but that would be childish."

He dropped the swimsuit onto a lounge chair.

"There's an Uber on the way... already paid for it through the app."

"Charles, you're overreacting. I didn't mean..."

"Look, Aisha, since you can't respect me and my lifestyle, then I think it's time you leave. Come on, get out of the pool and get dressed. Your ride should be here shortly. And just to clarify things, I'm not mad at you but I am really disappointed."

He offered me a handout of the pool and gave me a towel before turning and walking back to the house. He left so fast that I didn't have a chance to speak. I stood there naked, wet, alone, and speechless.

# Chapter 9
## The Night After

"Hey, T." I was still yawning, recuperating from the night before. I had to tell someone about my strange, yet exciting evening with Charles. Why not Tonya?

"Sooo…" I paused.

"So what?"

"Girl, we were right. That man is loaded."

"Well, even Stevie Wonder could see that," she sassed.

"But it's not only that," I added. "He's like a dream. He's the full package."

"Really? How so?" She yawned, sounding like she would rather have a conversation with her pillow instead of me.

"Well, for starters, he's successful, he's got money, he knows how to put me in my place, and on top of that, he has a big wanger."

"Whoa, wait, back it up… You slept with him? You skank."

"Wait a minute. Before you start calling me a skank, I did *not* sleep with him. I wanted to but I didn't. I did grab it though. It was big even when it wasn't completely hard. I bet he can put it down."

"The way he is looking, he's like a snack, entrée, and dessert. I bet he could too."

"There is something that's pretty weird though. He didn't want to sleep with me, even though I was practically giving it away. He didn't want to touch me, kiss me, or nothing."

"Oh, well then, that explains it - he's gay. I knew something was wrong with him. He was too metrosexual. You know - too smooth." Tonya laughed.

"Naw, girl, he ain't gay. He said he's celibate, which is just like being gay in my book. I'm gonna work on that though. I know he'll come around in the future; I just gotta work my magic."

"Celibate? That doesn't even sound right. I think he's lying. He's not ready to come out of the closet yet," Tonya implied.

"Why do you have to be so pessimistic, T? Can't you just be happy? I think I found the man of my dreams last night and you just gotta say something negative. You're the main one telling me to settle down. So, what's the problem?"

"I'm not talking negative. It's facts. What other logical explanation can you come up with? He had a huge crush on you in high school and were practically giving it away—what straight man wouldn't jump all over that?"

"Beats me, but he has a son, so obviously he has to be humping somebody."

"Okay, now things are becoming clearer. You left out valuable information. I think he still messes with his baby momma. She probably has a key and everything. He didn't want to get caught in the act."

"No, that's not it either. He said she doesn't even live here. She lives all the way in New York," I confirmed.

117

"Okay, Aisha, this is just strange. Besides, I thought you said you wouldn't ever be serious with someone who had kids?"

"I know what I said, but I just have to get over that. That doesn't have anything to do with me. Hell, I might want to have his baby too someday," I mumbled.

"What? What're you talking about? Aren't you the one who said you didn't ever want to have kids because you don't want them ruining your body? Girl, you wouldn't even know what to do with a baby." Tonya laughed.

"I know, but I got a strategy. I can have his baby and hire a live-in nanny. I'd have plenty of time to go to the gym and get my body back right."

"A nanny, Aisha? You're trippin' now. You said you don't make enough money to hire a housekeeper, so what makes you think you'll have enough to hire a live-in nanny?"

"Well, I'll definitely be able to afford a nanny. The man is filthy rich. He said his son's mother is a millionaire because of his child support payments. So, I'm sure he'd take care of me if I had his child. I'd be set for life."

I daydreamed, thinking of all the possibilities that come with having a fat bank account.

"Are you serious?"

"Yeah, I'm serious, that's what he told me."

"No, not about that. I'm talking about you having a baby. I thought you were just joking."

"No, I'm not joking. Of course, I want to have his baby. Why wouldn't I? That would be my way out. I wouldn't ever have to worry about money again. And you know it would be cute on top of that. I can push it around and have the nanny change it and feed it and all of that," I added nonchalantly.

"First of all, a baby is not an *it*," Tonya bickered.

"Well, I wouldn't know what I'd be having, so I have to call it an *it*. What else am I supposed to call it?"

"Call it a baby, Aisha – a baby."

"Well, I want to have Charles' baby, no matter if it's a boy or a girl. I'm gonna try to get pregnant by him. I might have to do something slick like poke a hole in the condom or something."

"You don't even like kids that much," she pointed out. "They get on your nerves. And poking holes in condoms? I can't believe you'd seriously consider such a thing."

"I'm sorry, but unlike you, I'm not about to be having babies for free. Maybe you didn't care about getting knocked up because you were in love… Okay, I get it, but I have a different game plan. I don't have time to be sitting around being broke, pregnant, and barefoot like some people."

"Barefoot and pregnant? Please, give me a break. How dare you. Yeah, I was in love. That's something that you obviously will never know about. Maybe it's because you're about as shallow as a stream with a teaspoon of water in it. Having a child is a serious decision; it's a life-changing event. Have you even considered the consequences? Better yet, how would you even get pregnant by Charles if the man is celibate? Did you ever think about that?"

"First of all, the baby would be fine. I told you; I'll have a nanny. She'll raise it, not me. It would be fun, dressing it up and stuff. You know it'll have the best of everything. My offspring ain't gonna be running around looking like no rag doll – especially if I'm a millionaire and the daddy is a multi-millionaire. I don't understand why you don't see where I'm coming from. This could work out for both of us. He might have a millionaire friend that you can pop out another little bastard for. Then we'd both be set."

There was an awkward pause and heavy breathing. T was trying to maintain her composure but couldn't. I could feel her eye-rolling through the phone. I knew I had to do damage control before she went off.

"I didn't mean it like that. Okay? I don't want you to be mad at me. I just want you to understand my logic," I explained.

"Well, I don't understand your logic, never understood your logic, don't want to understand your logic, and never *will* understand your logic. You're insane!"

"Well, everyone's entitled to their own opinion, I guess. I just wanted to let you know what a wonderful night I had and my plans for the future. I didn't know you were going to act like such a hater."

"A hater? Me? I'm not a hater. I'm just wondering how you can plan a future with someone who doesn't even want to have sex with you. Maybe he already knows how trifling you really are, and he don't want to go that route. Boy, I'll tell you, sometimes you make me ashamed to be your sister. We have the same momma and were raised the same way, but we turned out to be two totally different people. I don't understand it. I'm done wasting my breath."

Tonya hung up on me without the courtesy of saying goodbye. It didn't bother me though; I knew what I had to do. I wasn't going to let anyone stop me or ruin my plans. I was going to be with Charles and have his baby.

# Chapter 10
## Flat

"Charles, I haven't talked to you in a few days. Hope you're not still mad at me from the other night. I didn't mean to offend you. Please call me back. Thanks. Oh yeah, this is A."

It had been four days since the reunion and Charles still hadn't contacted me. I hoped he would call me back.

I started getting dressed to start my day at the office. Office Aisha was quite different from Party Aisha. I laid out a classic navy pantsuit on the bed with a ruffle-collared blouse to go underneath to make sure I wasn't showing too much skin. I paired the outfit with Jimmy Choo pumps that were just high enough to keep my pant legs from touching the ground, but not so high that I looked like I just came from the club. I took my job seriously and I wanted my counterparts to take me seriously as well. If I wanted to hang with the big boys, I needed to play the part.

I showered and pulled my hair back into a tight bun. When it came to makeup, I kept it simple—bronzer, mascara, and a bit of lip gloss.

I grabbed a banana and an energy drink on my way out the door and I was only on the highway for ten minutes when I noticed a thumping noise coming from the passenger side of my car. I pulled off on the next exit to find the nearest gas station, a place that shared a building with a barbershop and a chicken joint. The parking lot had a mix of the ghetto's finest—a few thugs, a couple of bums, and a wandering crackhead looking to get a fix. This place was not my cup of tea, but I had no choice. I pulled to the far side of the parking lot, hoping to stay as far away from the ratchetness as possible.

*Dammit!*

My tire was as flat as a squirrel run over by a semi. I got back in the car and called roadside assistance for help. I was holding for a representative when someone tapped on my window. I cracked it about a quarter way to address the stranger.

"Don't scare me like that! What do you want?" I said, grabbing the top of my head. The knocks frightened me so bad that I had hit my head on the roof of the car.

"I was jus seein' if you needed some help, shawty, that's all." The tall dark man sucked his gold teeth and slowly nodded his head. His slang, combined with his grimy, look made him seem a bit shady.

"No, I don't need your help, thanks… I guess." I turned my head and brushed him off. (He would've been better off asking to wash my windows.)

"Damn… It's like that? What, you think you too good to get help fromma brotha or sumpthin'? A bitch like you is why a good nigga like me don' wanna do shit. Try to be good to a sista, but nooo… it's neva good enough."

Frustrated, I slammed my phone down into the passenger seat. I didn't care if I had to call roadside assistance back and hold again, I had to give this dude a piece of my mind.

"Good to a sista? Dude, you for real? If you wanna help me, you'd get the hell outta my face, disrespecting me like that. Why are you still standing here anyway? First of all, I did not *ask* for your help. Second of all, I do not *want* your help. And third of all, I do not *need* your help! Call it what you want, but you need to get away from my car. Go learn to speak proper English and stop using the 'N word' before you talk to me."

"Oh, snaps! Sista tryin' to pop off at the mouth, huh? *Proper English?* 'N word?' Shawty, I speak what and how I feel, whether you like it or not," the man said, waving his hands back and forth.

He took short paces back and forth... like he'd made a point. Then he took a step back from the car and looked at me long and hard.

"Wait a minute. I knew you looked familiar... I 'member yo ass from the hood. You talkin' bout speakin' proper English and shit, but I know you had a lil bit a ghetto girl mixed under all tha' white bread. That curly-ass hair ain't foolin' me. Just cuz you a redbone don't mean you betta than nobody else."

"Think whatever you want, but I don't know you. So—"

"You used to mess with my man Tay. Your name's A, right? Tay and A. I 'member that *and* I never forget a face." He over-emphasized the word "and" like he was digging up some real dirt.

Although I ignored him, he was right. I did used to mess with Tay, but Tay messed with all the pretty girls on the south side of Chicago where I grew up. I didn't know this man from Adam, but I did know that he was frustrating me. (I just wished he'd leave me the hell alone.) I started fiddling with my phone and pretended to be texting to make it a valid point that I was ignoring him.

"Oh, I guess you think you all high and mighty now. I see you rolling good... uh huh. But don't act like you didn't used to flip back in the day. Prolly still do. Good ol' Aisha. That's your name, right? Aisha? Yeah, that's what I figured. Aisha do anything for that almighty dolla, huh? I remember you and yo mans used to set folks up."

By this point he was rubbing his hands together like his one-sided conversation was really heating up. He was getting too deep with the information, and I was getting pissed. Not because he was still talking, but because he knew way too much about me and I didn't have a clue as to who he was.

"Get the hell away from my car. I don't know you from the next hustler. You think you can judge me? You're the one who got on those dirty-ass Nikes. I may have done some shit back in the day, but at least I got something to show for it. You're a hustler and you're still walking. So how do you have nerve to talk? For all I know, you might be trying to set me up – You might be trying to jack my car or something."

"Whoa, baby girl. Obviously you don't know me like that. I got cars. I got houses. I got money. All of my shawties are taken care of... nah mean? Hustlas neva sleep, baby. I'm on my five-day grind." He sucked his teeth while holding up all five fingers.

"I hustles seven days a week. I been up twenty-six hours handlin' my business. I don't have time to worry bout dirty shoes. At the end of the day, I got more money than you, I don't got a flat tire like you, and I got better rides than you. I was just tryin' to help you out, but you're just an ol' raggedy-ass, flat-tire havin', stuck-up bitch. Don't forget, you came from the hood, shawty."

He walked away and pressed a remote to open a candy-apple '96 Impala SS and jumped in. He turned up his music and sped off.

"Stupid ass," I mumbled.

I refused to let him ruin my day even more than it already was. I picked up my cell to redial assistance but just as I was about to call, Charles' number popped up on the screen. My day instantly brightened.

"Hey, you... Been trying to catch up with you. How have you been?" I asked.

"I've been okay. Saw you called a few times. I was just real busy. You know, flying in and out of town for business," Charles said.

"Oh, yeah. Well, that's okay." (My words were unconvincing. He must have heard the tension in my voice.)

"No, no, no. That was rude of me not to return your calls. You just really threw me off the other night, you know? I wasn't expecting you to act like that. I needed some time to gather my thoughts because I didn't want to say the wrong things."

"Yeah, I apologize. I don't usually act like that with men. I don't know what came over me. I guess you're just too damn sexy." I giggled like a schoolgirl.

"You're silly, Aisha. Well, look, I just got back in town, so I was thinking we could meet up for lunch or something today. Grab a bite to eat and smooth things over? My treat. You down?"

"Well, I don't know. Right now, I'm down for real. I was about to go to work, and I just caught a flat tire. I don't think I'll be able to make it to work in time. I got a lot going on right now, but as long as I get everything together, we can have lunch. That sounds great."

"Alright, lunch it is. Now, you said your tire's flat… Do you already have someone coming to fix it?"

"No, I was about to call roadside assistance until this asshole came up talking crazy to me. But that's a story for another time."

"What? Are you stranded or something?"

"Sort of. Just sitting in my car."

"Girl don't worry about that car. Actually, don't even worry about work today. If you definitely can't make it in and you call off, I'll just give you the money as if you were working. I got you. Where you at right now? I'm gonna come get you."

"I'm at the Marathon gas station near my house. You're gonna come get me for real?"

I was so relieved; not because I didn't have to worry about my tire, but because I really wanted to see him.

"Yeah, why not? I can't just leave your pretty self out there stranded now, can I?"

"You're making me blush, Charles," I replied coyly.

"Well, that's the least I can do. Just stay right there and don't talk to any more strangers. You got that, missy?" he pretended to scold me.

"I'm definitely not going anywhere. I'll be here. I just got to call in to my job to tell them I'm not coming in, and then I'm all yours."

"Alright, don't get into any trouble now, A. I don't want you to lose your job over a lunch date."

"Boy, please, I am a valuable asset to that company. They are *not* getting rid of me anytime soon. Aside from that, I hardly ever call off."

"Alright, just making sure. Sit tight; give me about twenty minutes, okay?"

"Okay, I'll be waiting."

I sat patiently, anticipating Charles' arrival. I browsed the net and people-watched to pass the time. Exactly twenty minutes later he arrived to rescue me. Once that Bentley pulled into the lot, I knew it was him. He stepped out of the car looking like he just stepped out of *GQ*. He definitely stood out among the people hanging around the gas station. I got out of the car to greet him. He took me by both hands and gave me a quick kiss on the cheek.

"Well, look at you... all business-like. I like it," he said.

"Well, thanks," I said, smiling ear-to-ear.

He slowly circled my car, investigating the busted tire along with the others.

"Damn, girl... your tire is shot. Looks like your rim is bent too."

"I know, it's embarrassing. I just haven't had time to get new ones. I need to pay more attention. I'm well overdue for an oil change too. I hate car stuff," I scowled.

"Well, the only way God is going to bless you with something better is if you take care of what you got," he said as he popped the trunk to get the spare.

"That's true. Just like you were taking good care of you baby momma and now you blessed with something better. I might just be your blessing in disguise. Just sayin'..."

I flirtatiously leaned against the door and played with my hair.

"Hey, you never know; life is funny like that." He cocked a half-smile and began taking the lug nuts off the wheel. A few moments passed. I was hoping for something more. Maybe a little more convo, maybe a little more flirting, but he would not bite. From what I noticed from our brief encounters, it was always just a nibble, nothing substantial. I wasn't used to having to work for men's affections, yet there I was feeling like a little puppy dog begging for a bone. Once I realized he was only focused on the tire and not the hot, slim-thick, caramel latte standing in front of him, I changed the subject.

"So, when we get the spare on, then what?" I said pulling out a smoke.

"What are you doing?" Charles stopped unscrewing the lug nuts and looked at me with a mixture of confusion and disgust—the exact opposite of how I wanted him to look at me.

"What's wrong?" I questioned.

He raised his eyebrows and looked at the cigarette hanging from my mouth.

"Oh, Lord, Charles. Really? I thought you said not at your house?" I felt like a teenager being scolded by their parent.

"I did say that, but you shouldn't be smoking at all; it's not good for you. It shows you don't care about your body… And I care about you *and* your body."

I was like putty in his hands. (It's not what somebody says, but how they say it.) Without saying a word, I plucked the cig from my mouth, reached inside the car, and grabbed the brand-new pack of squares off the seat. I walked past Charles while keeping eye contact and pitched the cigarettes into a nearby trash can.

"Okay, I'm done. Cold turkey." I brushed my hands together and held them up in the air. Charles gave me a soft kiss on the cheek, and I felt a sense of achievement. I didn't get rid of the cigarettes for me; I did it for him. And I had high hopes that it would help break down his wall.

"We need to take your car to the nearest auto shop so we can get your oil changed and a new set of tires."

He removed the last lug nut, looking so manly and sexy. He made removing a tire look easy, despite his grunting between words. But hey, I wasn't complaining – his grunts were sexy too. It turned me on.

"I don't have any money to do all of that right now. Maybe I'll just get the one tire done. Payday is Friday. I got a new role, but the new pay isn't reflected just yet."

"Don't worry about it, A. I told you— I got you. We're gonna make sure it's in tip-top shape no matter what the cost."

"Charles, you are too sweet. You don't have to do that. I still feel bad about the other night. Hell, I'm the one who owes *you*."

"I know I don't have to do this, but I want to. I like to help people any way I can and whenever I can. Well, looks like we're ready to roll now," he said as he tightened up the last lug nut on the donut.

"That looks so ugly." I frowned.

"Girl, it ain't supposed to be pretty; it's temporary. But, since you're having such a shitty morning, I'll tell you what… You can drive my car and follow me to the shop. How does that sound?"

"Sounds good to me."

I didn't hesitate; I was excited to drive Charles' Bentley Continental. I jumped in his car faster than I could get the words out.

"Damn, A, that's a good look for you."

"It feels good too. I might be able to get one someday. This is my dream car."

"Only sleepers have dreams, baby. If you stay on top of your game, I'm sure you'll be blessed with one. Just be patient."

"Oh, I will. I still can't wait though." I gripped the wheel like I was revving the engine to a racecar.

"Don't hurt my baby now. I care about her a lot. She's almost as pretty as you are." Charles winked.

It was cute that he compared me to a car, but I knew I was prettier by far.

"So, I was thinking… while my car is getting fixed, we can grab a bite to eat - my treat. I need to redeem myself from the other night."

"Sounds great. But how are you going to treat anyone out? Payday is Friday, remember?" He laughed.

"I didn't say I was broke. I can afford lunch. I just can't afford the buffet of auto repairs you were trying to serve up."

He gave me a look like he didn't believe me.

"Aisha, like I said before, it will definitely be my treat. So, what do you have a taste for?"

The way the last words rolled off his tongue had me thinking all types of wild thoughts.

"Well, you already know what I got a taste for, but you won't let me have that."

I looked him up and down, softly biting my lip. He raised an eyebrow as if he was confused, but I'm sure he knew exactly what I was talking about. With lack of flirtatious response, I continued.

"As far as eating goes, anything is fine. I don't have a taste for anything in particular."

Charles shook his head and smiled.

"I never thought you would be this sweet on old Chunky Chucky."

"Well, I must say, you've grown up to be completely opposite from the way you were back in school. But I'm sure you know that. That's why you play hard to get – because you know you're worth it."

"If that's the case you should be playing hard to get too. Just remember that," Charles said as he brushed my hair away from my face through the window.

"But that's enough talking, sweetheart. Let's go. We can talk over lunch. We still have a lot of catching up to do."

# Chapter 11
## First Date

"I hope you like the food here." Charles quickly ushered me into the restaurant.

"If you like it, I love it. I'm sure I'll find something on the menu. Wow, this is a really nice place…"

I looked around and couldn't help but notice this was the power-lunch crowd full of business executives, doctors, and lawyers. It was my habit to scope the crowd for potentials. I prided myself on my knack for knowing a person's occupation based on their demeanor. (Eighty-five percent of the time I was right.)

"This is my favorite restaurant; I love it here. I come here so much they know me by name. I'd come in here with old raggedy jeans on if I wanted to. It's upscale but laid-back at the same time. Everyone here is so friendly and helpful; I've never had anyone cop an attitude or get my order wrong."

The hostess soon deterred Charles' attention.

"Good afternoon, Mr. Proctor… Madam. Will there only be the two of you dining today?" the hostess nodded to us as we walked up to the lectern.

"Yep, just me and the missus today."

"Delightful. Now I noticed that you didn't have a

reservation today, Mr. Proctor, so would you like a booth, center table, window…"

"That one right over there is fine." Charles pointed.

"Great, right this way."

Now seated, we ordered drinks and chatted while we waited.

"So, where do these clowns usually take you?" Charles asked.

I was too busy paying attention to the exotic aquarium nearby and didn't hear his question. He laughed. "Oh, so now you're paying more attention to the fish, huh?"

"Never. They don't even compare." I smiled. "Now, what were you saying?"

"I was asking where your dates usually take you. No one has ever brought you here before?"

"No. I saw this place and a few people invited me, but I turned them down because I didn't want to go with them.

"Oh, thank you," I said as I was served my glass of raspberry tea and Charles got his drink.

"You turned them down? Still the same old Aisha – breaking hearts. You must be messing with some real ballers if they can afford to bring you to a place like this." Charles took a sip of his margarita.

"If you want to say that. But you know me, I only deal with the best."

"Oh yeah, trust me, I know. So, what looks good to you?" He skimmed the menu.

"I think I'll have the fresh tossed greens and lobster tail. What are you getting?"

"I get the same everywhere I go - steak and potatoes. It's what I grew up on and it's what I love." Charles closed the menu.

At that moment, our server Hubert came out of nowhere. "Did I hear fresh-tossed greens and lobster tails for the lady and our best sirloin with potatoes for you, sir?"

"Yes, sir. That will be all. Medium-well on the steak, thank you," said Charles as the man scurried off.

"So, you might have to cook me some steak and potatoes one day. You know how to cook?"

"Of course, I do. I'll make you dinner one night and follow it up with breakfast in the morning." I placed my hand on top of his and stroked it slowly. (I know, I was laying it on thick.)

"I don't know about all that, but we can get together one day," Charles stuttered slightly.

I withdrew my hand.

"Why do you act like you're so scared of me?" I asked.

"It's not that I'm scared. I'm never scared, believe that, baby. It's just that there are some boundaries I don't want to cross, and I definitely don't want to give you the wrong idea. You know I always thought you were special even though you dissed me in school," he joked.

"That is the past, this is the present. Class dismissed." I tapped my glass of raspberry iced tea to make a ringing noise. "You won't regret if you have some of *this* desert. I promise."

"Okay, okay. You're right, the past is the past. But you just come to a point in life when you think enough is enough. I know there are certain things I should and should not be doing; there are things that I've done in the past that I'll be regretting until the day I die. There's a lot of stuff that makes me feel like just giving up; things both big and small remind you of the importance of those in your life and your relationships with them. That's why I think it's best if we just stay friends. I'd love to take it to another level with you, but you entered back into my life a little bit too late for all of that.

"So, none of that hanky-panky stuff like you tried to pull the other night, missy. You'll understand one day when I tell you the full story. It's really complicated. I just want to keep things platonic. I don't want to make any fatal mistakes."

"Fatal mistakes? How can having sex with me be a mistake? I might give you a heart attack because it's so good, but that's it. Fatal mistake... You act like you've killed somebody."

My heart immediately started racing and I stopped breathing for a moment. My eyes grew big as I leaned in over the table like I had a divine revelation. "You haven't, have you?" I whispered.

"No, woman. Do I look like a killer to you?" he laughed.

I sighed with relief.

"Well, I don't know. They come in all shapes and sizes these days. You know how those millionaires are – feel like they can get away with anything. I've seen enough *Lifetime* movies."

"No, no, no. It's not like that at all. I just don't want to get into it at this point because I don't want you to think differently of me, and I don't want you to feel bad for me. I hate pity parties. As our friendship grows and I feel more comfortable, I promise I'll let you know."

Hubert reappeared. (I promise this dude was like a little blond groundhog. He just popped up and you never saw him coming.)

"Lobster tails and tossed greens for you, ma'am, and a medium-well sirloin with potatoes for you, sir. Is there anything else I can get for you at this time?"

"No, everything looks fine, thank you." Charles nodded, looking at the spread.

Hubert gave a small bow and left.

"I'm starved," Charles started digging in before the waiter could walk away.

The food was fantastic; I savored every morsel. I hadn't had a meal so exquisite in a long time. I was happy I could share that moment with Charles.

After we finished our meals, we took a long walk in the park and talked about our pasts and what we've been doing since. It was a beautiful day, and everything was just perfect. We ended our day together when it was time to pick up my car.

"Thank you so much, Charles. You are truly a dear."

"No problem. Believe me, it's nothing. I wish I could do more."

"You always could; I wouldn't complain." I smiled. "So, when will I get a chance to see you again?"

"I have meetings for the rest of the week, so I'll be pretty busy. I'm sure we can arrange something though. I can always fit you into my schedule."

"Okay, well, I'll give you a call then."

"Cool. Drive safe, Aisha. I look forward to hanging out with you soon; maybe we can have lunch again. I'll give you a call and let you know."

I gave Charles a hug and a kiss on the cheek, got in my car, and drove off.

# Chapter 12
## Darla

I plopped down on the couch and began dialing numbers on Tonya's house phone.

"Who are you calling?" she asked as I compulsively pushed redial on her phone.

"Charles! I don't understand this man. He had a major crush on me in high school and now he has a chance to get with me and he won't even bite. We went out to lunch the other day, he got my car fixed, and then we went for a walk in the park where I tried to kiss him, but he moved away… I know there's nothing wrong with me and he swears up and down he's not gay. So, what's the problem? We finally spoke on the phone again yesterday and we're supposed to go on a picnic today. Now today he's not even answering my calls. This is some real BS," I exclaimed.

"Well, I don't know what to tell you, sis. Maybe you hurt him so bad years ago that he doesn't want you to get close to him in that way. Maybe he's afraid that you'll hurt him again. I mean, if he's not gay and he's not committed to anyone, then what else could it be?" Tonya sat on the edge of the couch.

"I don't know, but it's really starting to piss me off.

When I flirt with him or attempt to get close, he dismisses me so fast. How can we ever be more than friends if he doesn't even flirt back? How can I have his baby if doesn't even want to kiss me?"

"So, you were really serious about having his baby, huh?"

"Look, at first I wanted to have his baby just because I wanted to be rich. But to be completely honest, I feel like that's the only way I can keep him in my life. He comes around when he has time. I want to be around him all the time. You know what I think, Tonya? I think I'm falling in love with him."

"You love his money, not him. You only hung out with him a couple of times, so how can you love him already?" Tonya snatched the phone out of my hand in the middle of my redial.

"I don't know, maybe you're right. I might just be infatuated, but he's perfect in every way. If I had a baby by him, I'd never have to worry about money again. You see – it's a win-win. I'll have what I want, and he'll have the girl of his dreams. Face it, I live outside my means, Tonya. Doesn't matter how high I climb the corporate ladder, it's not enough. I can barely afford my house payment after taking out a second mortgage for all of those renovations, and I have credit card bills stacked to the ceiling. I'm so close I can taste it. The expensive foreign cars, the mansion, living debt-free, all designer clothes, a fine-ass man by my side. I don't want to keep working all of my life and Charles is my ticket to reaching my dreams and retiring early… like real early.

"You make six figures, Aisha. It's not like you're exactly poor. You just don't know how to manage your money. You can't just rely on this man as your way out."

"Look, I worked very hard to be where I am today. Going from rags to riches isn't easy, and still, I'm nowhere near where I want to be. With student loans and other debts, I still need more money. I'm striving to get to the top and I'm not stopping until I get there. I can't do it by myself. Don't you know there's a glass ceiling for minority women in the corporate world? I need help, dammit."

"I mean seriously, Aisha, how much money do you need? I'm sure it's not the student loans that are making you broke, but more so, your spending habits. If you didn't buy designer clothes every week then maybe you'd have money. You don't even save.

"Aside from that, what makes you think a baby is gonna make him stick around? I got two kids by the same man and where is he? With his newfound wife. And what about Charles? Didn't you say he has a son? He's not with the mother of his child - at least not that you know of. So, what makes you think having a baby would be such a good idea?"

"I'm pretty certain it'll be different with me. If not, at least I'll get the money. Money makes the world go 'round, right?

"Let's put it this way, Tonya – there's two different types of people in this world: the go-getters and the no-getters. Go-getters are opportunists – they see what they want and by any means necessary, they go get it. They're people like Donald Trump and Oprah Winfrey.

"On the other hand, there are the no-getters. No-getters are people that let life just pass them by; it doesn't mean they're not doing anything constructive with their lives, but they're not utilizing all their resources to reach their full potential - the people who are content with working their measly little nine-to-five jobs and don't feel it's necessary to seek anything greater.

"Now, there's nothing wrong with working a regular job if you're that kind of person, but see, the difference is that I am a go-getter. I realize that there's more out there than gangsters making money. I mean, of course, I can go back to dating drug dealers, but for what? Very few of them are rich, and besides that, dealing is short-lived. Now, with this situation I'm in, this is a life-long ordeal – and possibly one for generations to come. I'm sorry if you think I'm wrong, but I think I'm right."

"I see what you're saying, but you're going about it in the wrong way, sister. You can be a go-getter and not a gold-digger – there's a difference. I think you have your definitions twisted. I see a go-getter as someone who recognizes how successful people got where they are, and they apply that to their own goals. You know… having their own successes. That's why Oprah Winfrey and Donald Trump are go-getters. Do you think they waited until a billionaire came by and dropped money in their laps? No, they didn't. That's the difference, Aisha."

Tonya's face was flush with frustration as she raised her voice. "You're so spoiled, conceited, and selfish that you can't decipher reality from a dream world."

"Look, you have your beliefs and I got mine. I feel that this Charles situation is the only way out and that's what I'm sticking to. Things happen for a reason, you know. I'm a go-getter and I'm going to get what I want. I'm leaving. I'm going to do what makes me happy regardless of what you say. Matter of fact, why don't you just sit here and continue being a no-getter?"

I was furious. I couldn't understand why she didn't get where I was coming from. I got up and slammed the door on my way out.

~

Charles never answered the phone or returned my calls to confirm our picnic date. I just figured he was too busy or got sidetracked with work. He told me he would be at home most of the time making business calls, so I decided to go to his house to surprise him with an indoor picnic. I went home and packed sandwiches, fruit, and bottles of water.

I arrived at his house at eleven o'clock and when I pulled up I saw a new Bentley Continental GT parked in front of the mansion.

I walked around the car, admiring it from different angles. I waltzed up to the door with the basket and my purse in hand. Due to recent construction to the front foyer, the doorbell didn't seem to be working so I knocked on the door a couple of times, but there was no answer. I jiggled the handle just to see if it was unlocked, and to my surprise, it was. I felt like a kid sneaking open the cookie jar. I invited myself in and sat the picnic basket in the living room.

"Charles? Oh, Charles? Where are you?" I called out as I walked through the house looking around corners and into rooms. I freely sashayed up the long spiral staircase as if the mansion was mine. Nearing the top of the stairs, I heard the sound of running water from the shower in the master bathroom.

"Charles? Are you in there?" I whispered, hoping not to scare him. When there was no answer, I walked in and slowly pulled the steamy glass door open to see my baby's rock-hard body. A piercing shriek resonated against the bathroom walls.

"Oh, my god!" I yelled. "Who in the hell are you?"

In the shower stood the same lanky white woman who'd sat next to me in Lee's nail salon a few months prior. At first, I didn't recognize her as she'd traded her auburn tresses for long beach-blonde extensions. Her big blue eyes bucked from their sockets in fury. She put her hands on her naked hips as she began to rant. Her gangly posterior didn't match her pugnacious attitude. To my dismay, she didn't seem frightened at all – only angry.

"No, who in the hell are you? You're in *my* house. Are you the new maid or something? Where in the hell is Charles? Charles!" she bellowed.

She obviously did not recognize me from our previous encounter and neither did I mention it. It was already an awkward confrontation, and I was beyond pissed off.

"Excuse me? New maid? Bitch, are you crazy? I should be asking you what *you're* doing here. Where's Charles?" I combated.

"Oh, no, no, no. Do not talk to me in that tone. Who do you think you are? You have until I get out of this shower to tell me who you are, or I'll be calling the police." She stepped halfway out of the shower pointing her wet finger in my face. I smacked her hand away, showing her who was in charge.

"Lady, are you nuts? Call em', I don't care. You're the one taking a shower in *my* man's mansion," I confirmed.

*"Your man?"* The lady grabbed a towel and wrapped it around her naked body. "That is *my son's father.*

Technically, that is *my* man. So, with that in mind, I don't care who you are. You have no right to be lurking around this house unless *I* say so," she replied with sheer effrontery.

Her brash tone infuriated me, and rage ignited inside me. I felt hot blood rush through my veins like a rocket. I just knew this heffa didn't just say, *"Unless I say you can!"*

"Unless you say? Is that right? Oh okay, I get it now. You must be the whore who's been coming between Charles and I. Trying to wriggle your way back into his heart, huh? Well, I ain't going for it. And besides that, where's that son of yours at anyway, huh? Why are you even here? Don't you live across the county or something? If your son isn't here, then you shouldn't be here either. Tell me this: Are you sleeping with *my* Charles too?"

"Sleeping with him too? So, you're saying you're sleeping with him?" The woman seemed flabbergasted at the thought of him even being with another woman.

At that moment, the argument came to a brief halt as Charles barged into the bathroom, shocked to see both of us standing there.

"Whoa, whoa, whoa! What in the hell is going on here? Aisha, how'd you get in here?" he yelled.

"The door was open. I walked in, came upstairs, and saw this naked-ass lady in the shower. Don't question me like I did anything wrong. I should be the one asking you the questions. What happened to our picnic today? Why haven't you called me? Is it because you've been too busy screwing this bimbo?"

"Who are you calling a bimbo?" The lanky lady took two steps closer to me. We stared each other down like two cats about to pounce. Charles blocked her from getting any closer to me; he sensed it was about to be trouble.

"Darla, calm down, I can handle this. Look, Aisha, you're way out of line. What gives you the right to just come into my house uninvited? Do you know this is technically breaking and entering? I should call the police right now."

"You're going to threaten me? All because of this white, trashy, anorexic bimbo?"

"Trashy anorexic bimbo? You black bitch!" Darla leaped over Charles' arm and smacked me so hard I flew into the Jacuzzi.

I laid there a tad disoriented, waiting to regain my composure.

"This has gotten way outta hand. Darla, please, just go put some clothes on. Both of you are acting ridiculous." Charles directed Darla to the other room by pointing at the door. He offered his hand to help me out of the tub and shook his head in disgust.

I reached for the towel rack with my right hand and pushed myself out of the tub with my left. "I don't need your help, thank you very much. The only thing I need is for you to put her ass out. Instead, you're too busy doing whatever the hell you feel fit. Her over me? You must be crazy. You think you can play me, Charles? Who do you think I am? Do you think—"

"Look, stop. I don't want to hear another word out of your mouth, and I don't want to hear anything you have to say about Darla. I'm not saying that she was right, but you are definitely in the wrong."

"I didn't touch her though. If I'm breaking and entering, then what she did is battery. Tell the police that. She had no right to touch me. I would've been wrong if I'd have thrown her skinny ass into a wall."

"Look, Aisha, this is outta line. I need time to think.

You just need to go. We'll straighten this whole mess out later."

Charles rushed me down the stairs, making me stumble over my own feet on the way down. He didn't even give me time to speak.

"Need time to think? Wait… But I… Wait, Charles."

"Naw, naw, Aisha. I don't wanna talk to you today. You caused enough trouble already."

"You don't want to talk to me today? When *do* you want to talk to me?" I yelled in desperation. "Everything is your way or no way. You've been ignoring me, not answering my calls. You call me back whenever the hell you feel like it. Hell, I was trying to be nice and decided to bring you some lunch because I know that you've been working hard, and now this?"

"Wait, let's back this up. Not answering *your* calls? Like I told you before, I'm a businessman. I'm busy all of the time. I'm not obligated to answer your calls or to answer to you in any shape, form, or fashion. I can do whatever the hell I please and whatever I want with my phone.

"Who just pops up over someone's house that they barely know anyway? Are you crazy or something? You really crossed the line, Aisha. I don't want to deal with your crazy ass or any more of your drama. You are not about to bring any excess drama into my life. Hell, naw!"

Charles quickly guided me back to the front foyer.

I angrily spun around and pushed his hand off my shoulder.

"Businessman, huh? Is that the business that you have been handling? Is that why you've been dissing me? Because of that tramp? I understand she's your son's mother and all, but I'm a top-notch bitch. Nobody's better than

145

Aisha... Nobody. Remember that. You're retarded if you haven't recognized that by now." I snatched up the picnic basket and put one foot out the door.

Charles stopped me in my tracks. He leaned in close with wild, squinting eyes. His nostrils flared as hot air escaped his nose like a bull.

"No, Aisha, this whole ordeal with you popping up at my house is retarded. And let's get one thing straight... You may be a bitch, but you are *not* top-notch. Matter of fact, you don't even have a place in my future. Now get the hell outta here before I lose all my scruples and gentlemen-like ways. You'll end up witnessing a side of me that you wish you hadn't."

Darla, now fully dressed, suddenly appeared in the door behind Charles. "Excuse me, but what did you say? Did you call me a tramp? You don't even know me and I sure in the hell don't know you."

"Oh no, you know me. And if you don't, then you *should* get to know me because you're gonna see a lot more of Aisha 'round here, so you just need to learn to accept that."

Darla's eyes cut sharply to Charles.

"You better do some fucking explaining real quick and I mean it. Does she know? Did you tell her? About me? About you? About our son?"

"Look, Darla, it's not like that. Listen to me when I say, me and this girl are *not* together. We hung out and went to lunch once – That's it."

"Excuse me? *That's it?* First off, don't talk about me like I'm not standing here," I interrupted. "Secondly, *it is* more than that, Darla. This man has been in love with me since high school, and since the reunion we've sparked a

146

romance. So, don't act like it's not *like that*, Charles, when you were just all over me the other night."

Darla's mouth dropped. I could see the disgust and anger in her eyes. The overly tanned skin around her mouth began to wrinkle up. I knew she wanted to say something, but she didn't have anything to say.

"Yep, right in that pool back there." I pointed to the back of the mansion, embellishing what had taken place the night of the reunion.

"So, Miss Darla, you guys need to fix this situation real quick because I don't appreciate you lurking around here while I'm not around."

"You sick, twisted bastard. You're a trifling man. I should've smacked you, not her. Have you lost your damn mind, Charles? This is what started our life change in the first place – you cheating on me. You know what? I'm out of here. I can't take this anymore." Darla grabbed her jacket from the coat rack and headed out the door and to her car.

"Darla, wait," Charles wailed.

"No, Charles. It's over," she yelled as she stomped to the car. "And you know what, lady? You can have him. But I warn you to be careful; you don't want what happened to me to happen to you," she yelled at me out the window of the red Maserati that I initially thought belonged to Charles.

"No, I don't have to be careful, because he won't ever cheat on me like he did on you. Bye, have a nice life." I waved her off as she sped away.

"What in the hell has gotten into you? You're acting crazy right now. If I knew you were like this, I wouldn't have even invited you over that night. Something is wrong with you in the head." Charles tapped me on the side of my temple.

"Don't touch me, you damn liar. She's the reason you don't want to be with me. Just keep it real and admit it."

"Look, that's my son's mother. I'll always have a relationship with her if you're in the picture or not. That's not going to change. But this? This right here? What you are doing is going to change. I see I have to put my foot down with you. Don't call me anymore; I don't want to see you again. Now get off my steps before I really call the cops."

"The cops? Oh, it's like that? Call them then. You don't know who you're messing with, Mr. Proctor. You probably ain't even celibate; you just been sexing that white whore and you scared of being with a real woman," I exclaimed.

Charles clutched my shoulders vehemently and looked into my eyes. His nostrils flared again, and his grip was strong.

"That is my son's mother. Don't you *ever,* and I mean *ever*, talk to her or about her like that again. You hear me? We've been through a lot together. Me and you? We're nothing. You got that? Nothing. So leave A, before things get ugly. I really don't want to have to go that route."

"What are you going to do, Charles, hit me? So, you a woman beater now too? Hit me then, Charles. Hit me, I dare you to."

Charles clenched his fists and bit his bottom lip. "Stay far, far, away from me, Aisha. I'm through with your crazy ass. You just go about your life the way you been doing."

He stepped back in the door and slammed it in my face.

"That's okay," I yelled from the other side of the door. "You don't know me like that. Keep talking to me crazy; you got another thing coming. I'll be back."

I knew he was on the other side listening, so that was good enough for me. I threw the picnic basket at the door as I walked away; it made a loud thump, decorating his door with an array of meat, cheese, bread, and fruit. I jumped in my car and skidded off, angry and confused.

# Chapter 13
## Awakening

One month went by and still no answer from Charles. I left him apologetic messages on his voicemail, but still no reply. I'm determined to get him back into my life, no matter what it takes," I rambled over the phone to Tonya.

"Just hang it up. You went over the man's house, got him and his son's mother all upset, popped up without notice, invited yourself in, started a ghetto commotion, and lied about your relationship. *Now* you expect him to answer the phone? Come on, A. If someone came over your house doing all that, I know you'd be more pissed off than he is right now. If I were him, I wouldn't answer your calls either. Hell, I might even get a restraining order."

"I was just really mad. You know I can't control my temper. When I saw that lady, it seemed like my head was going to explode. I guess you were right all along. I knew it was something up with him. He's still messing with that wretched woman. That's why he didn't want to be with me like that."

"Yeah, well, I told you from the get-go it was something. You act like just because I'm a couple of years younger than you that I don't know these things. You may have dated more guys, but when it comes to relationships, I know how people operate."

"Oh, shut up, Dr. Phil. You always think you know something," I joked.

"That's because I do. Just leave the man alone and move on with your life, A. You're acting like a stalker or something."

"Yeah, maybe you're right. But I don't know what I'm going to do; he drives me crazy. You know that I'm not a quitter, and he's one of the things on my 'To Do' list. If he just gives me one more chance or would return just one of my phone calls, I'd show him that I'm truly a good woman."

"I call your bluff on that one, playa." Tonya laughed.

"No joke. If given the opportunity, I would be a good woman to him. As long as he was doing me right and taking care of me, that's all that would matter. I would be all the woman he wants me to be. We could get married, have kids… It would be perfect."

"You're ridiculous. First you were talking about having a kid by him, now you're talking about marrying this man? Wow, Aisha, you're really smart. You want to have kids with a man who won't have sex with you, and you want to marry a man who doesn't want anything to do with you. That's just spectacular. Now I see who the brainiac of the family is." Tonya laughed hysterically.

"There is nothing funny about this, Tonya. Why is it that every time I say something about my life you always say something negative? You don't ever take me seriously. What's your problem?"

"How can I take you seriously? You say the dumbest things. I just reply with real talk. Sometimes the truth hurts, dear. *Get over it!* If my truthful talk happens to come out negative, it's probably because you're saying something stupid again. You can't make somebody fall in love with you that don't even like you, and you can't have a baby by someone that you can't have sex with. That's just logic. What are you going to do, rape him or something?" Tonya paused, waiting for my response. "Hello?"

"Tonya, you're a genius. I'll talk to you later."

I hung up before she could say another word.

~

Later that evening I decided to take a walk in the same park that Charles and I had strolled together a month earlier. It was now fall and the once-green trees had shed their foliage, painting the ground amber and soft crimson. Crunchy leaves crumbled beneath my feet with every step, stimulating my thoughts. I sat on a swing, contemplating my next move as my legs dangled like a child. Perturbed and perplexed, I sat there until the sun went down, thinking about my future... thinking about what my sister said... thinking of Charles.

# Chapter 14
## Birthing a Plan

"Hey doc! How are you today?" I eagerly hopped onto the table. The lilt in my voice made it hard to believe I was at the gynecologist's office. Nevertheless, on this particular day I was ecstatic to be there.

"I'm fine, Aisha. You're in a cheery mood today. So, what are you in for? Annual PAP?" Doctor Fowler held her laptop and peered over her glasses as she reviewed my medical history. She had been my gyno for years and I felt completely comfortable with her. She knew almost everything about me - everything except what I was about to spring on her next.

"Well, first of all, I am happy to let you know that I'm engaged."

"Engaged, oh my. Congratulations, Aisha. Last time you were in you didn't even have a boyfriend. Who is the lucky fellow who's swept you off your feet so quickly?" Her cheeks were rosy, and she bared a smile that was bigger than Chester Cheetah's.

"His name is Charles, and he is a spectacular man; he's a millionaire mogul. He's educated, funny, and handsome." I clasped my hands together, smitten.

"Okay, now that sounds too good to be true. So,

what's wrong with him?" she joked, pushing her glasses back up on her nose.

"Nothing; he's just perfect. Oh, there is one thing I guess... He already has a son, so I'm stepping into a ready-made family. That's the main reason why I'm here today. Charles and I would like to have a baby of our own right away. I want to make sure that I'm healthy and my body is prepared to carry a baby."

Doctor Fowler seemed taken aback. She took a deep breath and folded her arms. By my years of knowing her, I knew she was preparing to give me a lecture.

"Aisha, stepping into a ready-made family isn't always a problem. There are plenty of blended families out there that are more functional than most nuclear families.

"Now, I must admit, there is one thing I'm concerned about - Why the rush for a family right now? You still have several years until you're even close to advanced maternal age. Don't you want to wait until after you are married to have a child? It's a big responsibility and conception should not be rushed. I get it, you seem genuinely smitten, but have you truly planned and thought this out carefully?"

"Yes, of course we have. We've had long discussions about what we want our future to be like, and having kids was one of the major discussions. I may not get pregnant today or tomorrow, but we do want it to happen soon. We're just planning a small backyard wedding with family and close friends. We've decided to do something very intimate so that only our true friends will be there. Actually, we're getting married next week."

"Next week? Wow, that's fast. *Very* fast."

"I know it may seem that way, but we've known each other for quite some time now. Friends soon became lovers, and he just popped the question, just like that. At that moment, I was overwhelmed with joy, and I said yes!"

I threw my arms up with excitement.

"Love has no waiting period, Doc."

"Agreed," she said, sounding doubtful. "If you're happy, that's all that matters. I wish you both the best.

"So, where's the ring? I would love to see it." She looked at my hand, noticing the bare ring finger.

"Oh, I was doing some housework today and forgot to put it back on. I don't know what I was thinking. I'll show it to you the next time I come in. It's beautiful – a rare pink diamond."

"My goodness. A pink diamond? That had to cost a fortune."

"It did, but he insists on only the best for me. Since we're having a small ceremony, he put a lot of money into the ring. He is so special."

"Yes, he sounds special indeed.

"Okay, well let's get to it then. Since you're trying to get pregnant, what I'll do is give you a PAP test and take some cultures to make sure you have a happy, healthy environment in which to carry a fetus."

"Yep, that's *exactly* what I want."

Minutes felt more like an hour before the doctor announced she was nearly finished with my exam. "You okay?" she asked.

"I'm fine, Doc. I just can't wait to get pregnant. I'm so excited."

"I remember feeling like that with my first. Those little suckers are a handful though, I tell ya. But, if both of you are mentally and financially prepared to have a baby, you'll be fine."

"Yep. Now I'm ready physically too, right?"

"So far, so good. I'm glad you're going about this the right way, Aisha. Most women don't care if their bodies are prepared or not. You're a healthy young woman. The only thing now is to get the test results and you'll be all set."

"Thank you, Doc. I'm sure my fiancé will be thrilled."

"I'm sure he will be. Congratulations again on everything. I'll be giving you a call by the end of the week with your results, or you can check the patient portal. Do you have any questions?"

"Actually, yes. I'm sure in your files it shows that I have abnormal periods; I usually have them monthly, but I never know when they're coming. Would that affect my chances of getting pregnant?"

The doctor skimmed over my history in the computer as she stuck her neck out, peering over her glasses.

"Yes, I see that here. Well, for most couples who are healthy and have no medical issues, the normal timeframe for conception could be up to six months, even when having sex during the time of ovulation. However, for you, it could be hard to pinpoint ovulation. I can give you a prescription for Clomid; that will help you become more regular. This should help you home in on the best days to conceive. However, before I do so, it's standard to check your fiancé's sperm count. I can recommend a good testing center for you." She started writing something on a small sticky note, but I stopped her.

"No!" I wailed.

"Is there a problem? I know men can feel a bit uncomfortable about it but if you guys are trying for a baby, I'm sure he'll be okay with it."

"No, it's not that," I began, "it's just that since he already has a son, we're confident he's not shooting blanks, if you know what I mean. I think he might feel insulted or like I'm doubting him."

"Ah, gotcha. Well, if you're both adamant about not getting the sperm count done, then I can't force you. But I will tell you this: studies show that being on Clomid for more than six months won't increase your chances of pregnancy. So, you need to make sure that everything else, including him, is working properly. Get my drift?"

"Of course, I hear you, but I assure you, I know what I'm doing and I'm willing to take that risk."

"Alright, alright. I can only suggest it. You can get the prescription filled today and then get the process going. We'll cross our fingers and wish for the best. You'll need to come in once a month while on the medication so I can check for any complications. Other than that, I think you're good to go. Take care, Aisha. We'll set you up for monthly visits until you get that little one." She winked before heading out of the room.

As soon as I got out of the doctor's office, I turned my phone back on and quickly scrolled down to Charles' number, hoping he would pick up.

Still no answer. I wasn't used to being put on the back burner and it infuriated me. My hand started to tremble, and I nervously tapped my foot. Charles was becoming a challenge - one that I so desperately wanted to conquer. The more he ignored me, the more a hunger rose up inside to make him mine by any means necessary.

I marched to my car and hopped in. Willing and ready to go to extreme measures, once my Bluetooth connected I said, "Dial Lil' Saab."

He and I didn't talk often; however, he always had my back when I needed him.

Lil' Saab got his name because he was only 4'11" and he only drove Saabs. He had gold on the entire top row of his teeth and he talked with a lisp. He always sported 'locs with a fresh line-up and wore long t-shirts that went to his knees. (It was hard to speculate if the t-shirts were long because he liked them that way or because of his height – who knows.) I really didn't care one way or another, I just knew that he could play a big role in getting me what I wanted – what I needed – and that was a baby with Charles.

Lil' Saab was a big-time drug dealer in my old neighborhood. Though I disassociated myself from the Southside, I never severed ties with Saab. His brother Mikey was the only real boyfriend I'd ever had. Unlike Saab, Mikey wasn't into pushing heavy weight; he only sold enough to pay his momma's bills, put food on the table, and take care of necessities. Mikey was kind-hearted and never wanted to be part of the game, but felt he had no choice. One night after walking me home, he was shot execution-style in a back alley. The murder was left as a cold case and rocked us to the core. Another black kid in the hood whose life was taken too soon. Since then, Lil' Saab and I remained close. Even though we never talked about him, I often reminisced about Mikey and the type of life we could have had together—if he was indeed in fact my *true* love.

"What up, A? What's goin' on?" Lil' Saab said when he answered the phone.

"Hey, Saab. How are you?"

"You know how I do… Chillin', chillin'. *Ay, Mane, hold down a hot second, Mane.* What's good, baby girl?" Lil' Saab was talking to me but holding side conversations at the same time. (He did that a lot – the life of a dealer.)

"Umm, I need to ask you a favor. I know it's kind of ahhh... never mind."

"Just spit... *One hunnid? Yeah, a'ight, I got you.* What was I saying? Oh yeah, spit it out, sis. You know whatever it is, I gotchu."

I sighed. "Okay, I need... I need... *something.*" I couldn't just come out and say exactly what I needed because that is a big no-no, even on a burner phone (which I knew Saab had).

"Somethin', huh? Well, whatever it is, you know I got you. It's fo you? Or it's fo someone else?"

"It's for a friend of a friend."

"A friend of a friend, huh? So, what *exactly* does this friend need?"

"How can I put this," I said, trying to be crafty with my words. "So, it's like they need... a... something to relax someone on a date... if that makes sense," I stuttered and silently cringed.

"What kind of friends you got that need sumthin like dat? That's cray-cray, folk. It don't seem like you be hangin' round people like that, 'specially nowadays. I dunno, A. Guess you know what you're doin. What kind and how much?"

"I don't know what kind; I didn't even know there are different kinds. They just asked if I knew anyone that had anything, and I told them I'd see. What kind do you have? How much is it?"

"The price depends on how much they want and what kind. If they wanna buy a lot, then I can do wholesale price, but if they only wanna buy a small quantity, then I gots to charge them a little extra. Know what I'm sayin? You know

159

how the game goes, A.

"Yeah, I gotcha. Nothing big, you know? But what kind do you have so I can tell them?"

"I have and can get all kinds, baby. You know I got the connects. I got what they need – just let me know what they want." Lil Saab choked between words. He stayed high as a kite; must've been in the middle of smoking.

"Alright, I'll do that. I'll talk to you a little later on."

Lil' Saab uttered, "Right on," before hanging up.

It was time to do a little research to figure out how to put my plan into action.

# Chapter 15
## One-Time Deal

"Hello?" I answered frantically. My house phone didn't ring often, so when it did it startled me.

From the time I got home, I'd been pacing my living room, consumed with putting my master plan into action. The noise of my thoughts muffled the subtle sound of my cell. Tonya decided to call my house since I wasn't answering, snapping me out of deep thought.

"Hey, what's up, girl? Whatchu doin? Is everything okay?" her voice radiated through the other end of the phone. (I guess she picked up on my uneasiness.)

"Yeah, everything's okay. I'm just thinking, that's all."

I went into the dining room to grab my laptop.

"You feel like hitting up some boutiques? I got some extra cash, and I feel like treating myself."

"Naw, I'm kinda busy right now."

"You? Too busy for shopping? Must be something serious. What's on your mind, sis?"

"Well, you should already know who I'm thinking about."

"*Who*? Oh brother, Aisha. Please don't tell me you're talking about Charles again."

"What do you mean? Of course I am. I can't get him off my mind. I want him bad and I'm confident that I'm going to find a way to get him to feel the same."

"Aisha, you might as well hang it up. You sound desperate – and it's definitely not becoming on you."

"Not desperate – determined."

"Hey, if that's what you think. I think you should let it be. I'm pretty sure you'll run into some rich, handsome, well-established, well-groomed, too-damn-close-to-perfect, multi-millionaire someday... Not!" Tonya couldn't control her laughter.

I couldn't chime in on her chuckles; I didn't think a damn thing was funny.

"You always think something's amusing. I know the chances of me running into someone of that caliber again are slim to none; that's why I got to get him. I can't lose out on that man. I'm for real." My tone was serious as I clicked the internet browser a bunch of times. It wasn't loading fast enough for my taste.

"What are you doing?" Tonya asked, hearing the multiple clicks in the background.

"Nothing," I snapped.

Reality was, I was on a mission, and she was bothering me. I didn't have time to be lollygagging with my sister. I had business to take care of. My eyes were fixed on my Mac as if they were being held open with toothpicks.

"Well, excuse me. Since you have a little attitude, I'm about to get off the phone. Holler at you later."

Without saying goodbye, I hung up and continued the task at hand. I didn't care if I was being rude; I had things to do. I proceeded to research almost every drug used as a "date rape drug" that I could. Most of them were odorless and colorless, which was good, making them easy to slip into a drink. I just had to think of some way to get a hold of Charles so I could make it happen. It had to be perfect timing. No Charles, no pregnancy. I decided to call up Saab to hopefully clarify some of the products. I was so confused.

I concluded my thoughts and worked up the nerve to call Lil' Saab to place my order.

"Hey, what's going on, Saab?"

"Man, what up, baby? My bad about earlier, but I was runnin' 'round takin' care of business, you know me. So, what up? Did you get in touch wit your peoples? You find out how much dey want and what dey need? I'm ready to make dis happen. New customers are the best customers. So, what dey want?"

I dilly-dallied around, trying to be crafty with my words. "They want a date on the roof, I believe." (I was sure Saab heard the uncertainty in my voice.)

"Ruffies?" he blurted.

"Saab!"

"Girl, ain't nobody checkin for ruffies. Nobody even use dat damn word anymo, folk!" He paused as if he wanted me to say something back. "Ruffies, 'you believe'? Either you do or you don't know, so which one is it? Didn't dey give you money or somethin' for what dey want? Why don't you just let one of my mans talk to them so we know fo sho. That's the whole reason why you didn't get it earlier, right? I like my customers to be satisfied so dey come back for mo, you feel me? You need to make sho you got it right or else I ain't givin' you nuttin' at all," Saab said arrogantly.

I huffed out of frustration. This was more complicated than I originally thought, and Saab's lisp combined with his ghetto gibber-jabber was hard to follow.

"Look, Saab, enough with all the questions. I only need this as a one-time deal. Do me this one favor and I'll be out of your hair."

"Favor?" Saab cut in. "Is this fo someone else or you? Keep it real, A."

"Does it really matter, Saab? That's beside the point anyway. I need—"

"Naw, that ain't beside the point. I wanna know what it's fo now. This whole situation seems stranger than an Eskimo eating a popsicle naked in Alaska… You jus call me outta the blue wanting dem thangs and you ain't talked to me in months. You might be sellin' to dem boys or somethin'. How do I spose to know? I ain't tryin' to get caught up in nuttin' like dat right there. I mean, me and you is cool, but your peeps… I dunno dem muthafuckas. Dis might be a set-up or somethin. Can't trust nobody nowadays, you feel me?"

"So, what're you trying to say? That I'd set you up? I would never do anything like that to you. I can't believe you'd think I would do something like that after all we went through with your brother. You're just paranoid as hell, that's all," I yelled.

"Calm down, lil' momma. I'm not sayin that *you* tryna set me up, per se. What I'm sayin' is, you can neva be too careful. I dunno who you givin this stuff to, mane… Might be a set up. Dey go through lil' people like you to bring the big boys down. You feel me? All I'm sayin' is, try not to get into nuttin' foul, A. I ain't bout to go to lock up fo nobody. I know how to play da game but dis game ain't no game dat you need to be playin' wit. I don't know what you tryna to do or what you into now, but a few bucks don't mean nuttin' to me. You know you like a sister. I don wanchu gettin in any trouble or gettin caught up in somethin' dat you don't know nothin' bout. Dat's why I wanna know who these folk is, cuz they might be dem boys. You dunno that fo sho, right?"

"Look, Saab, I'm getting a headache," I said, rubbing my temples. "This conversation went way left and it's turning out to be more complicated than it should be. So, I'm just going to keep it real with you."

"Yes, please do… Proceed."

"I'm not getting into anything crazy, okay? The truth is – it's for me. I need to do something. No one is getting set up; no one is getting hurt. I just need you to do me a favor and that's it. I don't need a million questions asked and I damn sure don't need a lecture. Just give me the stuff and let's be done with it," I demanded, realizing I sounded somewhat bratty.

"Damn. Okay, I'm just tryna look out fo yo crazy ass. Ya know, watch both our backs. But as long as everythang coo, then we straight. I got some other stuff that will blow yo mind though, or whoever it's fo, you feel me?"

"Okay, I'm listening. What is it?"

"Man, dis the best. It's new on the market… Well, round the midwest, at least. Take some of dis and you will be floatin' high as a kite. This came from across da water. Nobody got dis round the Chi. It's pricy, but I can letchu cop it fo wholesale. It's fo you though, right? If it's fo some otha folk, I gotta tax."

"No, Saab, it's for me," I reiterated.

"That's what up. So, is dat whatchu want den?"

"Yeah, yeah, yeah, that's what I want, I guess. You said it was the best, right?"

"It's the best, baby girl. I wouldn't stir you wrong. Whatchu lookin' for? An aphrodisiac or somethin?"

"Yeah, something like that. But not for me, for someone else."

"I thought you just said dis was for you, folk?"

"Oh, my god, Saab. What's with all of the got-damn questions? I need it to do something. Do I really have to let you know all of my business?"

"Naw, lil' one. I don't want to know all the biz. The only reason I was askin', baby girl, is cuz when you take dis, you might not 'member what happened the night before. So, if you take it, you betta be careful. You don't wannabe round a bunch a folk and somebody take advantage. Then I'd hafta *click-clock* and let the gun go *pop*, you feel me? You know I keep that thang on my hip and she's closer than my honey dip. So, if anythin' goes wrong, you need to let me know."

"Naw, don't be worried. Nothing's gonna happen to me. I'll tell you about it some other time since you're one of the only people I trust."

"That means a lot, A, cuz you one of da only bitches dat I trust – fo real, no offense."

"None taken. I know how we rock. So, getting back to this stuff, is it a pill or what?"

"Naw, it's actually sold inna lil' tube. It's clear, so most people jus drank it straight fo an immediate reaction or put it in they drank. If you put it in your drank it take bout twenty minutes to kick in, since it dilutes."

"Oh, okay, that's perfect. That's just what I need to get the job done."

"Git da job done? What the fuuuck! What you tryna do, A? Rip somebody off or somethin'? You know if you messin' wit some of dem rich boys or one of those folks that's high up in da game, I can just have my mans an 'nem run up in da crib and take whatever you want. Don't worry,

166

we won't kill 'em. Yo name won't even be brought up."

"Saab! You are saying a whole lot on this phone," I sassed.

"Naw, I'm sayin a whole lot of nothin. Long as nothin happens, nothin is nothin, you feel me?"

The way Saab always had analogies and spoke in riddles reminded me of an old pimp.

"Don't worry about it, Saab. This is a solo act. I want to handle this on my own. Besides, it's not a situation like that where I'm just trying to 'rip someone off' as you say. No one else need be involved. So, in saying that, when can I get the stuff?"

"Aight, hold tight, I'll make it right. Meet my mans at the gas station right ova there by 83rd and Racine in twenty minutes. He'll be in a black Caprice. Oh yeah, and no credit cards. I know how you roll," Lil' Saab laughed.

I disregarded his comedic gesture.

"Why do I have to meet up with somebody else? Why can't I meet up with you?"

"I'm all the way in Gary right now, baby girl. I can give it to you myself, but you gotta wait till later. Right now, I'm out in these streets doin my thang. You feel me?"

"Well, go ahead and do you. I'll just meet with him then. But damn, why do I have to meet with him all the way over there? You got me all up in the hood, don't you?"

"Baby girl, I know how you feel bout bein in da hood. But I know you don't think he gonna come out to the burbs, do you? You must be trippin' fo real. He don't have time to be runnin' all over. I be on some real money shit and I need him to go to—"

"Alright, alright, I'll be there. Which gas station?"

"Don't play, A… You know which one. Right der by

Aberdeen."

"Alright."

With no time to waste I snatched up my keys and jetted out the door.

# Chapter 16
## Lemonade

Finally, I had everything I needed to complete my mission. I lined up all my pregnancy-related contraband like a soldier preparing for war. Pregnancy tests... check. Illicit drugs... check. Ovulation kit... check. I strategically paced the floor, about-facing every few seconds to observe the items on the bed. I came to a halt as I visually inspected the ovulation kit. My curiosity could no longer wait. I snatched the kit off the bed, busted open the box, and grabbed an ovulation stick along with the directions. I knew my cycle would be coming up soon, so I wanted to do my calculations. I anxiously rushed off to the bathroom to begin the process.

I looked at the directions and followed them to a T. The minutes leading up to the results were painfully slow. I breathed shallowly and watched for a symbol to show.

*An O? That means that I'm not fertile now? That doesn't make sense. I'm supposed to come on in a few days. This is some BS.*

Upset, I chucked the test in the trash and stormed out of the bathroom and back into my bedroom. I threw the rest of the contraband in my panty drawer for safekeeping. I tried to call Charles' number again. Nothing. The only thing I got from his end of the line was the same damn tired ringing, which led to the same damn tired voicemail. Frustrated, I fell backward onto the bed. Several minutes went by without a blink as I was completely absorbed with my own thoughts. My eyes grew bloodshot, and I peered at the ceiling, feeling as if a speculum was holding them open. Anxiety rose inside me like a riot; I was adamant about making Charles mine. Snapping me out of my reverie, my phone rang.

"Hello?" I answered anxiously without looking at the number. I was excited, thinking it was Charles finally returning my call.

"Is this Aisha?" an unfamiliar voice projected from the other end.

"No, this is not Aisha. She isn't here right now. Can I take a message?" I changed my voice to a higher pitched, conservative voice.

"This is Tony Benser calling on a business matter. We've been trying to get in touch with her for some time now and she never seems to be home. She must be a busy woman. Do you know what time she will be back... Or will she *ever* be there?" The sarcasm was blunt, yet indirect.

"I'm sorry you haven't been able to get a hold of her; I'm the house sitter. I don't know what time she'll be home." I responded with twice the sarcasm.

"House sitter, huh? How do you not know when she'll be home if you're the house sitter? Seems odd. And what's even odder is that she would leave the house sitter with her cell phone. I'll tell you this, young lady. I hope you're not getting paid for doing that house sitting job because you won't have a job much longer. You want to know why? Because that friend Aisha of yours won't have a house for you to sit in. She shouldn't be paying anyone anything when she can't even pay her bills." The man fluctuated his voice on ever other word to make sure I understood everything he was saying.

"Excuse me? Where do you get off talking to me like that? You will not… And I do mean, *will not* bully me in this conversation." My anger and irritation grew the more he babbled.

"Wow, you're some feisty little house sitter, huh?"

"That's none of your damn business who I am and if I'm feisty or not. You shouldn't be discussing her house foreclosure with me anyway; that's against the law."

"Wow, that's interesting. I never said this was for a foreclosure. I said this was a business matter. So how would you know all of that 'Miss House Sitter?' Are you her accountant too?"

"No, it's common sense. You said—"

"Look, Aisha, cut the crap. I know this is you. We're done playing your cat and mouse games. We've sent you numerous letters and called all your contact numbers several times. You already know that your house is in foreclosure. Why don't you just pay up? If you don't pay your entire back mortgage, we'll be evicting you out of your nice little home. That's going to screw up your credit and no one will give you a loan. Hell, even apartment complexes won't want you there once we get done with you. I don't know how you could get this far behind. I can't even fathom how you live with your mortgage out of control like this. I need you to get that payment in ASAP. It better be all of it too; I don't want half, and I don't want a percentage. When I say all, I mean every little red cent. You got that?"

"Look, first of all, you don't even know if this is Aisha or not. Secondly—"

The man rudely interrupted. "I don't want to hear

171

your 'first of alls' or 'secondlys'. You've said enough. Please just stop talking and save me some hassle. I know your voice; I hear it on the voicemail every time I call your home, your cell, and your job. Speaking of job, I don't think they're that happy with me calling either. I'm surprised they haven't said something about that yet. I know that if I were your employer, I wouldn't put up with that crap. But on the other hand, if you pay your bills you wouldn't have to worry about the harassment and embarrassment. Now, I don't care if you're Aisha or not, even though I'm pretty damn sure you are. But if you're not Aisha, then you need to tell her to pay her bill, or it'll be curtains for her. No need to give you the number; I'm sure you already got it."

I didn't let the man finish his side of the conversation before I hung up the phone and threw it across the room. I didn't feel the need to speak to him any longer. Obviously, he said what he had to say and frankly I was tired of listening to him badger me.

*Uhhh, could my day get any worse? I can't believe that stupid bank is threatening me now. How in the hell am I supposed to come up with money like that? I have to get in contact with Charles; he's the only one I know who has the means to help me. I don't know what else to do. That damn Neal. I knew I shouldn't have stopped screwing him.*

I retrieved my phone from the other side of the room and immediately dialed Neal. He answered on the first ring.

"Hello, who's this?" he said.

"Who is this? It's Aisha. Who do you think it is? What, you don't have my number in your phone anymore?"

"Hell no. Why should I have your number in my phone? Knowing you has brought me nothing but misery. Anyway, I got a girlfriend now, so I definitely had to erase your number. She doesn't like me talking to other ladies. Or whatever you want to call yourself. With that in mind, you can't be calling my phone. So, lose my number."

"Damn, do you have to say it like that? To be quite honest, I don't care if you got a girlfriend or not. And I'll call you when I feel like it. I just didn't feel like calling you until now. I want to know why, for the past six months, your company has been breathing down my throat, talking about how they want payment. Some man today said my house was in foreclosure. What's that all about? I thought you were taking care of that."

"Correction: I *was* taking care of it until you started acting like a *puta*. You think I'd still help you out after you just used me? Yeah, right. Pay your bills, lady," Neal yelled.

"What do you mean? We had an agreement; you can't just do that to me."

"The hell I can't. I can do what I want. Agreement, my hairy ass," Neal argued.

"This isn't right, and you aren't right either. I thought you were down for me," I bickered.

"The key word is *were*. Look, Aisha, when you started treating me the way you did, I threw my hands up. I couldn't take it anymore. I didn't want anything to do with you. I even handed your account over to another rep. I washed my hands of you. I helped you get that house; you should be thanking me, but now I guess they backtracked to show how much you really paid. No es *mi problema, chica.* My hands are clean. That's your dirty bed, you lie in it. Now, I'm sorry, but I gotta go because my girl is waiting. Oh, and please don't call me again. I can't jeopardize my relationship with a real woman for you. And by the way, it's best if you pay my company the money because they aren't joking around. With back payments and late fees, I believe you owe them around ten grand. There's nothing I can help you with now. Adios."

"Bastard," I yelled into the phone, but it was too late; he had already hung up. I pulled my legs up to my chest and shed tears until my eyes were bloodshot and my head pounded. I headed to the bathroom to wash my face; my mascara looked like a small child took a black magic marker and went to town, my face being the canvas. I stared at myself in the mirror, dazed, wondering why all of this was happening to me. My life was falling apart at the seams. I didn't have anywhere to turn. I didn't want to lose everything I had. I'd been through too much and worked too hard to get where I was. I sucked up my tears and dried my eyes. *Get yourself together, Aisha. It's showtime.*

I ran some water in the sink to wash my face and to re-do my makeup. I needed to gather myself before calling Charles, yet again. I changed my clothes and went downstairs to make a fresh batch of lemonade. I normally would have chosen a chilled bottle of Chard from my wine fridge, but mentally, I needed to see that no matter how sour something is, it can turn into something refreshing. I stepped out on the deck and sat in my Swingasan, brainstorming on what I would say before calling Charles.

*What can I say to get him to call me back? I've tried to be nice, and I've tried being aggressive. I don't know what to do anymore. I'm just going to be honest and see where that gets me. All I need him to do is talk to me. After we speak, I know I can talk him into meeting up. God, please, give me the right words to say so that he can call me back.*

I dialed once more, wishing for a miracle and hoping that the words I spoke got him to call me back. I desperately needed to talk to him.

"Hey, Charles, it's me, Aisha. I know that you're tired of me calling, but I just wanted to sincerely apologize for any stress I caused. I really didn't mean to bring on all that drama and I definitely don't want to lose a good friend. I've really been going through a lot lately, and quite honestly, I could use a good friend right now.

"I'm about to lose my house; I'm about to lose everything I have. It makes me sick to my stomach to know that everything I worked so hard for is going to be gone. I only got about a week to come up with almost eleven thousand dollars, and I'm out of options. I know this is bold, but if you can help me out, I promise I'll repay you as soon as I can. If you can't do it, that's okay, I understand. I just want you to call me back, please. I don't care if it's to help me out, accept my apology, or just to say, 'Damn you.'

"I still want to be friends. I need you in my life more than you know. You're the only person that truly cares for me. Truthfully, sometimes I feel that not even my mom or my sister really care about me. Sometimes I feel like they just think I'm a shallow shell with no emotions or depth. But you, on the other hand, are a genuine and kind person who sees potential and what's within. Well, I hate to keep rambling. Hopefully I'll hear from you soon. Thanks. Take care." I sniffled and then hung up the phone.

I felt naked.

I laid all my emotions out there for him to see, even some thoughts I didn't know I had. Self-discovery comes at the oddest times.

# Chapter 17
## Turn of Events: All Smiles

Two days passed since I'd left the message on Charles' voicemail. Still, no response. With clammy hands and fumbling fingers, I fidgeted with my cell with high hopes. Distracted during my weekly work meeting, I hid my phone under the table to sneak a peek every few minutes in hopes of seeing his name flash across the screen. However, my optimism quickly dwindled and the reality that I may never talk to or see Charles ever again sunk in.

I was losing all hope. I was on the verge of losing my house and my grand scheme to have Charles' baby held slim odds. Without the funds that I so desperately needed, what could I do? I had to come up with a way to keep my home.

My mind was flooded with thoughts of how to get out of the jam that I'd put myself in. Even if I borrowed money from other people, it wouldn't be enough. It seemed like my feet were on fire because I'd burnt so many bridges. It was hard for me to call upon someone who would be loyal to me, possibly because I wasn't loyal to them. Due to the stress of the situation, depression nestled in my head. My chaotic thoughts were slowly killing me. I couldn't keep my focus on anything. Work was the furthest thing from my mind.

"Aisha?" my boss Mr. Morgan yelled from across the long table. "Did you hear what I said?"

"Oh, were you talking to me?" I quickly snapped back to reality.

"Of course, I'm talking to you. You are the only person in this room named *Aisha*, aren't you? Now, I said, what do you think about the new project in Country Club Hills?"

Not knowing how to answer the question, I sighed. I had no idea what he was talking about because I was too busy nervously checking my phone.

"I'm sorry, Mr. Morgan. What about the project?"

"I said, what do you think about it? I know you know a lot about those parts. So, what will it be? What do you think is best? Is it a yea or nay?" Mr. Morgan's face was grimaced with frustration.

I quickly looked at the charts at the front of the room to come up with an immediate answer. I didn't have a clue what the hell Mr. Morgan was talking about. My mind was so boggled with thoughts of Charles and the house that I had been a bit disoriented the past couple of days. This day was no different.

"Umm, let's see. Well, I believe if the company decides to tear down the abandoned apartments in Country Club Hills and build a park, they'll be losing potential revenue. That's a newly profitable area. We need to move fast with the renovations because even though it's not the quote unquote ghetto, soon enough, those abandoned apartments will turn into a catastrophe. In a matter of time, it will be flooded with squatters and kids trashing it, writing graffiti everywhere. I think it would be a waste to tear it all down and build a park. So, I vote nay."

"Negative, I object," said my colleague Jennifer, raising her pen in the air. (She was my archenemy at the firm.)

Jennifer always felt that I wasn't worthy of my position and made sure that she called me out on all my errors. She made several attempts to take my spot, but my role was one of a kind, and was created, just for me. In two years, I went from making $85,000 a year to making $120,000 a year. She, on the other hand, had a $5,000 pay increase in the same time period.

Speaking about pay rates are usually taboo. However, we still nattered amongst our peers, especially when given a new position. It was a bragging rite of passage. Once she caught word of my significant increase, she was livid. This prompted her to accuse me of sleeping my way to the top, which if I did, was none of her business.

"Excuse me?" I cleared my throat. "This isn't a courtroom, Jennifer." Everyone chuckled as I raised my pen in mockery of her.

"Well, I think that's a horrible idea," she said bellicosely while pushing her glasses up on her pale pointy nose.

"Well, Jennifer, why do you think that? Let's hear what you have to say. This firm is always open to fresh ideas." Mr. Morgan rubbed his chin with peculiar interest.

"Well, what I was saying is what Aisha proposed may be a good idea but it's not the best idea. Revamping those apartments isn't going to benefit the community and it will definitely be detrimental to us. See, Mr. Morgan, it takes money to make money. We can't just rebuild those apartments and expect to make immediate income or rely on potential revenue. There isn't a high demand for apartments in that area right now. Do you know how much money we'd be out?"

"You tell me, Jennifer... This is your point," Mr. Morgan urged.

"Millions." Jennifer slowly looked around the table and whispered as if she had just released a great secret.

"Oh, my God, Jennifer, you're so dramatic. Now back to what I was saying..." I was fed up with her proposal.

She held her pen up again, demanding to be heard. "No, not back to what you were saying - I'm not done yet." She was relentless. (She must have had a bowl of courage that morning. She was never that charged.) "Now, what I was saying, Mr. Morgan, is if we make a park instead, it will cost less money, be good for the community, and it would take us off the 'bad guys' list with competing businesses in the area. It will also be a great write-off. After all, we may just break even if we go with Miss Aisha's idea over here. So, what's the purpose in putting all that work, time, and money into some apartments whose revenue won't supersede the cost of rehabilitation? I think those apartments would just be another thorn in our side. We need to go with the park."

"Good point, Jennifer. I never thought of it that way. I think that's what we'll do. I do have to consult the partners, but I'll take everything you've said under advisement. Thank you for your insight. You never cease to amaze me; keep up the good work." Mr. Morgan closed his briefcase.

"Well, that concludes things for today. Good meeting guys, great ideas. You're free to go; see you all back tomorrow."

Everyone started closing notebooks, pushing in chairs, and hustling out the door. I was getting my things together when Jennifer walked by and whispered, "Seems you're mostly beauty with minimal brains. Must suck, I know."

Oh, I was about to wring her damn neck until Mr. Morgan interrupted.

"Aisha, I need you to stay. We have some things to discuss."

Jennifer smirked and walked off. Seemed I traded one shit talker for another. I knew I was about to hear an earful from Mr. Morgan.

"Have a seat," he said.

I flopped down in a chair and rolled my eyes like a student at detention. I always got in trouble for my behavior, but no one could tell me that much when I was sleeping with the boss. After everyone left the room, Mr. Morgan closed the door and sat on the table where I was sulking. He peered over his glasses as he spoke.

"Look, Aisha, I don't know what's going on with you, but whatever it is you need to fix it. You hear me? I'd rather you not come to work at all than to come and do a half-ass job. It's embarrassing that one of my juniors is showing up someone in a senior position. And let's get one thing straight… I don't give a fuck who you're fucking, you still got a job to do. Got that?" he said, pointing his finger at me.

I moved my face closer; his finger was almost touching my forehead. I wasn't afraid of him. I was so sick of him throwing our affair in my face. I cringed every time I had to sleep with the fat fuck, but it was necessary to break the glass ceiling and solidify the position I was in.

"Sounds like sexual harassment to me. Talk to me like that again and we'll see what happens. You don't intimidate me," I said.

Not taking me seriously, he chuckled, which escalated my anger even further.

"Is that what you consider a threat?" He folded his arms and leaned back in his chair. I mirrored his movements and twisted my lip as to say, *yes*.

"Don't be mistaken, Aisha… You *are* replaceable. And what you aren't willing to do, someone else will." He looked out of the glass meeting room into the office at Jennifer. "If you continue being like this in my organization, bet on not coming to work ever again. I'll blackball your ass, and you'll never have a decent job in the city of Chicago again. Forget about your degree or credentials, you'll be back in the slums where you belong. Now, I'm warning you. Take it or leave it because I'm not going to say it again. And that's not a threat, it's a promise."

His words make me shudder with anger. I weaved a web that I could not get out of unless I was willing to risk losing everything. I was a pawn in his twisted little game. It was just a bonus that I had book smarts as well. But I couldn't help to think that no matter how grimy this low-down bastard was, he was right. The minority woman is the lowest on the totem pole. It was a slim-to-none chance I'd get the type of position I had at my age when competing with highly qualified white males. I was beyond pissed but had to keep my composure. I could see people from the corner of my eye gossiping, trying to figure out what was going on this time. Of course, Jennifer was the ringleader, which made me want to go out and punch her in her damn face, but I had to suck it up as usual and put on my best corporate face. Without uttering another word, I got up and left the room.

He won again.

I decided to get some fresh air before my next meeting to clear my mind and get myself together. I thought it would do me some good to walk to lunch, so I did. I only had an hour before my next meeting, so I had to make it quick.

Once my four-inch Pradas were tired of stomping the pavement, I settled on Chinese. It wasn't what I particularly wanted but the aroma was great, and I was tired of traipsing around downtown Chicago.

Just before opening the door to the restaurant, my phone rang. I scrambled through my purse to answer. It was Charles. I stopped in my tracks and sprinted to the bench in front of the restaurant like I had a new pair of running shoes on. I was flushed with overwhelming thoughts when I saw his name flash across my screen. I sat down and took a huge breath before answering.

"Hello," I answered with anticipation.

"Hey, Aisha. How's it going? Sorry I haven't called you back, but I've had a lot going on."

"Oh, yeah? That's okay, I understand. I thought you'd never call me again. I really thought you were still mad at me." My voice regressed to a babyish tone.

"Naw, it's not like that. Well, I'm not going to lie to you; that was part of the reason. The incident at my house could've been handled more appropriately, but everybody makes mistakes and tempers were raging that day. I was a little out of line too, but you did make me mad. I had to take some time to clear my head. I just needed a little cool-off period from you, that's all. Aside from that, I've been a little flustered because my son has been really sick, and he was in the hospital. I had to take the first flight I could to go see him. When I was there, it was all about him; no phones or anything. I just wanted to care for him. That's why I'm just now getting back to you."

"Oh, I'm sorry. Now I really feel horrible for calling your cell like a mad woman."

"Oh, it's not a big deal, honestly. Since my phone was off, I didn't receive many calls. I'm just slowly returning voicemails when I get the time."

"I totally understand that. So, how's your son now? What was wrong?"

"He deals with a congenital condition. He seems okay for now. Even though he's weak, he's still trying to jump around and play. You know, kids are invincible. I pull so much of my strength from him."

"Well, that's good. Happy to hear he's feeling better."

"Yeah, I'm happy too. That's Daddy's boy. I love him so much." Charles paused. "Oh, yeah, I got your voicemail. Now, what's going on?"

"Well, yeah. I feel bad for even expressing my burdens when you have problems of your own, you know." Suddenly I felt like the scum of the earth, selfishly pestering Charles when his child was so ill.

"Hey, if I didn't care about your problems, I wouldn't have asked; I would've just erased your voicemail and let it be. But it's okay. I might be able to help you out."

I took a deep breath. "Alright, well, I'm just going to get straight to the point then. Things have been a little rough for me lately. It seems like when it rains, it pours. Work has been stressing me out. My boss is tripping. He's saying I got my head in the clouds, but he's just mad because I don't have my head up his ass anymore. My bills are the biggest issue though. I'm about to get foreclosed on any day now. It's just frustrating. I don't know how much more I can take. It's really taking a toll on me."

"Well, you know what, Aisha? I don't know what to do about your boss, but I can definitely take some worries off your back on the bills. Maybe we can get together tomorrow. I'll cut you a check then. I'm back in the city, so maybe we can do lunch or something? You said it's only eleven thousand, right?"

*Only?* I thought. "Yeah, around that. If I give them that, I'll be paid up."

"Okay, we'll get that done for you then. I'd hate to see you out on the streets. Not literally, I know you got places to go, but there's nothing like your own. You know what I'm saying?"

"Oh, yes, I know what you're saying. My god, I appreciate this so much. Without you, I don't know what would have happened."

"No problem; it's nothing. What I'll do is cut you a check for fifteen thousand. That way, you can pay it up a little more and do something special for yourself to relieve the stress, okay?"

"Well, of course. That's great. It's not like I'm going to say no," I giggled.

"Good. It seems like you have a smile on your pretty little face now. So, what time to you want to meet up? Should we say noonish?"

"Yeah, that would be fine. I don't have any meetings between eleven and two-thirty, so that should be perfect. Really, Charles, I hope there aren't any hard feelings. I don't want you to be mad at me."

"Right. I'm giving you fifteen grand but I'm mad at you," he laughed. "I'll meet you in front of your job at noon then."

"Sounds like a plan. I'll call you in the morning to confirm just in case something changes."

"Nothing is going to change on my end, but definitely let me know if it does on yours. I don't want to come downtown for nothing, *especially* at noon." His voice dragged as if he was already stuck in traffic.

"I feel you on that one. Okay, I'll call you tomorrow. And thanks again."

*Cha-ching*! I was back in the game.

After work I went straight home. No stops by Tonya's house and no stops by any stores. I needed to get my clothes ready for the next day so I could be looking extra fly when I saw Charles. I felt like a kid on the first day of school. I was ecstatic. I couldn't eat, couldn't sleep; I was just ready to see Charles.

I still had a little glimmer of pregnancy hope, even though I was just meeting him for lunch.

I kicked off my house shoes and undressed, flinging my clothes across the bathroom. My shirt landed in the sink and my Chanel skirt in the trash, knocking it over. When I lifted my skirt to clean things up, I noticed the ovulation kit I'd taken days prior.

*Oh, I almost forgot about that. Maybe I should take another one. I might get lucky this time since I'm seeing Charles tomorrow.*

I went to my conception stash and pulled out another kit. Before getting in the shower, I took the test and put it on the counter.

After showering I sat down at my vanity to do my night routine, but something told me to check the test.

I moseyed over to the sink and picked up the

ovulation stick, expecting another O. To my surprise, the unexpected happened.

*A smiling face? A smiling face! Well, I'll be damned. I can't believe this. This is too perfect. I can't wait until tomorrow. The simple part is done. I just got to build up the courage to do everything else.*

I snatched another kit from my stash just to make sure. I was able to conjure up a few more droplets of urine to take another test. Yep, there was that face smiling at me again. I held the sticks like they were winning lottery tickets. (Well, to me, they were.) They were the ticket to a good life, a worry-free life, a shop-til-I-drop life.

I walked downstairs through the laundry room to the kitchen, back to the living room and then back upstairs. I was so full of anticipation that I was all over the place. I didn't know what to do with myself. I finally plopped down on my bed, fantasizing about things to come.

# Chapter 18
## Checkmate

Waking up at six o'clock to prepare for my workday was vital. With the hustle and bustle of the Chicago streets, I liked to get a jump start on my long day at the office. Working late nights had me crashing, so I valued every moment of sleep I could get. When my phone rang at five forty-five, I was less than thrilled.

"Hello?" I answered groggily with a slight attitude. I didn't get a chance to screen the call since my eyes were still adjusting.

"Hello, Aisha?" A familiar uncertainty was on the other end of the phone.

"Hello? Charles, is that you?" I pulled the phone away from my ear to take a quick glance at the bright screen. Yep, it was him. I perked up as if he was in the room, rubbing my eyes and fixing my hair. I would have hung up on anyone else at this hour.

"Yeah, it's me. Sorry for calling so early and waking you up but I'll have to drop that check off to you this morning because I'm going to be busy the rest of the day. I have a nine o'clock flight to New York and I won't be back until midnight. My son is sick again and I need to see him. I want to stay out there longer but I can't due to obligations I have here. I'll probably fly back out there at the end of the week."

"Aww, I'm so sorry to hear that."

Yes, it was indeed sad that his son was sick, but I couldn't stop thinking in the back of my mind that I was fertile. Everything was perfect— I had to find some way to get pregnant by this man, ASAP.

"Midnight, huh? Well, I really wanted to spend some time with you. I didn't just want to take your money and run. I can wait until midnight when you get back if you want. I'll still be up."

"Well, I don't want you to get kicked out of your house. Don't you have to pay those people by sometime today?"

"Well, yeah." I hesitated slightly before reiterating my other comment. "But I still want to spend time with you."

"It's going to be kind of late, A…"

"It doesn't matter. It's fine. I told you I'd be awake," I interrupted.

"Tell you what… I'll drop by to give you the check and then later on when I get back, we will hang out for a little bit. I need some relaxation in my life, maybe a couple of drinks. How about it?"

"Okay, that sounds good. What time are you coming by this morning? You're kind of pushed for time, don't you think?"

"I was thinking I would come by in about fifteen minutes because my driver is taking me to O'Hare, which is by your house if I'm not mistaken?"

As soon as Charles mentioned that he would be there in fifteen minutes I flung the blanket off, jumped out of bed, and headed toward the bathroom to brush my teeth and wash my face.

"Yes, you're right. I'm very close to O'Hare. Do you need directions?" I attempted to discretely hold the toothpaste in the side of my mouth as I spoke.

"Nah, I don't need directions. Just give me the address and I'm sure my driver can find it."

"Okay, well just give me a call if you get lost. I'll be waiting for you." I gave him the address as he rushed off the phone.

~

*Ding dong!* The doorbell rang in the midst of me scrambling some eggs.

"Hey there," I opened the door and greeted Charles with a big hug.

"Hey there. I see you still look good early in the morning. *Mmmm*, something smells good back there. Are you cooking?"

"Yessir, I'm trying to whip up a little somethin-somethin. I made some eggs and bacon. I'm starving. What about you? You hungry?" I asked.

"Actually, I had a cup of joe before leaving the house. Not too big on breakfast."

"No problem. Well, you can have a seat if you want. It'll just be a minute."

"Oh, sorry, A. I can't stay long or else I'll miss my flight."

"Well, you know it's rude to just stand in someone's door like that." I walked back toward the kitchen to turn off the burners. He followed a few steps behind, studying my house.

189

"Nice spot you got here. I see why you don't want to lose it. You did a good job."

"Well, thank you," I curtsied, before wiping my hands on a nearby kitchen towel. "Nothing compared to yours though."

"Hey, look at me." He softly grabbed my chin and stared deep into my eyes. My heart started to pound, and my breathing became shallow. I wanted to kiss him right then and there, but I knew it wasn't time for that yet.

"Stop comparing yourself. Don't ever compare your house, your car, your job, or *anything* else to *anyone* else. Got it?"

I replied with a trance-like nod.

"You got it all, girl. Coming from where we came from, this is a whole helluva lot. You should be proud."

"Thank you, Charles. You are always so encouraging."

"No need to thank me. Pat yourself on the back. You worked hard and it shows. But even hard workers need help every now and again."

He passed me the check.

"Thank you so much. I don't—"

He put his hand up, halting my words.

"No need for all of that. Just go handle your business." He winked.

I smiled in return.

"Don't forget to call me when you get back. I can come over and we can have a few drinks. Let loose a little, you know? TGIF."

"Sounds great." He nodded. "Well not to rush, but I need to get going."

"I understand. I better get going myself before my

ass-of-a-boss has something to say about me not getting there early. On time is late to him." I huffed.

"Ah, the war of the corporate world. You got this though. You're strong and a hard worker. I believe in you. You might just be the boss one day."

*The boss of your dick,* I thought.

Charles held the back of my head and tenderly kissed me on the forehead.

"So true. I'll be on top one day." I grinned.

# Chapter 19
## Rescued

It was 11:45 pm and I kept checking the clock, anticipating Charles' call. I flipped through the channels staring aimlessly at the TV. My thumb continuously pressed the arrows on the remote in the same manner that it continuously pressed the top of my pen at a boring work meeting. Nothing to watch and nothing to do but to wait for Charles. I could have been out doing something, but I chose to stay home to ensure I wouldn't miss him. Of course, he would call my cell phone, but I didn't want to take any chances. I wanted to make sure I was available as soon as he flew in. After a while my eyes grew heavy. I eventually dozed off.

*Ring, ring!* I leaped off of the couch as if he was already standing in front of me.

"Hello?" I answered the phone clearly as if I wasn't just drooling down the couch pillow.

"Hey, doll, what are you up to?" Charles asked.

"Oh, nothing, just sitting here watching TV. What are you doing? I thought your flight landed at midnight."

The clock said it was 12:50 am.

"Well, you know how airlines can be. I just got off the plane. If it's too late to meet up, I completely understand.

We could probably do it another time if—"

"No, I'm wide awake," I blurted.

"Okay, well, I'll be up late anyway; I have a lot on my mind. A nightcap would be great."

By the sound of it, he really could use some company, and I sure wasn't going to deny him.

"Oh, really? Well, I took a long nap today. After dealing with the mortgage company and a grueling day at work, I'm ready to have a drink too."

"I hear that. So, everything's good with the house now?"

"Yes, it is. Thank you so much. You will never know how much I appreciate that. I don't think I can ever repay you for what you did."

"Sweetie, really, don't worry about it; it's nothing. I've known you for a long time and I've wanted to do something special for you ever since high school. So that's just a small token of my appreciation for finally accepting me as your friend. Whenever you need something, just let me know. As long as I got it, it's never a problem."

"Feels good having someone in my corner. That's awesome. Are you still at the airport? Do you need a ride?"

"Oh, heavens no, my driver is on his way. Do you want me to swing by and get you?"

"That would be perfect."

"You know, just in case you have one too many. We don't want you driving back like that," Charles chortled. "Oh, there he is, right on time. We'll be there to pick you up in about twenty minutes. Is that cool?"

"Yes sir, I'll be ready." I packed an extra set of clothes, my toothbrush, and makeup. I just knew that I'd be spending the night, and that this night was going to be *the* night. I put the small vial of clear liquid in my purse.

Finally, things were going as planned.

~

Charles' car arrived within a half-hour. I slowly strutted to the car like a fierce diva, but on the inside my excitement made me feel like I was a little girl on the first day of school, prancing in her brand-new clothes. As I approached the car, the driver opened the door, revealing a sexy, polished Charles in the backseat. I melted a million times at the first glance of his face. He gently took my hand as I got in, and I melted more. He looked so dapper and smelled so good it was hard to resist pouncing on him, but I kept my composure and play my cards right. Whatever it took to get this man, I was going to do it.

We arrived at his house a little shy of 2am. I was anxious, my heart beating like I just ran a marathon, and my mind was doing cartwheels. My imagination was running rampant, thinking of all the possible things that could happen on this night. I waited for a long time to have this opportunity to be alone with Charles again and this was indeed my chance.

"Make yourself at home. Don't be a stranger. Kick off your shoes." His voice echoed as he headed toward the wet bar. "What can I get you - Wine? Vodka? Cognac?"

"Whatever you're having," I concurred.

"Alright, rum and Coke it is. Do you want me to make you a glass, or do you want to do it yourself?"

"You can unwind and change your clothes while I play bartender. I know you had a long day, and you're probably stressed out."

"You're right, I'm beat. I'm going to go get changed and I'll be back down in a minute. And make mine strong; I'm feeling like double shots tonight."

"I will. I'm going to make mine strong too." I looked him up and down seductively.

"Aisha, Aisha, Aisha. You my dear, are relentless. I'll be back." He smiled and shook his head before sprinting up the spiral staircase.

I put ice in both cups and mixed the drinks before remembering the vial.

*Oh, crap,* I said to myself as I shuffled around in my purse. *Where is it at? What the f—*

"Hey there, Miss Bartender."

Charles reappeared in a t-shirt and sweatpants that left little to the imagination. I jumped so hard that I knocked over one of the drinks and dropped my purse. Everything fell out of my little handbag and the vial rolled across the floor. My eyes gave away the shock I felt.

"Charles, you scared the crap out of me!"

I hoped he didn't see the vial.

"Sorry, I'm light on my feet. You'll never hear me coming. Here, let me help you." He scooped up my lipstick and cell phone and started to search for other scattered items.

"No," I yelped, "I got this."

If he discovered that vial, it would've been lights out for me. I had to get to it before he noticed.

He threw his hands up in the air. "Whoa! Okay, I know how women are about their things. I'll just clean up this little spill and make another drink." As soon as he turned his back, I quickly grabbed the vial and hastily stuffed it into my bra. Too distracted to notice what I was doing, he proceeded to fill the entire cup with rum and splashed it with

Coke.

"Damn, you really do like it strong, huh?"

"Yup, that's the way I like it."

Charles looked at the glass, swirled it around, and took a big gulp.

"*Wffeww*, that's what I'm talkin' bout. This is like a strong cup of coffee; it wakes you up. You just don't know how bad I needed this."

"Sure, just like coffee." I playfully rolled my eyes. "Well, you're going to be drunk if you keep drinking like that."

"Girl, I handle my liquor well. You won't even know I'm drunk… most of the time." He laughed. "I have at least one more stiff drink calling my name after this one. But enough of that, let's go in the den and relax. You want to watch a movie or something? Listen to some music maybe?" he asked.

"Music would be nice. I'm not really up to the movie thing tonight; I've been flipping through channels ever since I got home today, so I definitely don't want to watch TV. What kind of music do you have?"

"I got whatever you want, baby girl. Even though I got all the technology I need in here to download music, I still collect a lot of CDs and records."

"Oh, really? Well, surprise me then."

I grabbed my drink and followed Charles into the living room. He popped in an Isley Brothers CD and two-stepped with his drink in hand. I soon joined him.

"Ooh, now this is what I'm talking about." I danced around the living room to *For the Love of You,* holding my glass in the air. Charles spun me around. my back was facing his chest and began to sway back and forth.

"Hmmm, you're a good dancer, Mr. Proctor."

"You're not bad yourself, Ms. Carmichael."

He took my drink out of my hand and sat it on the table along with his. We continued to dance. He softly dipped me.

"Did you know I originally went to school to be a masseuse?" he said.

"No way. That's very interesting."

"Lie down on the couch; I have a special treat for you." He lowered me onto the sofa and began to caress my body. I was taken aback by the sensual touch. I moaned softly.

"Does that feel good, A?"

"Oh my gosh, are you kidding? That feels amazing. No one has touched me like that in a long time. Your hands are like magic, I swear. If you didn't make money with your businesses, I'm sure you could have become a millionaire doing this."

"Well, thank you, thank you very much," he said in his best Elvis impersonation.

"You know, Aisha, I learned to be intimate with a woman without taking her clothes off. A lot of people confuse sex with intimacy. There's more to it than that. Being close, touching, caressing, breathing slowly, hearing someone's heartbeat next to yours, just pleasing someone else and enjoying their company is what intimacy is about. Just exploring a woman's body is so sensual to me."

Charles ran his fingers down the small of my back and then took another gulp of his drink.

I closed my eyes and enjoyed every second and every touch. I grabbed my drink and took a few sips to catch up with him. He was almost finished.

"Wow, I'm feeling a tad tipsy already. How about one more? We're almost done with this round. One more for the road?" I suggested.

"Yeah, of course, one more."

Charles picked up both glasses to refill them. I put my hand on top of his, stopping him from picking the glasses up.

"Don't worry about it, honey. I'll get it. You just gave me an awesome massage, now it's your turn to relax. I promise I won't spill it this time." I smiled.

"Alright, thanks. Now I can just kick back. Don't forget how I like mine - just a splash of Coke."

I was about to give him just a splash alright. A splash of Coke, a splash of drugs, then a splash of me.

The timing couldn't be any more perfect. After leaving to make drinks, I peeked around the corner to find him lying on the couch with his hands behind his head. He looked as if he was on vacation, sunbathing out on the beach. I then pulled the vial from my bosom and stealthily poured the contents into his drink, stirring it ever so slightly. I returned a few moments later and sat the drinks on the table.

"You're a good man, Charles. It's such a waste that you don't want to be in a relationship."

"Oh yeah? Well, I know I make wise decisions. Believe me, I know what I'm doing." He paused and took a long sip of his drink.

"Now, this is a man's drink. Make you grow hair on your chest." He laughed.

"That's why mine isn't that strong - I definitely don't need any hairs growing on my chest." I laughed while looking down into the plunging neckline on my dress.

Charles sat up on the couch and looked me square in

the eyes. "You know, I wish I would've met up with you years ago. You know what I mean, before I met my ex-wife. I mean, you're a little prissy, but that's what I like. I would've loved to take care of you. I would've spoiled you. You would have been ruined once I got done with you. Even if we would have broken up, no man would have been able to satisfy you. Your standards would have been so high that it would have been hard for anyone to even approach you."

"What do you mean? You can still spoil me. We can still be together. It's not too late, you know. I like you and you like me - What's the problem?"

"Life. Life is the problem. All this money doesn't mean anything. People treat me like I'm famous or something, but really, they don't know anything about me—the real me. My life is screwed up, Aisha. You don't even know the half of it. I don't want to drag anyone else into it; that's why I try not to get involved with anyone. I keep my distance and that's it."

He stared at me with a bobbled head and glassy eyes as he continued.

"Whoa, I'm really starting to feel this drink. I haven't really eaten much today. I should know better than to drink on an empty stomach." Charles held up his glass and looked at it, swirling it and splashing the contents.

"What, are you hungry or something? Did you want me to fix you something to eat?" I asked.

"No, I don't eat past midnight. Not good for my diet," he slurred.

"Oh, and drinking is good for your diet, right?" I sassed, rolling my eyes.

"No, but I... I don't know," Charles giggled.

"What are you laughing about?" I asked as I looked

into his glazed eyes.

"I don't know, I just feel weird. I haven't got high in years but that's the way I feel right now. That's what we should do, Aisha – get high and go skydiving. That's as high as you can get. Being high when you're high in the sky. Now that's what they should call the Mile-High Club."

"Okay, drunky, you're talking a little crazy right now. Let's get you upstairs and into bed. I think that you drank too much too fast on an empty stomach."

"That might be it," Charles yelled, drunkenly.

"Okay, just finish your drink so we can go upstairs."

"You's not feeling this here drinks? I am. Okay, let me just finish these last sips," he slurred.

Charles chugged the last quarter of his drink, indulging in every last drop like a thirsty scavenger in the middle of the Sahara. After he finished, I wrapped his limp arm around my neck and escorted him to the second level of the house. His feet were dragging like two large cement blocks. By the time I got him to the room I was sweating like I'd just worked out. His loose body flopped back on the bed.

"I'll be back. I'm just going to take a shower and freshen up a little. These drinks got me a little sweaty."

"Freshen it up, freshen it up," he yelled and laughed uncontrollably, falling off the bed. I huffed.

*Now I got to pick him up off the floor?* I was in over my head. Nevertheless, a girl has got to do what a girl has got to do. I wrapped his arm around my neck and lifted him back onto the bed.

"Now stay here. I don't think I can lift you anymore," I said firmly.

"Okay, okay. Your wish is mine commandments." He made a gesture as if to bow and then nose-dived into the pillow.

At least he was knocked out now. By this point, I eliminated the whole shower idea. I didn't see the point. After all, he wouldn't care one way or the other. I began kissing his motionless body and proceeded to ease his sweatpants off.

"Wait, wait, wait. What're you doing?"

"Don't worry, Daddy. Momma got this." I pulled him up to a sitting position and took off his shirt.

"Mmhm, look at those abs. That's nice." I caressed his stomach with one hand. My right fingers took a bumpy ride over his six-pack as I worked my way into his boxers with the other hand.

"No, no. Stop. What you doing?"

"Shhh, don't worry. I just want to make you feel good. I know you been waiting on this for a while now." I confirmed.

"Wait, can we do this? I meant, we can't do this." His voice was weak, and he fell back onto the bed.

"Why can't we? You need to stop having all of these rules and just let loose."

I stroked him until he was firm and erect, subsequently massaging his manhood with my mouth. After about ten minutes the taste of pre-cum coated my tongue. *Oh, no you don't, not yet.*

I hiked my dress up to my waist, peeled off my panties and prepared to straddle his cock. The more he said no, the more I thrust my wetness upon him.

Charles' denials became groans and moans as he climaxed. He was too weak to do anything but lay there and move his arms, so I made sure I took control. He grabbed my hips and rocked me back and forth as I rubbed against him.

I went faster and faster and our moans became louder. Finally, our juices collided as I felt him pulsating inside me. The sensation made my body tremble. I rolled off him and onto the bed, breathing heavily.

"That was so good. You shouldn't have held back this long. I see why you're celibate; anybody would fall in love with that. I'm about to get a towel. You need something?

"Charles?"

He was knocked out, already snoring heavily. I smiled as I looked at him, and then went to the bathroom to clean myself up. I quietly tiptoed back in the room so as to not wake him. I slid in the bed and wrapped my arms around him, then drifted off to sleep.

~

It was six-thirty in the morning and as the sun rose, so did Charles. When he opened his eyes and saw my naked body lying there, he immediately flipped.

"Aisha, get up! Get up right now! What in the hell happened last night?" he lashed.

I jumped at the sound of his voice and sat up straightaway. I was sleeping soundly until he went into a screaming frenzy.

"What do you mean what happened last night? And why are you screaming?"

"You know damn well what I mean. Did I... Did we? Umm... You know what the hell I'm talking about. Don't act stupid."

His eyes darted around the room. They went from me, to his clothes laying on the floor next to my panties, back to me, and lastly looking at his own naked body. I stretched and seductively crawled to his side of the bed to debunk his confusion.

"What do you think? We're both naked, silly. I can't believe you were so drunk that you don't remember. All I can say is that it was wonderful." I smiled.

"Wonderful? I wasn't *that* drunk. I may drink, but I remember things. I'm not stupid - something ain't right." He looked under the bed and then under the covers. He kicked clothes around on the floor then shook his sweatpants and shirt.

"What are you doing? What are you looking for?" I fixed my frazzled hair, pulling it back into a ponytail.

"Trying to see what happened to the condom. Where is it? Did you throw it away?" He continued to search for the non-existent condom.

I paused for a moment. "Well, I don't think we used a condom. I don't remember you taking one off and I sure in the heck didn't throw anything away. You went straight to sleep afterwards. I guess since you haven't had any in so long, you just kind of dove into it."

"What do you mean? I don't... That's not right, I'm telling you. I would never do anything like that. I'm not that irresponsible, especially after the whole incident that resulted in me having a son." Charles paced naked across the floor.

"Sorry about your celibacy. It didn't seem like you cared about that at the time." I crossed my arms.

"Now's not the time for jokes, Aisha. Obviously, what's done is done now." Charles paused and rubbed is goatee trying to recall what happened. "Did I cum in you?"

When I didn't answer fast enough, he felt the need to

shout out the question again. "I said, did I—"

"Calm down, I heard what you said. Quit yelling at me. How am I supposed to know? I was drunk just like you. You may have, I don't really remember. What's the big damn deal? Is it a problem if you did?" I retorted.

Charles was now irate. "Hell, yeah, it's a problem. You act like you don't care. We aren't even in a relationship, so why would we be having unprotected sex? You're on birth control at least, right?"

"Oh, I see. So that's what you're worried about. You get your rocks off and the only thing you're worried about is if I get pregnant. Charles, I can't believe you. So, are you just using me now? You play the sweet and innocent 'I'm celibate' role, but I see right through you. Matter of fact, you know what? I don't have to take this crap. I'm outta here."

I started gathering my belongings.

"Oh, don't try to turn the tables on me. You're the one who's scandalous, Aisha. You think you're slick, but you're just foul. I thought you were different. How are you just going to disrespect me like that?"

"Disrespect you? Really? You wanted it; I didn't force myself upon you. You stuck *your* dick in *me*. No one twisted your arm. You weren't complaining last night, Charles."

"See? You knew exactly what you were doing last night, and I didn't. You knew I was drunk. You took advantage of that. How could you?"

"Oh, quit acting like a little punk. Don't act like you didn't want it. You're putting on a show now. What man wouldn't want to be with me? Who wouldn't want to be with Aisha, huh? You were a nobody back in the day; I know where you came from. You should be happy that I'd even consider hanging out with you, let alone have sex with you. If anything, you should be honored," I antagonized, wriggling my way back into my dress.

"Naw, you should be happy that I wanted to kick it with *your* sorry ass. Are you kidding? I can have any woman I want… I'm well aware of this. I have brains, the looks, and the money. You're the one who's broke and don't know how to handle money. You're the one still a trifling-ass gold-digger. I was just trying to be a friend to you and help you out. Money is nothing to me, but apparently it's everything to you. I know your type. I've seen it a million times with a million different bodies and faces. I should have seen right through you, but I gave you the benefit of the doubt.

"I'm done talking. Just get the hell outta my house before I have to throw you out. You straight violated me. Oh, and here's some money for an Uber – I know your trifling, broke ass need it."

Charles reached into his pants' pocket and threw five twenties at me. Without a word, I picked the money up off the floor and headed downstairs to get my bag and shoes. He trotted down the stairs behind me.

"You know what? I don't need your punk ass anyway," I screamed.

"Just shut up and get the hell out. You disgust me and I have zero respect for you. I should've cancelled you from my life when you pulled that act with Darla, coming up in my house disrespecting. Every time you come over you disrespect me. This time, it's over. I don't want to see your face again. Oh, yeah, and take a Plan B too."

Charles pushed me out, threw out a fifty-dollar bill, and swiftly slammed the door.

# Chapter 20
## Null

One month went by since Charles ghosted me. I called and popped up at his house numerous times, but it appeared he pulled one hell of a grand disappearing act. I eventually gave up on hunting him down to keep my sanity. My life was an emotional rollercoaster, and I literally was counting down the days to take a pregnancy test.

I'd felt nauseous and fatigued, which gave me hope that my dream of carrying his baby had come true. However, it was hard to tell if it was from morning sickness or anxiety and anticipation. Finally, after four grueling weeks, I decided to pop open the test.

I peered at the result window waiting for two lines to appear. A single line faintly showed up after one minute. I concentrated on the second line to emerge like I was watching a magic trick. *Come on, Aisha. Everything went as planned. You have to be pregnant.*

After five minutes of observing, I slung the test across the room. The second line never appeared.

*All of that for nothing. All the time, effort and money I put into this and what do I get? Nothing. Everything was perfect. I don't understand. This can't be happening. I'm supposed to be pregnant right now. This is some bull.*

My face was red as a beet and my eyes were bloodshot. I fell over onto my bathroom floor and balled up in a fetal position. Everything I'd ever hoped would come to reality suddenly died. Was I asking for too much? Sure, I had a good paying job, but it was with a boss who made me cringe and added tasks (and sexual favors) that I did not sign up for.

From the outside my life may have seemed perfect, but I felt like a prisoner in my own body and Charles held the keys to my freedom. Having his baby would ensure that I would never have to work again, never have financial woes, and never have to have a prick boss telling what to do and when to do it. I was tormented to the depths of my soul wondering what could have been and what would never be.

I cried myself to sleep on the cold, hard bathroom floor. I stayed until there until the next morning, wallowing in the bleakness.

# Chapter 21
## The Boot

"Aisha, snap out of it," Mr. Morgan yelled.

"Yes, sir," I answered.

"Aisha, I told you before; I don't have time to be dealing with you and your shenanigans. The past couple of months you've really been going downhill. You're starting to be a waste of space."

My boss jumped out of his seat in exasperation, while the eleven other faces around the table peered at me. Hell, the way everyone gawked, you would've thought my name was Hester Prynne. I tried to get a few words out to plead my case.

"Please, Mr. Morgan, can we talk about this later? I've been having some problems—"

"I don't give a damn about you and your personal problems." (His turkey-like neck shook when he spoke.)

"Your problems are causing me problems, which causes the company problems, which causes my pockets problems. Do you see the pattern? The only thing that matters is the big picture and you are a little problem in the big picture. Your senseless little issues affect my bottom line. Get it? You come to meeting after meeting and you don't pay attention. Furthermore, you lack contribution to the company. It's like you've been in La-La Land the past few months. Tell me why we should keep you on payroll?" He waited for an answer.

"I'm a hard worker, Mr. Morgan, and I'm a great asset to this company," I retorted.

"The hell you are. You used to be, but not anymore. We only keep the top-notch elite around here, and you no longer fit the bill. I don't know what's gotten into you, but I gave you every chance to make corrections. And did you?" he asked pointedly.

"No. I didn't think so. My hands are tied here, Aisha. I don't need you tainting the group. One bad apple ruins the whole bunch. That's why I'm telling you this in front of everyone in this meeting room – so we're clear that no one else has their thumbs up their asses. What I need you to do now is excuse yourself, pick up your things, and leave. You're done here."

"Mr. Morgan, give me another chance. I have bills to pay. What am I supposed to do? What do you want me to do to make this right?" I acquiesced, hoping he would have a change of heart. To my dismay, he ignored my plea.

"No, Aisha. You just do exactly what you've been doing – nothing. I'm sorry, but no more chances. You're done."

I felt like I was in a courtroom, and I didn't agree with the judge's sentence. I defiantly sat in my chair and didn't move. I waited for him to change his mind and hoped that he would have pity on me. I folded my arms and crossed my legs, timeout-style. Then I impishly grinned, daring him to make me move from my seat.

"So, you won't leave, is that it? You're just going to sit there?" he said.

When I evaded his question, he immediately pressed the speakerphone button on the meeting table.

"Security, I need an escort to see Ms. Carmichael out of the office, please."

Within seconds I jumped from my seat like a Pop-Tart bursting from a toaster. I dashed over to my boss and smacked my hand on the speakerphone to hang it up. I swiped the whole thing clear across the table out of his reach. I slammed my hand on the table, demanding his undivided attention. I refused to be embarrassed by security.

"Now wait one damn minute, Mr. Morgan. Is that really necessary? Because plainly speaking, firing me is not an option," I stated contentiously.

He was used to me being aggressive, but he never saw this side of me. He grabbed the front of his jacket in the same manner that an old woman would clutch her purse when a street thug walks by.

"Not an option, you say? Not necessary? I'll tell you what *is not* necessary. It *is not* necessary for you to be sitting here wasting our time. This conversation would not have been necessary if you had done your job. So, firing you *is* the only option."

Two security guards entered the room, ready to assist me out of the building.

"Just in the nick of time." Mr. Morgan threw his hands up. His stumpy sausage fingers waved in the air as if he was thanking the heavens.

"Wait, so you're just going to have your goons haul me off like I'm some sort of criminal? All the years of service at this company and this is how you do me? What about my things? I can't even clear my desk? This isn't fair," I bawled.

"We'll box up your things and send them to you. Oh, don't worry… Your office will be cleared by the end of the week. Now please, just go!" Mr. Morgan waved me off as the security guards awaited me at the door. One guard attempted to grab my arm, but I swung it in a circular motion to break away. He waved me off as the security guards waited at the door.

"I'm fine. I don't need this shit. I can walk out by myself," I snapped. Yes, I was a little embarrassed, but I knew I would bounce back from this setback just like I had from other stumbling blocks in the past. I stormed out of the building with security following me and made my way to the parking garage.

"Oh, for Heaven's sake! Do you really have to follow me out here too?" I lashed out.

"I'm sorry, Ms. Carmichael. It's company policy. We have to ensure that you're safely off the property before we let you out of our sight."

Both guards stood there with their arms folded and waited for me to get in the car.

"Oh, trust me, I am so ready to leave this place - damn rent-a-cops," I yelled.

I couldn't get in my car quick enough. As much as I hated losing my job, I felt a strange sense of relief. I put the car into drive and skidded off like I was on a racetrack, drifting out of the parking garage. I grabbed my phone from my clutch and called Tonya. I needed to gripe to someone about my hellish day and she was naturally the first person who came to mind.

"Hey, A," she sighed, answering in a less than cheerful voice.

"Hey, T, whatchu doin?" I asked. Tonya paused a

few seconds before speaking again.

"Hello?" I said.

"Uh, yee-a-yeah," Tonya's voice quivered as if she was about to cry.

"What's wrong with you?" I huffed. I was consumed with my own issues. I didn't feel like hearing her problems.

"You don't even wanna know, girl. I don't even wanna say." She took a deep breath.

"Look, Tonya, I'm having a bad day too. I don't have time for your guessing games. Now, what's wrong with you?" I asked directly.

"How can I say it? I'm... I'm pregnant," she exploded and began to bawl.

*Great. Now it's the Tonya show.*

"Really? Oh, okay," I replied nonchalantly.

"Is that all you have to say? *Okay?*" Tonya sniffled.

"It's not that I don't have anything to say, but I got problems of my own. I'm sick of having to listen to you and your problems all the time. Why can't you ever listen to me and my problems, huh? You're always pregnant, Tonya. That's not new news. Wooptie-fucking-do! What's new?"

"You? You always listen to *my* problems? Oh, please. You always got some kind of new drama going on in your life. You always have something to say. You don't ever listen to what I have to say; you don't care about what's going on in your niece's lives or mine. You're not a good sister or auntie. To hell with you."

"Oh yeah? Well, if I'm not a good sister or auntie, what am I then?"

"I'll tell you what you are. You are one evil, self-centered bitch," Tonya yelled.

"Yeah, yeah, yeah. Bitch is my middle name. So

what? You're pregnant. That's life, right? I mean who cares? Not me. I'm sure it's by Jordan. Congratulations, you will be well taken care of. My problem is that I'm *not* pregnant, I just lost my job, and Charles doesn't want to talk to me. Now what am I supposed to do? Who do I have to turn to? Who can I lean on? No one. At least you have Jordan. I'm a 28-year-old loser."

Tonya sighed. "This is just stupid. Look, these are both touchy subjects and our emotions are heightened. I'm sorry if I made you upset, but I'm upset too. We both have problems, and we need each other right now."

"No, Tonya, the hell with that. You live your happy white-picket-fence life with you and your kids and your sugar daddy to support you."

"Aisha, I'm pregnant by a married man. What are you thinking? He doesn't even want to speak to me right now. He's furious that I'm pregnant, like I did it by myself. I just don't understand it; I thought he loved me," Tonya wailed.

"Look, I'm sorry, T. I really want to feel sad for you, I really do. But right now, I can't. Your problems aren't real problems to me and I'm not joining your pity-party pack. I gotta get off this phone."

I pressed the end button and sped home.

~

After the grueling drive-in city traffic with a ton of stuff on my mind, I finally arrived home. All I wanted was a long hot bath and a nice glass of wine. Yet, I pulled up in the driveway and to my surprise Jordan was sitting on my front porch looking like a lost puppy. As soon as I got out of the car, he jumped off the step and walked over to me.

"What a coincidence. What else could go wrong today? What do you want?" I walked past him, sticking my key in the door.

"I'm sorry for just popping up like this, A, but I got a bunch of craziness going on and you're the only one I can talk to about it. Your sister's pregnant again. My wife's pregnant right now too; I don't know what to do. I mean, I told Tonya if she gets an abortion that would be best for both of us and—"

"Jordan, are you serious right now? What is this, Everyone Pour Their Problems Out on Aisha Day? What makes you think you can come over to my house, unexpectedly at that, and talk about this? I have issues that I need to deal with too, okay? Now please leave." I stood in the doorway, blocking the entrance.

Jordan grabbed my arm. "No, I can't leave. I can't go home right now and I'm not going over to Tonya's. One of my homeboys just clowned the hell out of me and the other one is a pastor, so he does not condone any of this at all. I have nowhere else to go. Please, just let me crash here for the night. I've been sitting here for two hours waiting for you to get home. I need time to think, and I don't want to be in a stuffy hotel room. Please, Aisha," he pleaded.

I snatched my arm away. "Okay, okay, you can stay. It's not attractive for a man to grovel like that. Damn, get yourself together," I scoffed.

Jordan immediately sat down on the couch once we got inside. "You just don't know how much I appreciate this. I will repay you one day."

"Well, how about you repay me with some money right now since I lost my job today. How about that?" I stood with one hand on my hip and one hand extended.

"Oh, man. I'm sorry to hear that, A. I'll help you out. You're helping me out, so that's only fair. I'll give you something tomorrow."

"Yeah, okay, we'll see about that." I walked into the kitchen to figure out what I was going to prepare for dinner. "Are you hungry?"

"Yeah, but we can order some take-out if you want. That's not a problem. We both had a long day."

"Sounds great to me. I didn't feel like making anything anyway," I said as he joined me in the kitchen.

"I'm going to start calling you Mr. Virile," I laughed, looking at him to lighten the mood. "Two women at the same time? You might as well be having twins. I can't believe it. I'm sure it's not a big deal - you can afford it."

He shrugged. "Yeah, I'm sure that I can afford to take care of twenty kids, but my wife is gonna kill me if she finds out Tonya's pregnant again. It's not a matter of how many I can take care of; it's the situation itself that's all messed up."

"Well, sorry for you, bud, but that's your slip-up. You weren't ever able to keep your dick in your pants anyway." I pushed him playfully on the shoulder.

We both smiled bashfully like school kids with crushes. We were both hurting and confused, and through our uncomfortable situations we found comfort in each other. Our smiles slowly dissipated, and we stood face-to-face with shallow breaths. He stepped closer to me, mere inches from my face—almost close enough to kiss.

By this time, I was holding my breath, knowing the inevitable would happen. Then it did. His lips touched mine. It was the softest, sweetest kiss I had felt in a long time. I closed my eyes and imagined he was not who he was. I knew it was wrong, but it felt so right. My flights of fancy were abruptly interrupted when he pulled away to finish our conversation. With a half-smirk, he proceeded.

"Naw, that's just when it came to you. Did you ever tell your sister about that? I know for a fact that she doesn't know about those rims I bought you."

"Hell, no. That girl is in love with you. I wouldn't ever tell her that you were my *buddy* back in the day. It's not something I'm necessarily proud of either. Oh, and as for the rims, I meant to tell you, don't ever try to be slick and say anything like that again."

"Like what?"

"Oh, don't play coy with me. You remember that day when you came over to Tonya's house and you said, 'Those new? I see you got some sap sucka to get them for you cause you damn sure didn't get them yourself.' So, do you think that was cute? What if I had outed you as the sap sucka who bought them? I bet your mouth would've dropped. Luckily, you're somewhat my sister's man, because if she was someone else, I would have said it, and you know it. You know how I am."

"I know how you are. That's what's so sexy about you," he said, brushing my hair away from my face.

"You always know how I felt about you. It's just after Tonya and I had Sicily, I knew that you would never be with me."

"You're damn skippy. You have kids by my sister. What we had was just a little fling."

"Yeah, I know, but I admire your sex appeal and your sassiness. You literally go out and get anything you want. I would have given it to you to." He inched closer.

"What did you come over here for? I mean, why are

you telling me this now? It's too late; you messed up with me a long time ago when you started sleeping with my sister, buddy. Now with a wife, two kids, and two kids on the way, you want to rekindle some sort of romance with me? Boy, please. Let's just forget this conversation happened. Can you order something to eat now please?"

I opened a drawer, picked up a stack of delivery menus and shoved them into his hands.

He abandoned the conversation and ordered Chinese. Once the food was delivered, we sipped on vodka and cranberry for the rest of the night to loosen up a bit and cast our worries aside. Needless to say, we sipped a little more than intended.

"Ooh, I'm so full… and sleepy. I think that drink got me relaxed." I yawned.

"Me too. Vodka and cranberry is my favorite; that's the only thing I buy at the bar. That's what we should have done tonight – went out," Jordan suggested.

"Nah, I was too tired to be doing all of that. Plus, if someone saw us out and told Tonya, we both would be dead tomorrow."

"Yeah, you're right, A. I think it was a good idea for us to stay in."

"Well, I'm about to jump in the shower before I go to bed. Do you need anything?" I said, making my way up the stairs.

"Naw, I'm cool. Go do your thing." Jordan kicked his feet up on the coffee table, folded his hands behind his head, and stared at the TV.

After I got out of the shower, I threw on some boy shorts and a tank top. I proceeded downstairs to take Jordan a blanket and pillow, placing the items on the edge of the couch as he poured us one last nightcap. Hell, since I didn't have to go to work in the morning, I took two shots.

"Okay, I'm going to bed now. If anybody comes to the door, *do not* answer it. If the house phone rings, *do not* pick it up. If you hear something outside, *do not* look out the window. Capiche? Even though nothing's going on, I don't want anyone to know you're here. I don't need any excess drama. I'm pulling the blinds on the door so no one can see in. Matter of fact, where did you park your car? I didn't see it outside anywhere."

"See, I'm two steps ahead of the game. I parked it at my job and took an Uber here. I didn't want anything to look suspicious either. My car, in front of your house? All night? All hell would break loose."

"You're right about that," I said, yawning again.

I stretched and my shirt rose to reveal my toned belly and small waist. Jordan looked me up and down.

"Damn, your sister used to have a body like that but now that she has all of those stretchmarks and loose skin; her body just isn't appealing anymore. Don't get me wrong, she looks fantastic when she's dressed, but when the clothes come off, it's a different story."

Jordan got up and walked toward me.

"Shut up. My sister looks fantastic. I've seen her with her clothes off and she don't look anything like the way you say she does. And if anything, it's your fault because you made her that way. You're a little inappropriate and blunt tonight, don't you think?" I snarled.

"Stop acting like that, Aisha. Hey, I'm just calling it like I see it. I know it's from the babies, but damn. Now she about to have another one. Her body's gonna be completely ruined. But that body of yours is just like new. Every inch of

218

you is perfect. I bet you taste sweet too. Can I taste you?"

I shot Jordan a look that could kill an assassin. *Was he crazy?* I chalked his behavior up to the alcohol and grabbed a pillow to create a wedge between us.

"Look, you can either sleep on the couch or sleep in the guest room. There's no TV in there, so you might as well sleep on the couch."

"What about option number three— Your bed?" He put the pillow and blanket on the couch and moved a few steps closer; close enough to kiss again. I turned my head away this time.

"Jordan, please. Let's not start this. Couch or guest room – you pick."

I pushed him away and made my way upstairs. He followed closely behind.

"Aisha, come on. Quit acting like you ain't down. I remember how you were back in the day, and I know how you are now. Don't act like you're holier than thou now or like you don't want it. You know it's been a long time coming anyway. It's a shame that we can't do anything about all of the sexual tension we have between us because your sister and the kids are around. We got to let it out; it's just not healthy to live this way. I'm here and you're here. Nobody else is around. So, what's the problem? You know we have that certain vibe between us. So, what's it gonna be?"

I turned sharply. "Jordan, please! My nieces are your daughters, asshole. Let's just stop this conversation now because it's leading nowhere fast. Anyway, that was a long time ago and I'm way more mature than that now. I don't just give it up to anybody. Enough said. Good night. Now go back downstairs."

I flipped off the light and got into my bed. Within seconds he turned the light back on.

"Oh, no, no, no. It's not like you have to work tomorrow or something. You already let that cat out of the bag. You're not getting off that easy, A. It's funny that you're always preaching that you don't do this and that, but truth of the matter is, we both know it's not that way – especially between me and you. And my daughters being your nieces… Let's not act like that's ever stopped us before."

"I was drunk that night - it doesn't count."

"You mean those *nights*, plural. I mean, hell, the last time was just a month and a half ago. Quit kidding yourself, Aisha. We're both grown. We know what we want. It's not like I'm asking you for a lifetime commitment or anything. I'm just asking for one night. And if you want to blame it on the alcohol, what better night than tonight?"

Jordan caressed my face and pushed my hair back. The slight nibbling on my ear made me squirm as he walked his fingers down to my moist hole. I'd rejected his advances long enough. He was right - who would know? Who would find out? No one had ever found out before. This was between him and I—our dirty little secret. I tried time and again to resist but gave in each time. This time was no different. Hell, I wanted it so bad. Quite frankly, I *needed* it. It had been a month with no pleasure because I had Charles on the brain. I needed someone to satisfy me, and as cruel as it may sound, I didn't care if he was my sister's beau, my niece's father, or married to someone else. I just knew he could get the job done.

"Wet already? That little talk must have turned you on, huh?" He pushed me back onto the bed, pulling my boy shorts to the side. Although I was timid at first, I quickly warmed up to his touch. Soon, he spread my knees and buried his face in my goodness. His velvet tongue licked me softly, slowly, seductively, enjoying every drop of my creamy delight.

"Stop, stop." My words were weak as he tossed my legs over his shoulders. I didn't really want him to stop but I had to put on a show so he wouldn't think he was in control of the situation.

"You want me to stop? You know you like that, don't you?" He took a lick between every few words. Between my squirming and heavy breathing, I moaned softly. Jordan slid up and wiped his face against the sheets before plunging into my slushy waterfall.

"Wait, wait, whoa!" I stopped him, pushing on his chest. "You got a condom, right?"

"Naw, do you?" he asked nonchalantly, pushing further into my walls.

"No, I don't. We can't do…"

"*Shhh*, don't worry about it. I'll pull out. It feels too good to stop now," he said as he penetrated deeper.

Jordan went at me like an inmate fresh out of prison. He twisted me up into several different positions like I was a little pretzel. Initially, I had one leg over his shoulder in a scissor-like position, then he stood up and bent me over the bed to pound me from the back. My cheeks jiggled against his pelvis, giving us both ultimate pleasure. Before I knew it, I was lying back on the bed with my legs straight up in the air before he rolled me on top of him. We both grinded against one another as he sucked on my erect nipples. Then he grabbed my hips, rocking me harder against him. The strokes became long and hard and soon he exploded inside me.

"*Wooo*! That was a long time coming. Man, that was good," he said, concluding our sexcapade.

"Excuse me? What the fuck was that?" I exclaimed.

"What, you didn't think it was good?" he panted.

"It's not that; you know what in the hell I'm talking about. I know you didn't just do what I think you did?" I sat straight up on the bed and waited for an answer. Jordan didn't respond, wiping sweat from his face.

"I know you heard me. I said, you didn't cum in me, right?" At that very moment, I started to feel warm secretions seeping from me, creating a puddle beneath me.

"Oh, hell no, Jordan."

"Sorry, baby girl, but I couldn't help it. It was too good. I couldn't pull out if I wanted to; you were on top. You'll be alright though. You're on the pill or the shot or something, right?"

"No! No, I am *not* on any birth control. *Ugghhh*! I'm really pissed at you right now. Get out of my bed and go somewhere else. Anywhere but here." I snatched the blanket and rolled over.

"Come on, don't be like that." He put his arm around me.

"Get out of my bed." I pointed to the door.

"You serious?"

"Yep. Just like I seriously didn't think you were gonna cum in me. You got me messed up. I'm not Tonya; I don't play that shit."

"Now, why you gotta bring up all that? Hell, the last time we had sex the condom broke anyway, so what's the difference? Just lie down and relax. What's done is done. We don't even need to talk about her right now. It just makes it seem… wrong. You're always so tense. Do you want me to give you a back massage or something?"

"Jordan, please. No back massage, no cuddling, no talking. It was only a fuck. Take it for what it was. Now please, get out of my bed. You've already made me mad enough as it is."

Jordan threw his hands in the air as if someone was holding him at gunpoint.

"Alright, calm down. I'll leave you alone then. I'll go. I got what I wanted anyway." He laughed as he grabbed his clothes. Without any more questions or comments, he went downstairs and went to sleep.

# Chapter 22
## The Good News

Restlessness woke me up around 5am. My stomach was rumbling, and the room was spinning. I tried to shake it off by going back to sleep but the queasiness wouldn't let me rest. By 7am my throat was tight and dry. I walked downstairs to the kitchen and grabbed a glass of water, hoping it would help.

*Maybe it's all that vodka I drank last night.*

I stumbled to the living room. Jordan was gone.

"Jordan? Jordan! Where you at?" I looked in the downstairs bathroom, then upstairs in the guest room. I ran back downstairs to the front door to find that it was unlocked.

*Son of a bitch,* I grumbled as I dialed his number.

"Hel..hello," he answered in a finicky voice.

"What are you sounding all pissed about? I should be the mad one. You must be back with the wifey." I made my attitude apparent.

"I'm not pissed, Aisha, and I'm not with *the wifey.* I'm at work. I got a meeting in an hour that I'm trying to prepare for. What's up?"

"I don't know what's up, but I can tell you what's *not* up. My door only locks from the inside. Why didn't you wake me up to lock the door? Anyone could have just walked in on me while I was sleeping. Anyone could have robbed me, or raped me, or anything. Are you stupid or something?"

"So, somebody's gonna pick some random house and just walk in? In your neighborhood? I highly doubt it."

"Don't get smart with me. Things happen to people every day in all kinds of neighborhoods – unexpected and terrible things," I exclaimed.

"Well, first off, I left around six-thirty, and I didn't want to wake your snoring ass. So, I just left."

"You could've called me or something to let me know. I mean, that's common courtesy, don't you think? Uh, hold on."

I dropped the phone and ran into the bathroom to puke. Before getting back on the phone, I swished some mouthwash around to kill the aftertaste.

"Okay, I'm back," I said, letting out an airy burp.

"What're you doing?"

"I was… Hold on." I started throwing up again, this time with the phone in my hand. "Okay, sorry about that."

"Okay, now that's just nasty. Why didn't you just hang up the phone? Nobody wants to hear all that," he fussed.

"Well, if it bothered you that much, you should've hung up the phone. I think I got a hangover or something."

"It may have been that Chinese food we ate because I'm feeling a little queasy as well. Or maybe it was a combination of the drink and the food," he suggested.

"I think maybe you're right. Either the food or the vodka, or maybe both. Uh oh, hey, I gotta go."

I belched loudly before more chunks escaped my mouth. I found myself lying on the bathroom floor to regroup. The cool tile somehow soothed my nausea. After a few minutes, I got up and made a cup of Alka-Seltzer. Once my stomach settled a little bit, I headed over to the hospital to be sure that I didn't have food poisoning. On the way, I called Jordan back.

"What, A? I'm in the middle of a meeting," he whispered.

"If you're that damn busy then why are you answering the phone?"

"Look, I don't have time for this. What's up?"

"Do you still feel sick? I've been throwing up all morning and I think that food last night wasn't right. I'm almost to the hospital now. I want to get checked out just in case."

"Well, I feel fine now. Sometimes food just doesn't agree with certain people's stomachs. That's probably what happened to you. But look, A, I really gotta go. I'll talk to you later. Tell me what happens at the hospital."

"Okay, talk to you later."

I hung up and pulled into the emergency room parking lot. I checked myself in, got my wristband, and watched TV in the waiting room until my name was called.

"Isha? Ayesha?" the nurse called, not knowing how to pronounce my name. I rolled my eyes. I hate when people get my name wrong, even if it was spelled differently.

"No, it's Aisha – like the continent."

"Sorry about that, Aisha, right back this way."

"What's your name? A-reeka?" I mocked. I stared at the nurse's name on her badge: "Airika."

"It's pronounced, Erica," the nurse politely responded, guiding me into the room. I wanted her to catch an attitude about me saying her name wrong, but she didn't. I needed someone to take my aggressions out on.

"Here's your gown. Make sure it's on where the front is open. All undergarments can stay on. The doctor should be in here in just a few moments. We aren't that busy today, so it shouldn't be long."

"Thank God," I replied.

The nurse pulled the curtain and shut the door. About fifteen minutes later the doctor appeared.

"Got some stomach issues, huh?" he asked without making eye contact, looking down at the chart.

"Yeah, I ordered Chinese last night— I've been throwing up all morning. I could hardly sleep last night. I think I may have food poisoning."

"Okay, well, lie back and let's take a feel. Any chance you may be pregnant?"

"Umm, no, I don't think so."

"'Umm' doesn't sound too reassuring. We might have to run some tests and take X-rays that could harm a baby if in fact you are pregnant."

"Well, I took a pregnancy test just a few weeks ago and it was negative, so I'm assuming that I'm not."

"Have you had unprotected sex since then?"

"Yes, but it was the other night, so I don't think that would be a factor."

"Well, just to be on the safe side, we need you to take a test. Sometimes home tests don't catch the hormones at the beginning stages. I want you to take another test just in case, okay? I'll be right back and there's a restroom right around the corner here. When you're done, stick your cup in the window and the nurse will run the test for you."

The doctor opened one of the cabinet drawers and handed me a small plastic cup with a lid.

Holding the front of the gown, I dragged myself to

the bathroom to handle my business. Upon returning to the exam room, I turned on the TV and continued watching daytime television. I heard two rapid taps on the door before the doc swung the curtain back.

"Well, good news. First, I should ask if you want to be pregnant."

"I do. We've been trying, why?"

"Well, in that case, we have double good news. We don't have to run any tests because we found out what the problem is… You're expecting. What you are feeling is morning sickness, which is totally normal. I'm assuming this is your first baby?"

I stared into space.

"Ms. Carmichael?"

I couldn't believe this was happening. Damn those home pregnancy tests.

"Yes, this is my first baby. I'm just shocked because I thought I wasn't pregnant. Oh my! Wait until I tell the father. We've been trying." I smiled.

"Are you married or…"

"No, engaged. He'll be so happy though. Do you know how far along I am?"

The doctor chuckled.

"Now that, I would not know. You need to set up an appointment with an obstetrician as soon as possible. Do you have a regular OB-GYN, or do you need a reference?"

"No, I have one. I'll make an appointment right away."

"Okay, well let me get your discharge papers ready and you're free to go. Have a great afternoon, and again, congratulations."

"Thank you, doctor."

Suddenly the nausea wasn't as bothersome anymore. I was smiling ear-to-ear.

# Chapter 23
## Bearer of Bad News

"Hold on a minute, geesh." Tonya squinted through the peephole to see me on the other side beating the door down.

"Aisha? My God! What is going on? Is everything ok? Come in…come in." She ushered me to the couch.

I plopped down on the nearest couch.

"Oh, everything is great! But you *will not* believe this."

"Believe what?"

"Just guess." I glimmered.

"Well, it has to be something good since you're sitting there with that big, dumb grin on your face," she said nonchalantly.

"Yes it is. I'm pregnant," I blurted out, unable to hold my excitement.

"Pregnant? By who? Not by Charles?" A contorted look came over her face.

"Yes, by Charles. Isn't this great? Now we'll have kids who will be almost exactly the same age. Best of all, I don't have to worry about working another day in my life. It feels like I hit the jackpot!"

Tonya flopped down on the couch, disenchanted by

the news.

"What? Are you not happy for me? Can I get a congratulations? A handclap? Two thumbs up? Damn… Something?"

"Well, you weren't excited when I told you I was pregnant, so why do I need to be excited for you? But I guess you got what you wanted; you always get what you want." Tonya rolled her eyes.

"Well, first of all, why would I be happy when it seems like you're *always* pregnant? Second of all, this is my first baby – you should be happy. I mean, you're going to be an auntie for the first time. Doesn't that count for something?"

"Okay, well, congratulations, Aisha. Bravo, good job." She sarcastically applauded.

"Whatever. I can't be mad that you're a hater, T. Obviously, you were just born that way." I made my way over to the full-length mirror and imagined how my belly would look once my stomach grew.

"Sure, whatever you say." Tonya paused as if she had just had an epiphany. "Umm, Aisha, honey, when is the last time you saw Charles?"

"Uh, it's been a while. But, after I tell him about the baby, I'm sure he'll come around more. He's a stand-up guy like that, you know."

"Hmm, interesting. So, does Charles still live here in Chicago?" Tonya grilled.

"I think so. Why wouldn't he? Why would you ask me something like that? That's a silly question."

"Just wondering. When is the last time you talked to him?" she interrogated.

"It's been a while. But he's gonna have to talk to me

231

now. He has no choice. If not, I won't hesitate to get paternity and lawyers involved."

I stopped poking out my stomach and stood up straight. It dawned on me that she must've been asking these questions for a reason and not just to be nosey. "Wait a minute. What's going on? Is there something you know that I don't? If so, you need to tell me, pronto."

"Okay, A, I think you need to sit down for this one. Let me talk to you for a sec." She patted the couch cushion next to her.

"I don't need to sit down. Just tell me," I asserted.

"I said *sit,*" she insisted. This time, I sat on her command.

"Well, since I'm having another baby, I figured that I might need a bigger house. So, I picked up one of those real estate magazines and saw this big, beautiful estate for sale on the front cover. You know, a girl got big dreams. I know I could never afford that house, but I was just browsing through…"

"Tonya, get to the point. What are you talking about?"

"Well, to make a long story short, A, I saw Charles' estate up for sale."

"What?" I exclaimed, popping up from the couch like a hot potato. "What do you mean his house is up for sale? He can't do that. No, no, he wouldn't do that. He told me he invested everything in that house."

I paced Tonya's living room like a lunatic before shuffling *Cosmopolitan* and *Elle* magazines around on the table, knocking a few to the floor. Tonya's eyes bulged looking like she just unleashed a beast.

"Where's the damn magazine at?" I yelled.

"I don't have it anymore. I thought you knew. I didn't feel like it was my job to keep it. I wasn't for sure anyway, it just looked—"

"Don't speak on things that you are not sure of then, honey," I cut in.

"Oh no, I know for sure. It was the same location that the driver said he was going that night after the reunion. And you showed me a picture of his place, remember?"

"What picture? I never took a picture of his house."

"I know. It was the picture that Charles gave you with him standing in front of his house with one of his friends."

"Oh yeah, I forgot about that. I bet I know what it is - I bet it's that damn baby momma of his. Yep, that's it… and his damn sick son.

"I'm tired of this. I'm tired of all this drama. I'm tired of them two being in the way. I got a baby on the way too. Once he finds out, he better treat my baby equal, if not better than his other sick little bastard."

"Aisha, that's a terrible thing to say. You created most of this drama anyway," Tonya exclaimed.

"I know, but I don't care. He's always running to New York doing this and that for his son and he hardly gives me the time of day."

"Well, that's his job. As a father, that's what he's supposed to do. You don't see too many men out there like that anymore."

"Whatever, Tonya. All the stuff you're trying to preach to me right now is irrelevant."

"How is it irrelevant? When your baby is born, you'll want Charles to do everything in his power to take care of that child. Even if you lived in China, he should take care of that child as if you lived right here in Chicago.  You can't down a man for doing what's right. You should be happy you found someone like that."

I pierced Tonya with my eyes. "Whose side are you on anyway? You're my sister; you're supposed to side with me no matter what."

"Aisha, right is right and wrong is wrong. I sided with right because you are wrong."

"It's enough that I have to put up with crap at work, then with Charles, but you too? Give me a break. I don't have to take this from you. I got to go. I have some business to take care of." I stormed out of the house and slammed the door.

I was halfway home when Tonya called me. (She probably wanted to apologize. She knew I rarely apologized, so she usually did what she thought would smooth things over.)

"Yep," I answered.

"Get your ass back over here right now," she demanded.

"Excuse me?"

"Ironically, Jordan just called. We have to get something straightened out over at his house. I'm not going to talk about it right now, I just need you to get back over here," she said and hung up.

*That damn, Jordan. He better not have opened his big mouth about what happened the other night. I swear I will kill him. I didn't need any more drama between me and my sister.*

When I got back over to Tonya's house, she was already standing outside. Before I could come to a complete stop, she jumped in.

"Drive," she blurted.

My heart was beating fast. Without hesitation or questioning, I took off. The entire way to Jordan's house, Tonya was silent. I didn't know what to say to her, so I didn't say anything at all. I felt it was best to keep my mouth shut.

When we arrived at Jordan's house the kids were playing with him outside. Tonya jumped out of the car and stormed over to them. I rolled my window down to listen.

"Give her here. Matter of fact, Sicily, go get your things - you're leaving with me," Tonya yelled and snatched Grace from his arms.

"But, Momma, I don't want to leave," Sicily whined.

"Look, you're getting too spoiled over here. You do as I say."

Sicily ran off with tears in her eyes when Tonya yelled at her. (Sicily wasn't used to her mom laying down the law.)

"Whoa, whoa… All of that yelling isn't necessary in front of *my* home. You keep your messy little life over there in the city," Jordan's wife yelled, appearing in the doorway.

"You just shut the hell up, Denise. No one was speaking to you," Tonya exclaimed. Denise cut her eyes sharply at Jordan, waiting for him to take control of the situation.

"Tonya, why did you just pop up like this? I told you on the phone that I was going to bring Gracie back to you later," Jordan hissed, pulling Tonya to the side.

"Bring her back later? Oh, hell, naw! You are not going to be treating my daughters differently."

Denise interrupted. "Exactly… *Your* daughters. Jordan needs to take care of his *one* daughter that he has with you; not any other little offspring that you bring into this world. That's what her daddy is for. Jordan's responsible for Sicily and that's it. I'm tired of Sicily coming over here and Grace tagging along. I know they're sisters, but Grace is not Jordan's responsibility."

"Denise, just go in the house," Jordan urged, but his wife continued.

"Look, I don't mean to cause a commotion. I've been trying to keep the peace with you ever since Jordan and I got married. I keep my tongue, and I don't say anything when it comes to those kids. But enough is enough. I'm not going to have your other daughter over here all the time."

"Wait, what? Jordan, what in the hell is she talking about?" Tonya looked perplexed. It only took her a few moments to make sense out of the situation. She slowly shook her head in disgust.

"She doesn't know, does she? You never told her. That's why you never wanted to take Grace with you, huh?" Her voice slowly accelerated.

"Look, I can explain," Jordan relented.

"Wait a minute, explain what? You need to be trying to explain something to me, Jordan? I'm your wife," Denise lashed.

Tonya intervened before he could say a word. "Both of these kids are his. Grace looks just like him. You'd have to be a fool not to know."

"No, that can't be. Grace is only a year old, and we've been married for a year and a half."

Everyone went silent. Denise took a deep breath as reality hit.

"So, what you're saying is that you've been screwing my husband? You filthy low life. You're just a breeder; that's all you're good for. He just wanted to have another baby by you because he thought we couldn't have any. Surprise, bitch, I'm pregnant." She inched within an arm's length of Tonya with her hand on her belly.

Jordan immediately wedged himself between his wife and Tonya.

"Jordan, move out of the way," Tonya demanded. "Get the car seats and put the girls in Aisha's car."

"No, Tonya, I'm not leaving y'all out here. Look, we can straighten this out later."

"Go do it... now," Tonya yelled while pointing to the car. Tonya shot him a look that put fire under his ass. Jordan immediately picked up the two girls and sprinted to the car, trying to make it back to the two women in a hurry. Before Jordan could put the girls in my car, Tonya hauled off and punched Denise in the nose. Denise stumbled backwards, blood trickling down her top lip.

"That's for disrespecting me *and* my daughter," Tonya exclaimed.

"You damn psycho! Who in the hell do you think you are? You can't hit me like that – I'm pregnant," Denise wailed, wiping the blood from her lip.

"Well, surprise, bitch, I'm pregnant too," Tonya screamed and walked away with a strut that exhibited confidence and achievement.

Jordan's mouth dropped. He was flabbergasted.

"Get out of my way," Tonya said, pushing him away from the car.

"I'm sorry, Tonya, I just didn't—"

"Pull off, Aisha! Ain't nobody trying to hear his damn lies."

I sped off without question and took Tonya and the kids back to her house.

# Chapter 24
## Momma

With so much drama going on, it was hard to keep my head straight. Tonya and Jordan, Charles, the pregnancy, and losing my job was all taking a toll on me. My mind felt like a tornado of destruction. I felt so alone—my back was against the wall. With no real friends, I didn't have anyone to call on and I didn't want burden Tonya with my troubles; she had enough going on as it was. I had a 'Come to Jesus' moment and decided to humble myself enough to call Momma. I was scared about becoming a mother and she had no idea she was going to have a new grandchild. It was time I let her know about the baby, as well as a few other things that were on my mind.

I decided to invite her over for dinner, which was rare. But she was unprepared for all of the conversation I was about to dish up to her. To start, we had an awkwardly silently dinner; you could literally hear the forks scraping the plates and the gulps as we swallowed. As an adult, my encounters with Momma had always been with Tonya or around other relatives. We never had official mother-daughter time. Most times when I saw her, she spoke to me as she saw fit, usually in a negative light. As the years went by, I grew accustomed to it. After all, that's just the way she was. After dinner, I invited her in the living room for a one-on-one talk.

"Aisha, what's all this about? Give it to me straight." She folded her arms. I took a deep breath, feeling like a teenager revealing an unplanned pregnancy to her mother. I didn't want to beat around the bush, so I just said it.

"I'm pregnant."

She just sat there with a stale face and looked at me with arms still folded.

"Okay. Are congratulations in order?" She raised an eyebrow. "Who's the daddy? Do you even know?"

"Yes, I know who the father is, and no, you don't know him. And thanks for the half-ass congrats."

She stood up right away and pointed her finger in my face. "Watch your mouth, girl."

"I'm grown," I retorted.

"You still need to respect me. Now sit down somewhere. You're not too old to get smacked. I don't care if you're pregnant or not."

"No, not this time, Momma. You gonna sit down and you gonna listen."

I slowly walked toward her, backing her into the couch until she plopped down. Her eyes grew big, almost fearful. I may have talked back in the past, but I never addressed her in this manner.

"Quite frankly, I'm tired of your overbearing ways. You never have anything good to say to or about me. Why is that?"

"Aisha, really? What good is there?" she huffed.

"Really, Momma? Look around. Look at all I've accomplished. I put myself through school, bought a nice

239

home, achieved a senior position at my job, almost thirty with no kids –"

"You mean the job you got fired from? And now you're knocked up by God knows who!"

I slammed my hand on the coffee table. "See that's what I'm talking about. When it comes to me, you only see the negative."

"Aisha, what else is there to see? All of these material things don't mean nothin. You've just always been fast, and I'm not just talkin bout sexually. I mean wanting fast money, havin a slick tongue and using your body to get what you want. I'm not slow, Aisha. I'm your Momma; I know how you are."

I was infuriated. Did she not notice her little angel Tonya had two kids out of wedlock and had one on the way? Tonya didn't do anything for herself and had to rely on her children's father for everything. Why was I the bad seed? I was tired of her shit-talking; I'd heard it all my life. It was time to say what I had buried inside.

"Do you want to know why I am the way I am? Why I felt the need to escape and get out on my own at such an early age? Why I may have been a *bit* more promiscuous than Tonya and other girls? Well, it's because of you downing me all the damn time and Daddy *using* me."

She waved me off as to dismiss my conversation as nonsense, but it was time she heard it from the horse's mouth, and I was just getting started. Even though she seemed to ignore me, I continued.

"Daddy, the man you once loved, used to touch me every chance he got. And he called that *love*. He led me to believe that those touches were supposed to happen and the only way to win a man's affections. But what hurt most is when I told you and you did nothing. You sat back and called me a liar, like I was making it up. When he moved out, I thought it would stop, but you made me go visit him and that's when it got worse. I'm glad cancer killed him slow; I'm glad he's dead."

She shook her head and curled her lip. "Don't talk ill of the dead, gal. That's not true. He would never—"

"Yes, he would, and he did," I maintained.

"But that's not it, Momma, I'm not done."

Momma breathed deep and rolled her eyes as to say, *What now?* I figured if I was going to let her have it, I was going to hit her with everything.

"Vance, the boyfriend you thought was oh-so-perfect, who ended up hurting you and cheating on you, had been cheating on you with your own daughter - in my room, right under your nose why you were exhausted from working twelve-hour shifts, taking naps. He used to force himself on me and threatened to kill me, you, T, and Drew if I said anything. So, I shut my mouth and spread my legs like a nice little girl. I took the pain to spare my family. But when enough was enough, I had to get up the courage to tell you, despite his threats, despite his lies. You still chose to take his side. And after you told him what I had said he left. So not only was he blowing smoke that he'd cause us harm, but he knew that if he didn't leave that he would end up in a penitentiary somewhere if anyone discovered the truth."

Momma gasped and put her hand on her head. Seemed like she wanted to say something, but I didn't give her a second to intrude. This was a long time coming and I had to get it out - all of it, for the sake of being a better person and a better mom. This was like my therapy; I couldn't go into motherhood carrying all this toxic baggage.

241

"And lastly, your boss... I almost feel like I got this from you as far as doing anything for the dollar," I huffed. "You know for fact that he raped me. I laid up in the hospital for three days with stitches from my vagina to my anus. He tore me open. There was so much pain— mental, and physical, that can never be erased. All of these so-called *men* turned me into this... this person that I am today. The person who is unable to love, unable to feel, and one that only sees men as pawns. Why should I see them any other way when all my life they just been using me as they see fit?"

"Aisha," she yelled, this time in tears. "Please stop it."

"Stop? Are you fucking kidding me? Don't you dare try to turn a deaf ear, Momma. You've been doing that long enough. Do you know how many tears I cried? Do you know what I had to endure? All because I grew a little bit of curves at an early age and these sick-ass, grown-ass, nasty-ass, perverted-ass men saw me as some type of sex object. Naw, Momma, this conversation is long overdue."

"I think I've said enough, and I feel like a weight is lifted off my shoulders, but you gonna have to deal with this. You gonna have to face the fact that you did not save your daughter and did not come to my rescue when I needed you the most. You were supposed to be my safe haven. You were supposed to keep me safe. Don't you understand that?! And now you have the nerve to act all holier than thou now when you were sleeping with the enemy then? I'm not buying it."

"I may have been a liar, and I may have been fast, but being molested and raped was no lie and I didn't ask for it. The adults I thought I could trust betrayed me and all those men took advantage of my innocence. This fucked me up in the head, Momma. Don't you get it? Or don't you care?"

I clenched my fist, shaking with anger. My lips were tight, and my eyes were red from withholding tears. I choked back words as we stared in each other's eyes for several seconds. Then, I exploded again.

"Say something," I yelled.

Momma fell to her knees in front of me and held on to my thighs. Her tears puddled close to my knees, and she screamed out repeatedly. "Lord, please forgive me. I'm sorry, I'm sorry."

Without remorse I replied, "Indeed you are. You're sorry. I'm glad the Lord can forgive you, because I can't."

I pulled back and walked away, leaving her sulking in her own misery.

Having Momma as a role model made me undeniably frightened to be a mother, but at the same time I was overwhelmed with joy. Coming to terms with my past gave me a chance at a clean slate. I wanted a chance to prove myself to someone who would have real love for me - my child. I realized I didn't want to be like Momma; I wanted to be a better person, a better mother. It was time for a change; time to grow up (*really* grow up). No longer did I care about Charles' money, but only what was in the best interest of the seed growing inside of me. Sure, he could provide great financial support, but if I were to be with Charles, it needed to be more than that. I wanted substance. Tonya was right - Charles was a good father, and I wanted to be a good mother. The next time I talked to Charles I wanted it to be open and unselfish. I wanted a fresh start and the best life for me and my baby.

# Chapter 25
## Is This the End?

A few months went by and there was still no word from Charles. Apprehensively, I searched real estate sites to see if his estate was really up for sale like Tonya had said. I was in denial; I didn't want it to be true. However, his lengthy absence led me to investigate. As I began my internet search, anxiety bubbled up inside me like lava in a volcano. My hands were clammy, and I couldn't stop my knee from shaking. I dreaded the thought of Charles permanently leaving the city without saying a word to me. Moreover, I dreaded him not knowing I was carrying his child. After searching numerous real estate sites, my worse fear rang true. His estate was indeed up for sale.

At that very moment, something inside me snapped. I went berserk. I started throwing pillows off the couch and stomping around like a child having a tantrum. I called Charles back-to-back on his cell and home phone, leaving sixteen messages within a single hour. I lashed out on some messages and apologized on others. Then I asked why he was moving and begged for him to stay. When he still didn't respond, I demanded that he call me back right away.

I couldn't take it anymore. As crazy as it sounds, I

couldn't stand the thought of Charles leaving me and the baby. (Yes, the baby he knew nothing about.) I really didn't want to leave that type of news on a message, but he had to know. I knew he was a stand-up guy who took care of his responsibilities, so I figured the last message to him would be different; I would grab his attention and get him to call me back. He wasn't the type to turn his back on his own flesh and blood.

"Charles, this is Aisha again. Please, please, just pick up the phone. I know we left on bad terms, but there's something I have to tell you. I wanted to tell you in person, but I... I thought you would be mad. I don't know how to say this. I... don't want to get an abortion. Charles, I'm carrying your baby. Please call me back. I don't know what to do, I'm so scared. I can't imagine doing this alone."

I hung up hoping that this message would soften his heart and get him to call me back. I sat back on the couch and I rubbed my now-five-month pregnant belly.

After about an hour of blank stares at the wall, I got up and threw on some jeans and a sweater. I jumped in my car and went for a ride to try to clear all of the emotions I had conjuring up inside. I rode downtown near Lake Shore Drive and throughout the heart of the city. Even though the streets were slick from the ice storm earlier in the day, I wove in and out of lanes like I was on the Autobahn. I stopped at Harold's Chicken to get some wings and fries (to satisfy my craving) and downed them as I drove.

Subsequently, I ended up in front of Charles' estate. Something led me there; I just had to see with my own two eyes. I parked my car at the gate's entrance. I got out and walked to the locked gate, hoping that this was somehow a nightmare. Tears welled up in my eyes as I peered at the abandoned home through the icy-cold iron bars.

"How could you do this to me, Charles?" I wailed as I grabbed the gate. My fingers were like popsicles, becoming slightly frost-bitten from holding onto the chilled wrought iron. I stood out there as long as I could stand it with bipolar emotions. I never felt such anger, confusion, loneliness, and desperation simultaneously. The frigid temperatures made my tears prickle against my cheeks as they fell. My face soon became numb like the rest of my body, matching my soul. Exhausted, I got in my car and made my way back home.

Upon entering the house, I noticed the message light on my house phone. Before checking my messages, I dug around in my purse for my cell phone to see if I'd missed any calls. My phone wasn't there; I'd been in such a rush that I'd left it on the coffee table after I went on my "calling spree." I rushed to the table to retrieve the abandoned phone and found that I'd missed four calls. I hastily scrolled through - they were all from Charles. I raced to the house phone and checked my messages. They were also from Charles.

"Aisha, it's me, Charles. I got your message. We need to talk immediately. Please call me as soon as you get this, no matter how late. It's important." His voice was shaky; he sounded concerned.

I nervously paced the floor as random thoughts flew through my head, wondering what I was going to say once I called him back. Did he want to talk about the baby? Did he want to talk about our future? Did he want to work things out or did he not want anything to do with us? Maybe he just wanted to pay me off. I didn't know what to think.

I put the pillows back on the couch and got the house back in order before calling as I tried to collect my thoughts.

I took a deep breath. The phone rang once and then there was silence.

"Hello?"

"Yep," Charles answered.

"Are you mad at me?" I asked.

"No, I'm not mad, I'm just disappointed. I don't think you know to what extent this will affect our lives. Not only our lives, but the baby's life too. That's why *there will be no baby.*"

His words terrified me. This is not the response I thought I'd get from him. He continued. "I don't even know how this happened. I don't know how I got into this. Aisha, let me get straight to the point: there is no easy way to put this, so I'll just go ahead and say it… You *have* to get an abortion. It's the only way."

"What?" I gasped, almost losing my breath. "What do you mean? I am not killing my baby. It's too late anyway - I'm five months along," I shrilled.

Charles replied nonchalantly. "I know somewhere where you can get an abortion up to six months. It will be quick, discreet, and no one will know. Just act like you miscarried."

I began hyperventilating and a hot flash come over me. It was like all of the sudden he didn't care; like he was a shell of the man I knew him to be. He wanted me to kill our child? No way! This was definitely not the Charles I knew, or at least the Charles I thought I knew.

"What? I don't understand. What you're implying is ludicrous and I'm not doing it. Why are you saying these things?"

"Well, first of all, I'm not *implying* anything; I'm *telling* you what you are about to do. Look, Aisha, having this baby is not good. There's a lot to it, and there are a lot of things that we've never discussed…"

"You keep telling me that, that we need to 'discuss things,' but you never tell me anything, Charles."

"Oh, you don't even need to go there. I would've told you everything you needed to know in due time, but you just made the situation way more complicated with, with this little baby charade."

"Excuse the hell outta me… Baby charade? It takes two to tango, Mr. I-Didn't-Do-Anything."

"Whatever, Aisha, cut the crap. It's because of your narcissistic attitude and deceitful scheming that you're in this predicament right now. You chose to do this, not me. But I'm about to step in and make some choices of my own. And my choice is that there will absolutely be *no* baby, end of story."

"Oh, yes, there will be. I've already heard our baby's heartbeat, and I already felt it kick. This is *my* baby too and I'm not getting rid of anything.

"Oh, I know, you must be going bankrupt or something. That's why you're putting your house up for sale and that's why you want me to get rid of the baby… because you can't afford it? Just scandalous."

"Scandalous? You're the one who's scandalous in every sense of the word. You are a scandalous, low-down, conniving, foul, ratchet, good-for-nothing skank. You're a joke. You're no *real woman*, because no *real woman* would need to trick a man into having sex. You need money? Is that what it is? That's why you want to keep this baby? You think that baby is going to bring you some kind of wealth? Well, you're dead wrong because you aren't keeping that damn baby, and you won't be getting another damn dime from me."

"You can't tell me what I will and won't do with my body. I can do what I damn well please and if I want to keep the baby, I will keep it, dammit," I yelled.

"Oh, really? Well, are you even sure it's mine?" Charles sarcastically questioned.

"Yes, it's yours. What kind of stupid question is that?"

"Well, hell, how loose and desperate you act, I'm shocked that you'd know."

The screaming match continued.

"And what in the hell is that supposed to mean, Charles? You're the one who kept turning me away. You act like you didn't like me, or that you never wanted me. I gave you what you wanted and now you're acting all scary trying to get me to get an abortion because you're scared of the truth. Get out of here with that crap."

"The truth? I can handle the truth very well and this is exactly what I didn't want to happen. You don't even know the half of the truth, or you wouldn't have done what you did and you wouldn't be pregnant right now."

"Whatever. Don't try to turn this on me like I'm the bad guy. The truth is, I'm having the baby and you're going to take care of us. That's it, end of discussion."

"Take care of you? I can buy your whole entire life ten times over - money isn't an object. Contrary to your irrational theory, I'm not bankrupt – far from it. But how about this... How about we keep things simple? You want me to take care of you, right? That's what this is?"

I didn't answer because I didn't know if this was a trick question, so I just waited for him to continue.

"I don't mind it; it's a small price to get you to do

what I want. Regardless, I'm going to have to take care of you after this anyway to get you to keep your mouth shut. But that's beside the point. I'm telling you… Get an abortion. I can't even take the chance and wait until the baby is born to see if it's mine or not; you have to get rid of it."

At this point I was completely confused. I didn't know if Charles wanted me to get rid of the baby because he didn't want another child, if he didn't want his son's mother to be upset with him, or if he just plain hated me. Whatever the reason, he was adamant about not having the baby. Why would he give me money if he didn't have to pay child support? Did he feel guilty about aborting the baby and thought money would ease my pain, or was he just trying to pay me off?

"What do you mean? That doesn't even make any sense. Why would you have to take care of me if there is no baby? I don't get it. I mean…"

Before I could say another word, Charles butted in. He answered all of my lingering questions in a few brief sentences. What came next was beyond anything I could ever imagine.

"Aisha, I don't know how to say this. I should've just come straight out and told you when we reunited, but I thought it irrelevant at first. I just wanted friendship, that's it. But since there's obviously a baby in the midst of this now I'm just going to come out and say it. Aisha, I have AIDS."

Silence fell over both ends of the phone. My phone fell to the ground, and I stared at the wall. I could still hear his voice in the distance, but my mind drifted elsewhere. Those four letters kept ringing in my head like a never-ending school bell: AIDS, AIDS, AIDS. I felt like dying right then.

"Aisha?... Aisha? Are you still there? Are you okay? Aisha! *Shit*, I'm coming over," his voice echoed.

I slumped down to the floor in disbelief and lay on my back. Staring at the ceiling, tears rolled from my eyes, down my temples and into my hair. The tears made my hair wet and heavy, nearly as heavy as my heart felt now that I knew the truth behind Charles' celibacy.

How had I not put two and two together? How could this happen to me? I was so wrapped up in my own selfishness that I never imagined this would be the endgame. I felt like I was going crazy. I stayed on the floor until Charles arrived.

Half an hour later the doorbell rang. Reluctant to get up, I lay motionless for a few moments. Charles knocked on the door, his rapping growing heavier and insistent. Soon, I heard him yelling. "Aisha, open the door. Please, come to the door?"

I picked myself up and went to the door. A gust of bitter wind brushed against my body, sending chills through my soul. The blustering air that blew through the Windy City that night was foreign to me, providing a discomfort that I'd never felt before.

Upon seeing Charles' face, I dropped my head, turned away, and sat on the couch. He followed me into the living room without saying a word. The room was silent for about two minutes before he spoke.

"I don't know what to say, or what to tell you. On one hand, I want to tell you I'm sorry and everything is going to be okay, but I know that's not the truth. I'm not sorry and everything is not going to be okay."

He stood in the middle of my living room in a black furry Kango hat and a black leather coat with matching

251

gloves. It wasn't cold enough outside to wear gloves, but he had them on. He looked like the Grim Reaper, and in retrospect, he was.

"What? You're *not* sorry? How could you say something like that?" I snarled with disgust.

"I told you time and again that I was celibate. It was none of your damn business as to why. I told you that I would tell you one day, but you wouldn't listen. You continued to try me and push up on me, and now you know why I wouldn't react. But somehow, that night you slipped me on—"

"Excuse me? Slipped you on? You're taking this too far now, Charles. Why would I do something like that? I would never—"

"I don't know why you would do something like that," he cut in, "but my doctor confirmed my suspicions that very same day. I know my drinking limits; there was no way I would've gotten drunk enough to sleep with you, condom or not. I was somewhat coherent, but it was like I was floating at the same time. I couldn't believe that you would do something like that. You are one trifling bitch."

"Don't call me a bitch or trifling. *You* are the one who gave me AIDS. Obviously, you're the one who's trifling." I jumped from the couch and pushed him aggressively.

"How could you? How could you do this to me? Why didn't you tell me?"

My pushes grew weaker as I broke into tears. Charles grabbed me and held me in his arms, almost as a reassurance that everything would be okay, even though I knew it wouldn't be. He looked down at my growing belly and shook his head.

"Aisha, I don't... I didn't know what to tell you. You

viewed me as a human being, not someone who has AIDS. You were, in some way, my breath of fresh air. After some of my close friends found out, they never treated me the same. I was shocked. Hell, some of them never talked to me again, like it would just rub off on them. The ignorance was outrageous!"

"The only person in this world who understands is my son's mother – that's because she's sick too. We ended up suing the hospital because out of all the tests they ran when she was pregnant, they never told us she was HIV positive. Then, when our son was born and had a routine blood exam, that's when we knew. We lost the suit because they said she contracted it during her pregnancy. Then she told me that she'd cheated on me with some random guy. She initially thought he was my son's father, so it was a toss-up, I guess."

"She claims to have cheated on me because I cheated on her, which was not true. I think she made that up so she could go out and do whatever the hell she wanted. That's why I don't trust women; that's why I have relationship issues; that's the reason I have AIDS - because that punk gave it to her. I was just HIV positive for years, but somehow, even with all the meds, my body still couldn't fight it. Now I'm in the final stage… Now it's full-blown AIDS."

"I love my son to death, but if I would have known that he would be HIV positive when he was born, I would've insisted she get an abortion. No ifs, ands, or buts about it. He's sick, Aisha. Every day, no matter how many drugs he takes, his little body is just breaking down. It tears my heart in two just to know that my flesh and blood is suffering like that. It's overwhelming. Every day I wonder how many more

253

days I have left; how many more days my son has to live. I don't know how much more I can take; it's like the world is on my shoulders.

"Yeah, I have the cars, the mansion, the money, but all of that means nothing. I'd rather be broke and have a happy and healthy son than to live like this. People tease him at school because they don't understand. They say he has the cooties and no one wants to sit with him at lunch. There's no way to really educate kids on things like that; you can tell them that they won't get it just by being someone's friend or holding their hand or even sitting at the same lunch table with them, but their little minds can't understand things like that. Even some grown folks don't get it because they aren't educated on the subject either.

"We took him out of his private school and began home schooling him. No one needed the added stress and difficulties of dealing with this sickness. He has no friends now, just family. Sometimes I feel like I'm shutting him off from the world, but I don't know of any other way to protect him.

"One day, my little man told me that he didn't want to live anymore. I couldn't believe what I was hearing, but at the same time I knew exactly how he felt. He's all I got; he's all I live for. He wanted to know how if God really loved him, why would He make him so sick. We prayed for a long time that day. Daddy has to stay strong for him. If I don't, who will? I'm his hero. I'm his father, no matter what."

"My life is one big struggle. People may think I'm living the life, but they have no idea. I just wanted a friend, Aisha. And I thought you were that person. I wanted you to trust me first, and then I was going to tell you I was sick. I didn't want you to run out of my life like everyone else did.

I'm sorry that this happened to you but at the same time you shouldn't have done what you did. Why did you do that, huh?"

Charles grabbed my shoulders and shook me. A tear dropped from his eye as he bear-hugged me.

I had no words for him, no explanation to right my wrongs. I broke away from his embrace and walked over to the ashtray where a half-smoked cigarette was nestled in one of the grooves. Being that I hadn't smoked in months, it was stale, but I needed something to calm my nerves.

"So, what now? What am I supposed to do? What about the baby? What about us? What's going to happen?" I asked. Puffs of smoke escaped my mouth between words.

"What? What do you mean? Were you not listening to that long-ass story? Did I just waste my breath? I don't know what's going to happen from here, but what I do know is that there's not going to be any *us* or any *baby*," he asserted.

"What do you mean? I can't do this alone. I can't go through life like this by myself," I exclaimed.

The concern on his face turned into a grimace.

"Let me make this crystal clear for you... I don't want to be with you. I don't care if I have AIDS or not; I'm not that damn desperate. Look at you— you're a mess. You act like you want to keep this baby so bad, but you're smoking? At this rate I don't need to make you get an abortion; you're doing a fine job of killing this baby yourself. I guess you really deserve a 'Mother of the Year' award right now, don't you? Round of applause..."

Charles began to circle me, clapping loudly. He really struck a nerve, especially with all of the changes I'd been trying to make since the confrontation with Momma.

"Oh, no, no… Don't you even go there. According to you, this baby is already doomed. And according to you, I'm *only* after your money. So why would you care if I smoke or not? You don't give a damn what happens to this baby, but I do. I'm going to be the best mother I can be."

"Look, Aisha, I know it's hard to process, but I don't care what you say or how much you yell – you brought this upon yourself. I have enough issues with the son that I already have. Once the baby is gone you can start getting some help— all expenses paid. I'll pay for the best medicine and care that money can buy. They also have meetings that you can go to, you know – support groups. You can still live a full life."

"Really, Charles? Really?" I snapped. "It's all your fault, Charles. You did this to me. I'm going to be a nobody now. Who will want to marry me now, huh? Tell me that. You did it and now you're the only one I can be with. We're going to be together until one of us dies, and that's final. No one else will want to be with you, so you might as well be with me," I insanely declared.

"Bitch, are you crazy? I wouldn't want to be with you even if *both* of us were *well*. You're sick, alright— sick in the head. What in the hell is wrong with you? No, Aisha, we are *never* going to be together. Never!"

Hearing this, I flipped. I wasn't myself anymore. From then on, I don't remember much; everything is a blur. It felt like I was in some type of evil nightmare; the kind where you're running from someone, but you don't know who you are running from or why. I went completely out of my mind without a care in the world.

"Okay, you want to play hardball? Okay, let's play. If you don't want to be with me, I'm keeping this baby.

There's nothing you can do about it. You can't make me get an abortion. What can you do about it, Charles? You can say what you want, but you can't make me do anything!"

"Do you hear what you're saying right now? Are you fucking retarded? I mean, what do you want, money? What?! I'll take care of your medical bills or whatever, Aisha, but…"

"But what? You want to keep living a life like you're fine? Well, reality check, Charles: You are not fine, you will never be fine, and you never were fine! You were a broke-down little nerd in high school that no one cared about and now you're a man living with AIDS and still no one cares about you." I shouted furiously.

I poked him in the forehead with my finger to emphasize my point. His head bounced with every poke, and with every poke he grew angrier. After one poke too many, he smacked my hand out of his face and heatedly drove me into the wall. He pushed me with so much force that the hung artwork fell to the floor. I couldn't move; I was pinned to the wall like a boutonniere on a lapel. And just like the pretty flower on a jacket, I was already dead, withering slowly.

"Don't you ever put your hands on me again, woman." His voice was deep and indifferent. I could feel the heat from his nostrils against the side of my face. I couldn't bear to look at him. He was like a wild animal whose prey was precisely where he wanted.

"I tried to make things easy for you, Aisha, but you have to be difficult. I gave you options, but you wouldn't oblige. You're so damn self-absorbed that you don't care who you hurt, even if it's an innocent child. But you know what? I'm not going to let you do that to this child. I won't let you let him or her suffer a life of sickness because of your

257

negligence and greed."

"No Charles, this is different. This baby inside of me offered me a new life. I can attest to you, I'm not the same person. I'm just mad. Mad that you won't be with me…mad that you won't acknowledge your seed. I didn't mean those awful things I just said. I swear." My words came tripping out over themselves, one after another, each filled with a different emotion.

My chest swelled as my heart beat a million times per minute. I desperately wanted this night to end. For him to say he was sorry too and that he took it too far. I wanted him to hold be in his arms and tell me everything would be ok and that we would work through it. I wanted to turn a new leaf, but from the look in his eyes, I knew this was a false reality of what I hoped would come. He wasn't going to change his mind; he didn't have any love for me, and he wanted nothing to do with the baby.

"Whatever you are thinking about doing… don't. Don't do this. You'll hurt the baby… *our* baby." I pleaded. My soul has never ached in the way it did at this moment. My eyes glossed over with tears and despair.

"*Our* baby?" He drew back. "I don't even know who you are Aisha, I thought I did, but I don't. And after you pulled the stunt you did, I don't know whose baby that is."

"It's yours, I swear. *She…is…yours.*"

The room fell silent, as if he was thinking what his life would be like with a baby girl. He gulped hard and breathed shallowly. I could almost see his heart beating through his chest...contemplating. Then like Mr. Hyde, he turned. He looked at me blankly and that emotional moment was over. I could tell he doubted everything I said, even doubted my existence, and he was ready to end it all. He grabbed my shoulders so hard that it felt like my bones were breaking.

"Charles, stop, you're hurting me," I cried out.

My cries for mercy didn't help. The more I cried out and tried to wiggle free, the more pressure he applied to my shoulders. He wanted me to feel the pain – his pain.

"I'm not letting you go until you agree to get rid of the baby."

"No," I yelled out.

"No? You say no? Well, I'm going to keep... throwing your ass... into this wall... until you... say yes! Or until... you lose it!"

He jolted me against the wall several times. My back was screaming like I got jumped and a bunch of people stomped me. Charles looked like a mad man. My only option was to use my legs somehow.

I kneed him in the groin as hard as I could and he fell against the coffee table, knocking a lit candle onto the floor and the curtain burst into flames.

The irony of it all... the same baby that gave me the reason for new life is the same reason why my life is being taken away. And the same man that once took my breath away figuratively, is now taking my breath away...literally.

Fleeing the fire, I bolted through the house, trying to escape through the back door. My hand was on the doorknob when Charles hurled a picture frame at my back, stopping me in my tracks. I fell face-forward to the ground and held the middle of my back where the corner of the frame hit.

Charles walked over to me slowly— the flames in the other room didn't concern him. He rolled me onto my back and stared at me, almost as if he was studying my next move. But I was tired of fighting. My body was weak; I was in pain.

259

Then, in the most solemn voice, he spoke.

"I really didn't want to do this, Aisha. I didn't want it to end this way, but you pushed me to this point."

I saw him pull something long and shiny from his inside coat pocket. I thought it was a gun at first, but it was too flat. Reality struck; this was really happening. Surrendering, I held my hands up as I slowly sat up through the pain.

"Whoa, wait a minute, Charles, just calm down. What's going on? Whatever it is, we can work it out."

"I'm sorry, Aisha, I tried working things out with you, but you're so damn selfish that you can't see things any other way. So, I guess we've gotta agree to disagree. Wish things could've been different. Sorry it had to come to this."

Charles quivered as he grabbed my arm and quickly pulled me toward him. All I felt was cold steel rip through the flesh of my belly. I let out a low piercing squeal, while clenching my hands tightly over my stomach. Charles vehemently plunged a blade into my abdomen, forcing it upward into my ribcage. He cradled me with one arm until I fell to the ground.

"What have you done, Charles? What have you done?" My voice was faint as I shivered in his arms.

"I'm so sorry. I didn't want to do this. I just can't have another child growing up with this illness. I wouldn't be able to live with myself."

He quickly withdrew the knife, ran out the back door, and left me in the burning house. The flames lapped around me like the pit of hell was waiting to engulf me, ready to punish me for my sins.

I finally realized what I was running from in that bad dream. I was running from death; I was running from karma.

I grasped my wounded belly as my life flashed before me. I messed up, I *really* messed things up. My life and my decisions had always been a bit messy, but I would have never thought I would cause search turmoil that would affect many people lives.

I had potentially ruined seven lives, starting with my own and my unborn child. And since Jordan and I had unprotected sex after I'd been with Charles; Jordan, his wife and their unborn child were three more added to the list. Conjointly, if Jordan slept with my sister again, he could possibly spread the virus to her and their unborn child.

Altogether, that's seven lives.

Although I say seven, realistically I can't even put a number on the lives that will ultimately be affected. The catastrophic web that I spun will span across many lives in a way that I can't even imagine, issuing devastating blows of fear, anger, disgust, and sadness. Nonetheless, it was too late to warn anyone of my deceit.

I pulled myself across the kitchen floor, slithering through the trenches of my agony. I gripped my belly with one hand as coagulated blood spewed from my mouth. My internal temperature was dropping rapidly, and I could feel my body turning cold. My body felt like the wrought iron bars that I'd held on to at Charles' estate earlier that day. Except this time, I was holding on for my life.

I unclenched my belly to reach for the phone on the counter to dial 9-1-1. Every time I attempted to pull myself up, I slipped in my own blood. I finally knocked the phone to the floor, but it was too late. The room turned black, and I could feel my soul departing from its shell.

Left alone to die, my body quivered as I took my last breath.

Karma finally got her revenge.

# Acknowledgements

First and foremost, I would like to thank God for my existence, my talents, and all the wonderful things and people I've been blessed to encounter. I see your beauty and marvelous wonder in even the smallest things— I'll never take that for granted.

I would also like to thank and recognize my husband, family, and close friends for all their support, love, and encouragement. Thank you for believing in me.

Special thanks to my editor Sutton Mason. We go together like peanut butter and jelly; you're stuck with me now sister! I have a million more books headed your way.

Big thanks to my sister Gabrielle Harris (Elle Harris Studios) for shooting the front and back cover. You are indeed a talented soul.

Thank you to the models: Jayla Hoffman (Aisha) and Trae Watson (Charles), as well as the truly gifted makeup artist and stylist— Jerra Jameson and Montel Sawyer. All your hard work and dedication is most appreciated.

Thanks to Ray Poindexter, Omar Jones, Nick Hull, Bob Ullery, Cathy Kennedy, and Patrick Love. You guys were there in the beginning, and I truly appreciate you.

Last, but most importantly, much love to everyone who took the time to read this book. Thank you for all your support and remember to always live in the present.

God Bless